I0691642

BLOOD SKY

THE AFTER SERIES
BOOK 4

TRACI L. SLATTON

parvati
press

If you purchased this book without a cover you should be aware that this book is stolen property. It was reported as "unsold and destroyed" to the publisher and neither the author nor the publisher has received any payment for this "stripped book."

This book is a work of fiction. Names, characters, places and incidents are either the product of the author's imagination or are used fictitiously. Any resemblance to actual persons, living or dead, or to actual events or locales is entirely coincidental.

Blood Sky

Copyright © 2015 by Traci L. Slatton. All rights reserved, including the right to reproduce this book, or portions thereof, in any form. No part of this text may be reproduced, transmitted, downloaded, decompiled, reverse engineered, or stored in or introduced into any information storage and retrieval system, in any form or by any means, whether electronic or mechanical without the express written permission of the author. The scanning, uploading, and distribution of this book via the Internet or via any other means without the permission of the publisher is illegal and punishable by law. Please purchase only authorized electronic editions and do not participate in or encourage electronic piracy of copyrighted materials.

The publisher does not have any control over and does not assume any responsibility for author or third-party websites or their content.

Cover designed by Gwyn Kennedy Snider
www.gkscreative.com

Cover art: Brilliant Eye/Shutterstock
Copyright © iStock

Published by Parvati Press

www.parvatipress.com
Visit the author website:
www.tracilslatton.com

ISBN (eBook) 978-1-942523-03-1
ISBN (Paperback) 978-1-942523-02-4

Library of Congress Control Number: 2015912264

BOOKS BY TRACI L. SLATTON

IMMORTAL

BROKEN

FALLEN

COLD LIGHT

FAR SHORE

BLOOD SKY

THE LOVE OF MY (OTHER) LIFE

DANCING IN THE TABERNACLE
(poetry)

PIERCING TIME & SPACE

THE ART OF LIFE
(with Sabin Howard)

THE BOTTICELLI AFFAIR

EL INMORTAL

CAIDO

HOW TO WRITE, PUBLISH AND MARKET YOUR
BOOK, YOURSELF INDEPENDENTLY

EL AMOR DE MI (OTRA) VIDA

For Sabin, YES!

BLOOD
SKY

1 THE SEEDS OF ALL TIME ARE PLANTED IN EVERY discrete moment. If you pause, breathe, and come to presence, you'll discover this marvelous truth: that all of time is contained within each single instant, just as a giant oak is contained within a fragile brown shell. It's all laid out for you, all of it—the past and the future, events and people and destiny. All you have to do is come to awareness.

So I should have known that there would be trouble. I, Emma, should have known that love would fail, that it wouldn't be enough to protect us all from the very person who had plunged us into the apocalypse a few years ago.

It was all there, in plain sight, right from the first moment we met, when he saved my daughter Mandy from the obliterating mists and then accepted my trade: myself for his protection of the band of orphans I was shepherding around France. We talked about food, and I pointed out that he was eating well. One notices such things after a global ecological cataclysm that has destroyed most of the planet's buildings and people and all its manufacturing capabilities. One cares about who is eating well when one has been scrounging for scraps for several months. Priorities come into sharp focus.

He spoke of the mists and of rebuilding. I wanted to take Mandy back home, to my husband and older daughter Emma in the Safe Zone of Edmonton, Canada. He had his goals and

I had mine; his were lofty, mine were personal. I should have known a conflict was inevitable, but could I have predicted that the fate of the world would be tangled up in it? Could I have foreseen that he would be taken by madness, a madness that had slept within him since before the day his invention erupted to scour the Earth clean of human beings and structures? Even with all the mindfulness of the world, could I have known in advance that Arthur would be possessed by madness?

WE LEFT MIST-RAVAGED Outpost City and traveled east, mostly along the old Trans-Canada Highway. It was summer, and we were en route to Quebec, where a boat was waiting to take us to Europe. "We" consisted of Arthur and me and our beloved friends from the original camp in Europe: warrior woman Jeannie; Robert, her Irishman; their infant twins; the sharp-tongued French beauty Laurette; her companion, Charles Nwokocha, a famed linguist in The Before; Serbian Theo; and young Marco, the Italian whose madness had been cured by Arthur mere seconds before the mists swarmed around us. Other comrades from Canada had joined us: Donny, who had once been a cop; inscrutable Kangee his Sioux wife; pretty but feral Susie, saved from a band of raiders; the sly pickpocket Gaff from Outpost City.

We were riding at a good clip, about fifty kilometers a day, moving south and west of Winnipeg. In the late afternoon, we rode along a flat, straight road into a small community by the name of Starbuck. It seemed deserted. There was no movement, no wild dogs or skinny cats or desperate rats scrounging for food. It felt empty and lifeless in spite of leafy trees and tall grass, desolate like all the ghost towns in The After. Even when a town hadn't been devoured by the mists, people didn't want to live outside the Safe Zones, where mists never encroached.

"Let's check houses for food," Arthur called from the front of our peloton of horses and riders. He swiveled around in his saddle and nodded to Theo and Donny, who peeled off together, trotting toward a small brown cape on the right with an abandoned car in the driveway. He then turned toward me and Laurette and nodded again, and we picked up our reins to veer off to the left.

"Some of these homes look sweet to me," Jeannie called. A worn expression scrolled over her lovely, dark face with its pronounced cheekbones. "How about we find a place with food stock and settle in for the evening?" She was as staunch in the saddle as ever, but since she'd given birth to twins a month ago, she tired more easily. She pressed her lips gently to the forehead of the infant strapped to her chest.

Arthur eyed her without responding.

"Aye, come on, Big Mister. Let's take a breather," suggested Robert. "It's not often me lady asks for one."

"Every break slows us down, lengthening the time it will take to get back to Europe and make a stand against the mists once and for all," Arthur said.

"Arthur, we have two babies with us," I called.

Arthur stared at me and abruptly nodded. He could still see reason at this point. He called, "Fine. We'll find a place big enough to accommodate us all. Then we'll send scouts out for food."

Theo and Donny rejoined the group, and Laurette and I stayed tight to the flank.

We rode along Arena Boulevard, past a school and a recreation center, to Birch Street. Tall, fragrant pines planted in neat rows and colorful perennials showed that the inhabitants had once taken loving care of their yards.

"Arthur," Theo called, "big yellow house ahead, green Ford truck out front. Looks good. Check out?"

Arthur waved his assent.

Theo and Donny trotted out ahead of us to a sprawling yellow place with a spacious yard. I watched them dismount and take out their guns; it was The After, and they couldn't be too careful. There was no telling who might be hiding in the house and how sane they might be. Billions had died on The Day, that terrible Christmas Eve when the mists rolled across the globe and devoured structures, people, animals, objects—anything with the wrong balance of metals in their chemical composition. Luckily, millions of people, perhaps hundreds of millions, had survived, but some percentage of them were mad and were a threat to the rest of us. The mists had taken their sanity.

"Emma . . ." said a quiet voice from my elbow.

I turned, and it was Susie. Her heart-shaped face was solemn. She jerked her blonde head to one side, wanting to speak to me privately. I guided my horse a few meters away from Laurette, and Susie followed so close that my horse danced anxiously beneath me.

"Quit!" I said firmly, dropping my heels in the stirrups. I looked over at Susie, who was practically at my shoulder now. "So?"

Susie frowned. "Something's wrong, something . . . in this town."

"You saw something?"

"Not exactly."

"Felt something?"

"Not really."

"Then what?" I pressed, my voice low. For all I knew, the mists had stimulated her sixth sense. All too often, they left strange psychic symptoms in their wake, extrasensory abilities that both tormented and enhanced the recipient. We all feared the gifts, because they often preceded madness. I had a gift, the gift of healing with my hands, but I kept careful watch over my internal state, lest I descend into a chaos from which few people emerged.

Susie shook her head ferociously and uttered, "Yah!" Her horse quickened its pace, and she rode off toward the yellow house without answering me.

I stared after her in bemusement. Susie, who lived to kill raiders, was uncomfortable with something in Starbuck, yet she couldn't or wouldn't explain her feeling to me. *Perhaps it's ordinary intuition,* I thought, *or perhaps . . . something more.* I looked around carefully, steering my horse in a tight clockwise spin when my neck wouldn't turn anymore. I saw nothing out of the ordinary. Streets were empty, and houses were quiet and dark. There was no movement apart from our group.

"What's wrong?" asked Arthur, who had guided his horse close to mine. He studied my face.

"Susie feels uneasy," I murmured, still scanning the surroundings.

"She has good sensitivity. She's open psychically," he murmured back. "I'm certain she'll be a key piece of the equation when we mount an attack on the mists." He looked around. "I don't see anything. Do you?"

"No, me neither." I frowned as I caught his eyes. "That's what worries me."

His gray eyes lit up, the way they always did when his genius struck. Before the mists, Arthur was a professor of sorts, a polymath inventor involved in military research and development. "I know what you mean. It's all a bit too quiet."

"Why are the yards all so tidy? And where are the dogs?" I wondered aloud. "Packs of wild dogs run through every ghost town. We should have seen some."

He scowled and gathered his reins in one hand, then pulled out his pistol with the other.

I followed his example.

"What are we fearing?" Robert asked, riding up to us. He didn't wait for us to answer but drew his weapon and held it firmly in his hand, despite the baby nestled on his chest.

"The quiet," Arthur answered.

"Is good!" Theo yelled from the house, breaking the unnatural silence of the sunny afternoon.

Arthur motioned the rest of us ahead while he took up the rear and scanned the countryside.

The yellow house was spacious enough. There was a living room with a fireplace, as well as four bedrooms, and a nicely appointed den. We were eleven adults and two babies, and Laurette assigned us all to rooms. She delegated bedrooms to couples and gave Donny his own, in case Kangee showed up. She put Susie in the den and told Marco, Theo, and Gaff to figure out their accommodations in the living room.

"I like this place. It is very well kept," Laurette said approvingly, standing in the kitchen with her arms akimbo.

"*Too* well kept." I was going through the pantry. There was little in it, though it was very well organized and spotlessly clean.

"I know what you mean, but why question it, it is so pleasant? You are so suspicious, Emma," Laurette said. She peered over my shoulder, looking into the cabinet. "There are dried beans, we can use those."

"Someone will have to hunt something. There's not enough."

"We can look in nearby homes for more," Laurette said. "Susie—"

"I don't want to go out." Susie said. She seated herself at the kitchen nook.

I pulled out a box of Earl Grey sachets. "Cup of tea anyone? If I can get some water boiling."

"There's no electricity," Susie said, laying her head on her arms.

"The water runs," Laurette said, turning on the faucet for a few seconds.

"We don't need electricity. We've got a fireplace," I said.

Jeannie walked into the kitchen with a twin on each hip. "I'm so thankful to be off that horse. Emma, what have we got? Anything to snack on?" She slid into the nook opposite Susie, who didn't pick up her head.

"Not much yet. I'm still looking," I said.

Shaggy and awkward, Gaff stood in the doorway. "Arthur is sending us to scout for food in nearby houses."

"Don't go anywhere alone," Susie murmured.

"I know. He said we should travel in pairs. I'm going with Marco," Gaff said. "You okay?" he said, looking at Susie curiously.

"Shut up," she answered, but her voice sounded listless, without its usual snap for Gaff.

"Go on, then, Gaff," Jeannie said, unbuttoning her shirt so she could nurse the babies.

Gaff shrugged and scowled at Susie, then made a face at me before he went outside.

I took his point: something was up with Susie.

Something more than what was usually up with her, that is. Susie was often quiet, depressive. She had been kept by a group of raiders after the mists had ravaged her hometown and killed her family. The raiders had used her badly, and the residue of their cruelty lingered with her. I had helped her find freedom after a mist incursion, so she was closer to me than anyone else, but she was still often remote.

"I will start a fire in the fireplace," Laurette announced. She pulled a large pot from the cabinet and filled it with tap water, then walked out of the kitchen.

"It won't matter," Susie said. "Even if she gets the fire going and boils the water, it won't matter. Nothing matters."

I leaned back against the sink, scrutinizing the girl. "Susie, you want to talk about it?"

She turned her head to look in the other direction.

"So . . . Food? Supplies?" Arthur asked as he walked in. He made his way over to me and put his hands on my hips. "Didn't we have our first encounter in a kitchen?" he asked, smiling. He touched my hair and lifted a blonde lock to his lips. Then he leaned into me, his tall, muscled form lithe and warm along the length of me. He breathed deeply, as if inhaling me, and then he kissed me, running one hand along my neck and the other along my bottom. He lifted his mouth from my flesh to murmur, "We'll have our own bedroom tonight. Privacy. Finally. It feels like a long, long trip to Quebec without any time alone together." He kissed me again, more hungrily this time, and his hands roamed over me.

I felt myself melting at his touch, as always. Always with Arthur, there was an instinctive physical surrender that I was unable to stop. I couldn't help myself.

"Yuck," Susie muttered.

Jeannie chortled.

Arthur pulled back and threw a glance over his shoulder at Susie, then raised an eyebrow at me.

I shook my head.

He stood back and reached past me to open the pantry door. "It's tidy."

"*Too* tidy," I agreed. "Not a speck of dust or an insect carcass or anything. From what I've seen, the whole house is that way, like it's been hermetically sealed since The Before. Which is not possible."

"There are no cairns commemorating the dead either," Arthur observed, his voice deep and thoughtful. "We see them everywhere. But not for the last dozen miles, not even in town."

"So . . . little food, clean homes and yards, no dogs or cats or dead gerbils, and no cairns," I summarized.

"Someone's here," he decided. "We don't see them, but they're here. They're taking care of these homes."

"Why didn't they greet us then, one way or another? I doubt they've gone mad, if they're handling upkeep like this. Maybe they're a little OCD, but they can't be crazy, doing this much housekeeping."

"Perhaps they're concerned about our sanity or our intentions," Arthur mused. "We're an armed group riding in tight formation. It would be a reasonable concern."

"They know you're not crazy," Susie said, her voice hollow. "They'll come." She refused to say more even when Arthur and I pressed her.

MARCO TOOK A deer with his bow and arrow, his first since returning to sanity a few weeks earlier. Theo and Robert dug a shallow pit in the front yard and made a fire to roast our venison, as they'd done many times before when we were on the road both here and in France, traveling hard and fast on a mission. Tucked away in the cellar of a house down the street, Gaff found a stash of food, including some canned goods. The big score was ramen noodles. Laurette used a cast-iron skillet in the fireplace to make a feast of noodles, which had an expiration date sometime in the next millennium. Of course, we wouldn't have cared if the expiration date was five years ago; the piquancy of the seasonings made the noodles such a treat. We all appreciated simply having food, but delicious, well-seasoned food was cause for special celebration.

It was a warm dusk under a vast azure and plum sky. We sat outside around the fire to eat our meal. Gaff and Marco had dragged chairs out for us, and Laurette and I had found and lit citronella torches to discourage mosquitos, so we sat in comfort. Crickets trilled, cicadas whirred, bats streaked overhead, and moths fluttered and the air smelled bright and fresh beneath the smoky pine of our kindling. Poplar and birch logs, pilfered from a stack behind a neighboring home, streaked the orange flames with dancing blue, red, and green nymphs of light.

"I had no idea so many stars existed," Robert said, gazing up at the sky. "Could anyplace have more?"

"Aye, France, where we met," Jeannie said, exchanging smiles with him.

"Less light pollution here, I think, because the spaces are so vast," Arthur commented. He was chewing a piece of venison backstrap, the succulent meat, tender yet lean, from along the spine of the deer. "Theo, your recipe gets better all the time."

"I use what I find," Theo said. He shrugged modestly but looked pleased. He'd found some spices in the cache of noodles and used them with great efficacy.

"Something's off," Donny said. He set his plate on the ground beside him and stood up. His dark, pockmarked face wore a brooding expression. He was a portly man of African descent, always grounded, calm, and steady; he'd been a cop in The Before, and we all trusted him implicitly. He muttered, "I feel it with . . . my other sense."

We all grew quiet and a little tense. The mists had given Donny a special ability to sense other minds, sometimes even influence them. We had relied on that unique mental power in other, prior missions.

"Do you feel a presence?" asked Nwokocha.

"Alexei?" Arthur asked, sitting up straighter.

Donny shook his head, indicating that it wasn't the Russian psychopath who had bedeviled us over the past few years.

"Alexei will come to us eventually," Arthur stated. He was counting on it, in fact.

"Maybe it's Kangee returning," I said, eager to reunite with her.

Kangee had been given a mysterious ability to travel great distances. When she walked, the air would morph into red streaks, and she suddenly turned up miles from where she started out. I had experienced it myself once when she carried me on her back. Since she was unfettered by distance, she came and went as she pleased. We kept her horse with us for the occasions she joined us.

"Not Kangee. I can feel my wife from . . . well, wherever she is when she starts to come back," Donny rumbled. He stroked his chin hard, as if trying to rub something sticky off it. "I can't tell. I don't know. What's wrong with me?"

"We are all curious, Donny, but don't fret over it," Nwokocha said. He pushed his glasses up on his nose and smiled at Donny.

"I don't know," Donny repeated in frustration, "but they're here. I can feel them."

"They who?" I asked. But I didn't wait for an answer, I withdrew my gun from my backpack at my feet and rose.

Arthur and a few others rose, also.

Susie buried her face in her hands.

A small voice piped up and said, "They, us."

A rustle of movement intensified until it saturated the space around us. Scattered gossamer ribbons of light twisted in the firelight like DNA helixes, and several small forms slowly became visible, first as columns and then as people.

I yelped, and exclamations flew up from Laurette, Jeannie, Gaff, and Marco.

"We're here to talk to her," said the small voice. It belonged to a dark-haired, dark-eyed girl, about nine years old, one of dozens of children who suddenly encircled us in the yard. The girl pointed a slim index finger at Susie.

Arthur took in a quick, startled breath. "Talk to her about what? What do you want with her?"

The girl looked at him and tilted her head in a birdlike pose. "She can do it. You can help her, maybe. She can do it. Susie, come."

"Do what?" Arthur asked, baffled.

The girl turned away from him to gesture to Susie. "I am Irina. Come with me. You're the one we've been waiting for."

Susie got up and walked toward Irina.

"No, Susie——" I started.

"Susie, stay where you are," Arthur said, in his command voice.

Susie kept walking. Her face was blank, expressionless. She took Irina's hand, and the two of them vanished.

Theo, Laurette, and I lunged toward the now vacant spot. Gaff yelled, "Susie!"

"Bring her back this instant!" I yelled. I drew myself up, placed my hands on my hips, and made a ferocious face of command. I had two children of my own, Beth and Mandy; I knew how to scowl effectively.

"Don't worry," said a boy near me. He couldn't have been more than six or seven, with ragged red hair and missing front teeth. "Don't worry, Emma." He patted my arm, and then he vanished too.

All at once, all the children were gone.

Robert squeaked. "Where'd the little birds fly off to with our girl?"

The rest of us stood aghast, unmoving. The appearance and disappearance of so many children completely befuddled us.

On high alert, I almost jumped out of my skin when Arthur touched my shoulder. "Arthur, we have to get Susie back!"

"Shh," he said, cocking his head. "Listen."

I froze, straining to hear what Arthur did. It was a steady susurration, a kind of syncopated snicking that receded into the ethers. Then I got it: It was the sound of many bodies breathing as multitudes of little feet pattered over grass and pavement.

Arthur saw the comprehension growing on my face, and he nodded. "Yes, they're cloaked. They're not teleporting the way Kangee does."

"Grab one?" I asked under my breath. "Make them tell us what's going on?"

He shook his head.

"Why do they want Susie?" I wondered aloud. "Where did they take her?"

"They have to bring her back," Gaff said. He lifted his hat

off his head and scraped his hands over his thicket of dirty-blond hair. His narrow face was set and stern. "I mean, she's a heinous bitch and all, but they can't have her. She's one of us."

"I think she knew they were here all along," Laurette said slowly.

I nodded. But now what?

2 WE SEARCHED THE YARD OF THE YELLOW house, the neighboring yards, the homes nearby, and even the adjacent streets and alleys, but we found no sign of the children or of Susie. We were experienced at working together, so we fanned out and moved in pairs, checking basements, attics, toolsheds, living rooms, and bedrooms, but none of us found the slightest clue as to where she went or where the children were. There were only empty homes in a state of unnatural neatness, as if holding their breath until their absent owners returned.

Eventually, we went back to the fire and waited as the sky darkened into deepest indigo and the fire in the pit dwindled to a red-orange glow. Only Gaff kept eating, picking bits of venison from above the dying embers, though Jeannette nursed the twins.

Laurette kept giving us water, insisting that we hydrate ourselves. "You know how it is. Water can be hard to come by," she said.

"I didn't feel *people*," Donny said, pacing in a tight line.

"They were all children, *non*? Not a single adult," Laurette said. She sat down in a straight-backed wooden chair and clasped her hands over her stomach.

"Whatever they are, I don't feel them now," Donny said. He lifted his head and trained his eyes outward, sweeping around in a full circle. "I don't feel them. Don't see them."

"Still, they are probably present, watching us," Nwokocha said in his controlled way, "even if we can neither see nor sense them."

"I think so," Jeannie said wearily. "I think they've been spying on us since we got to town. We can't see them, but they're out there."

"Jeannie right," Theo said. He darted his eyes around, as if peering at the unseen entities. "Little ones listen, keep watch, report to others." He rose to his feet and walked to the edge of the yard. His hands were curled into fists as he surveyed the dark street. Theo was fiercely protective of our group.

We all looked around warily. There was nothing to see, of course, at least nothing we hadn't already seen during the day, even as it waned into evening: just the same ordinary houses, roads, trees, and cars.

"This will impede our mission considerably," Arthur said, his tone filled with a frown.

"Jeannie, go to bed," I said, before giving Arthur a sardonic look.

Arthur had the grace to shift in his chair, as if he was uncomfortable. The firelight threw flickers of amber light onto his beautiful, symmetrical face, still perfect even when stubbly with a few days' growth of beard and smudged with the grime of hard travel.

Would I ever be able to resist the forcefulness of his male beauty, coupled with that charismatic personality?

"Aye," Jeannie said. She rose, and Robert went with her, both of them too tired even to coo at their babies.

I hoped the babies would sleep and give their exhausted parents some rest. I remembered all too vividly the fatigue of the first few months with a new baby. With Beth, my oldest daughter, in particular, it stood out in bold relief in my memory, illuminated by my surprise that I could love as fiercely as I loved her. I had never loved anyone so deeply. It was another shock when Mandy was born and my heart lit up again with that extreme vastness of a mother's deep, imperfect love.

It caught my breath, thinking of my girls. Beth and Mandy were never far from my thoughts. They weren't with me physically, but they were always present with me; in some way, it was as if my mind was always pregnant with them. Sometimes it was a physical ache in my breastbone or a fever in the pit of my stomach.

Months ago, their father had vowed that I would never see them again if I left our home to help Jeannie and rescue Arthur. Haywood, my husband, who did not deserve my disloyalty to him, had finally had enough. I couldn't blame him. Nor could I fail to try to rescue Arthur, who was then the captive of Alexei, the Russian sociopath who had followed us from Europe to wreak vengeance on the man I loved. Arthur.

It had been an impossible dilemma: stay with my children while pregnant Jeannie died and Arthur was tortured, or try to go to help Jeannie and Arthur—but never see my children again.

I must have sighed aloud, because Arthur clasped my hand in both of his and drew it to his lips to kiss my fingertips. "Dreamy, let us rest too. It's past midnight. Theo and Gaff will take the first watch."

I felt the frisson of desire running down my spine, as I always did with Arthur, but I wasn't about to give up the vigil. "Arthur. Susie is one of mine."

He gave me a wry look. "Is that no, because I really think you and I could rest some together, in that nice bedroom on the second floor, in private,"

He didn't have rest in mind. I smiled with half my mouth. "One of mine, Arthur," I repeated.

He sighed and lolled his head back onto the high wooden back of the dining room chair in which he sat.

"Is okay, Emmy. You rest. We watch," Theo said earnestly.

Sweet Theo had promised in France that he was my

brother, because I had helped his brother. More than helped: I had saved his brother's life via the healing gift the mists had given me.

I shook my head, refusing to leave the yard until Susie returned.

"Go rest, people," Arthur said. "Em and I will take the first watch."

I WOKE UP with first light and found myself curled into the chair and damp with dew. I was also scratching from a dozen insect bites.

Susie was peering down at me.

"Susie!" I scrambled up and hugged her. "Are you okay?"

She didn't speak. She pushed me away, held out her hand, and dropped something into mine: a dead butterfly, its orange wings stiff and closed.

"Ah, so the prodigal daughter returneth," called Robert, who was walking out from the house toward us. "Susie, lass, are you well?"

"I'm fine," Susie finally said. For a moment, she let herself snuggle against my shoulder, as if she was a young girl instead of a sixteen-year-old who was taller than me.

I clutched her a little tighter and let the dead insect fall to the ground.

"I thought I heard some commotion," said Arthur, who came out into the yard at a fast pace. He joined us and laid his hand on her back. "You had us all worried, young lady."

Susie pulled away. For a moment, she looked into my eyes, and her young face was drawn into sober lines, as if she wanted to tell me something. Then she shook her head. Her usual cool, distant affect returned. "I'm fine. They took me to dinner, and that was all."

"The little birds fed you?" asked Robert, wearing a curious expression.

"Next time I tell you to stay, stay," Arthur rumbled. "Don't go off with strangers like that."

"They were little kids. There were no grown-ups with them, so you weren't invited."

"Susie, listen to me. We don't want to lose you, and—"

"And you didn't."

"Still, I expect you to obey a direct command," Arthur persisted. He paused a beat, searching the girl's face. "It's better for all of us if you listen to me. We care about your safety."

"I can handle myself," Susie said. She probably would have said more, but Jeannie and Laurette hollered out the window for her to come in for breakfast and a hug, whether she liked it or not.

Arthur wore a worried expression as he watched her go indoors.

Robert slapped his back. "Your turn to change the nappies, ole chap," he said. "I fear you haven't been pulling your weight with the wee ones."

I wondered what Susie had wanted to tell me that she wouldn't say in front of the others.

WE SADDLED UP to ride out of Starbuck by midday, none of us any the wiser as to why the children had taken Susie or where they were living. She wouldn't talk about it, and when we questioned her, she just stared straight ahead, her young face frozen in a mask of resistance. We finally stopped pressing her.

"She'll say something when she's alone with you," Arthur said quietly to me. He had come over to redo the girth of my horse, a youngish, prancyish fellow named Count.

"She keeps eying me," I agreed.

"She needs to talk." Arthur gave the girth a last firm tug. "You have to check this one, always. He's young enough that he'll blow up his belly when you place the saddle on his withers."

"It's not that he's young. It's that he's ornery," I muttered.

"You said the same about Edgar," Arthur said, referring to the horse I rode before Count.

"I have bad karma with horses."

Arthur grinned. "Edgar's good with Jeannie. He's a sweet old guy who needs a firm hand, and Count is a sweet young guy who needs the same thing."

"What is it with you guys needing a firm hand?" I asked, with a playful lilt to my voice.

Arthur circled my waist with his arms. He kissed my mouth hard but briefly. "If you'll come into a room alone with me, I think I can explain it to your satisfaction." He stepped away and handed the reins to me. "Let me know what she says, when she talks."

"Will do. I promise," I said. I had no way of knowing that I wouldn't be able to keep my word.

We headed east, along the Red Coat Trail that had once been used by Mounties to bring law and order to the Canadian wilds. Arthur rode in front with Nwokocha, Gaff, and Marco; Robert and Jeannie rode with the babies in the middle of the pack and Donny a bit off to their side; and Theo, Laurette, Susie, and I took up the rear. We had evolved to that formation, partly to protect the infants, in case we encountered armed strangers, and partly to keep Susie in reserve. She had a preternaturally accurate way with a bow and arrow. We all suspected that her skills might one day save our lives, and if we needed to deploy her, we wanted her to have the extra minute it would take her to nock her arrow and aim.

"Emma, we should avoid Winnipeg," Susie said. She rode close to me, causing Count to get antsy.

I wrestled with the reins, knowing I was handling the horse all wrong, as usual. "Why? What's wrong with Winnipeg?"

"The grownups are all mist crazy," she answered, shaking her head. "He just doesn't respect you, Emma," she said, looking at my horse.

"It's mutual. I don't respect him either." I dug my heels into Count's sides. Damn horse was now balking.

"You don't control him."

"Is your name Arthur?" I demanded. "I can't control him because he's, like, a thousand pounds of his own opinion about what he wants to do."

Susie broke out into a giggle, soft and reluctant. "He'll only have his own opinion if you let him." She drew her horse away and trotted out on her own.

I had to know what she meant about the adults in Winnipeg, so I trotted after her. I managed, despite myself, to steer Count up alongside her. "Susie, c'mon. Tell me more. What's going on in Winnipeg? Does it have anything to do with why there aren't any adults back in Starbuck?"

"The adults in Winnipeg are all mad, from the mists. They're dangerous." Susie shivered. "We should go around the city."

"Is there even any of the city left?"

She tilted her head. "Big patches still stand, I guess. It's never been completely swarmed by the mists, even though it's outside the Safe Zone."

"What else did those children say about Winnipeg and the adults there?" I asked.

Susie gave me a quick, piercing glance and shook her head. "Just that we should go around Winnipeg."

"They must have said more than that."

"I, for one, believe them," she said defensively. "Will you talk to Arthur?"

"Susie, can't you give me something more to go on?"

She shook her head. "And don't say more to Arthur than you have to. He's . . . Well, I don't think he's . . . you know."

"No, I *don't* know," I said. "He's what?"

"He's not quite right either," she said, then fell back into the obdurate silence she'd been keeping since her return.

A half-hour of pleading with her didn't inspire her to loquacity. I finally left her side and rode up to join Arthur.

He grinned at me out of one side of his mouth, keeping his eyes on the contact of my legs on Count's sides. "What is it with you and that horse?"

"I should've picked the old nag, back when I had the choice. She'd have been a lot less trouble."

"Em, you must figure this out. Even when we defeat the mists, it'll be decades before we have automobile manufacturing again, maybe a century. We're on horseback now. You have to master the skill."

"You say it like you enjoy it," I muttered.

He looked away, his face hardening. "I enjoy horses, not the apocalypse." He didn't say, *the apocalypse I created,* but I still heard it in his mind.

"It's easy for you. You're an expert equestrian. Some of us aren't." I scanned his face, wondering if Susie was right. What did she see that I didn't? "Arthur, Susie wants us to go around Winnipeg. She says the adults there are mist mad."

His gray eyes narrowed. "Is that why all those children are in Starbuck? They're orphans on the run?"

I shrugged. "She won't say. She just says she believes the kids."

"Damn it." He didn't speak for a few beats. Finally he called, "Nwokocha, we must stay well south of Winnipeg."

Nwokocha, riding in the lead, raised his hand to indicate he'd heard.

Arthur turned back to me. He was, as always, effortlessly poised in his saddle. "Get what you can out of Susie. I need to know what's going on. I can't make good decisions with only part of the information."

"I'll do my best," I promised.

He reached over and stroked my face with the back of his

fingers, then scooped away a windswept lock of my hair and tucked it behind my ear. His face softened. "I really would like some time alone with you, Emma. I miss you."

I turned my face to brush my mouth against his callused palm. "We'll make it happen."

THE FLAT, RICH-SOILED terrain of the Red River Valley provided little cover, in the event of unfriendly interest, so we waited to stop for a meal in Sanford, which must have once been a bedroom community of Winnipeg's. We stopped in the parking lot of Jeni's Food and Hardware and tied our horses to rusted cars, sections of metal gate, and old pylons embedded in the concrete.

The store had been picked through and vandalized repeatedly. Windows were cracked, and the front door hung down on its hinges. The shelves were empty except for the detritus of open boxes of goods, and the floor was littered with plastic wrap, broken dry pasta, raccoon droppings, and used up cans of spray paint that had been used to decorate the walls.

"It's good to know that art lives in The After." I picked up a can of Krylon Cherry Red. "Someone put this to good use." I lifted it toward a large design of whorls and cubes next to the window.

Robert asked, "You mean that portrait of something or other?"

"Abstract art. Bah!" Theo said. "Never like it. Is stupid. Child with crayon can do better."

"I prefer landscapes, still lifes, and figures myself," I murmured. For a moment, I remembered that I had once been an artist and an acclaimed illustrator in my own right. That was in The Before, which seemed like centuries ago now. It had been so long since I'd held a paintbrush in my hand, my former favorite activity, the times when I felt the most alive.

"It's a moose with a squirrel sitting on its withers," Robert decided, in a musing voice. "It's not abstract at all." He walked over to stand beside me and started to shrug off the baby carrier. He tilted his chin up at me, indicating that it was my turn to carry little Emily.

"Where you see moose?" Theo demanded. "No moose. Is curly, Like Delaunay in Orphism years."

"Delaunay? No, lad, it's Juan Gris, with those bright colors," Robert argued. He slipped the makeshift baby holster over my head and shoulders, settling the infant against my bosom and then moving behind me to tighten the straps. The baby mewled a little, and he clucked soothingly. "Also, it bears a resemblance to synthetic cubism, but like I told you, ultimately, it's a moose."

"More mosaic style of Delaunay," Theo insisted. "No moose."

"Since when are you two connoisseurs of fine art?" I wrapped my arms around little Emily, enjoying the tender warmth of the infant against my chest. "All these years, I thought you were only interested in . . . Well, I don't know. Maybe hunting and fishing and riding horses?"

"Survival, you mean," Robert said in a big, jolly voice. "That has left us precious little time for aught else." He kissed the baby's head, then gave me a friendly peck on the cheek. "I'll take a look around, see if I can't find us something good for the road."

"Robert know nothing about art. His taste all in his mouth," Theo muttered, then trudged off in the other direction.

"Score!" Gaff called.

Everyone turned and saw him in the back of the store, in the manager's office.

He emerged, waving a can in each hand, as if he'd just won the prize trophy in some athletic competition. "Peaches and green peas, lots of cans. Found 'em in a hidey hole under a board. And three bottles of peppermint schnapps."

"I *love* schnapps!" Nwokocha said, with some jubilation.

"I know, right?" Gaff said, then darted back into the office.

"That is a strange combination," Laurette said. She moved to join me and stroked the baby's cheek. "I cannot even remember the last time I drank schnapps."

"Find anything?" I asked.

She shook her head. "Not really. A bottle opener, we have those. But we can trade it later."

"There's a cellar. I'll see what's what," Robert hollered. "Maybe I can find some real liquor to go with that schnapps. Some Jameson would be nice."

"Don't go down there alone," Arthur warned. He stood not too far from me, his tall form bent over as he picked through a heap of detritus. He looked up, saw the infant on my chest, and smiled.

I smiled back but then ambled outside to avoid a confrontation. Whenever Arthur saw me holding one of the babies, a misty look seeped into his eyes. He wanted more from me than our arrangement as lovers and traveling companions, he was open about that. But I was married to Haywood and had two children with him, so I was reluctant to commit to Arthur. I could not explain to Arthur about the cleft in my heart, which remained even after Haywood's ultimatum and the choice I had made to leave home and rescue Arthur. It had been a point of contention between us for a long time.

I wandered to the edge of the parking lot and looked around the street, which was still in surprisingly good condition, despite the snows of last winter, its pavement flat and free of potholes. Clearly it had once been a well kempt, oft-trafficked thoroughfare. In The Before, Sanford must have been a nice little town, with its rich farmland and family businesses and the commuters who were happy to return after working in the nearby city.

Down the road, a mysterious gray stone cairn, commemorating the dead, rose at least ten meters into the air. They were everywhere now, though I'd never seen anyone building one. Crazy Alexei had told me his followers were now the keepers of the cairns, but that didn't speak to the question of their builders.

"Do you think we're far enough away from Winnipeg?" asked Susie, walking out from in front of a line of our horses.

"We're ten or fifteen kilometers southeast, Donny said," I answered.

Susie's mouth tightened.

"It's far enough away to discourage casual interest," I said in a cajoling voice; I hated seeing Susie so dour.

Susie didn't soften.

"Guess what. Gaff found peppermint schnapps and canned peaches. They'll be delish. Maybe they'll find more in there. You never know. Maybe chocolate. Wouldn't that be nice?"

"Emma, please take me out of here."

"They'll be done looking through the store soon enough. We'll have lunch, then be on our way," I said uneasily.

"Not *here*. I mean . . . here." Susie sidled over to stand right at my shoulder. "I want you to take me out of the group."

"What!? Why?" I exclaimed.

"We don't need them. We can get to France on our own," Susie said defensively. "You said your husband was a pilot, that's how you got to Canada from France. He can take us back."

"Susie, hold on. What's going on?" My dismay woke the baby, whose tiny hands and feet scrabbled on my torso.

"Arthur's going to want to use me for his own ends," Susie said. "You can't let that happen. You have to take me out of here, get me back to Europe, without Arthur."

"What are you talking about?" I asked, confused. "Why do you have to go to Europe?"

"That was what the kids in Starbuck told me, that I'm not safe with Arthur."

"Why not?" I demanded, feeling the heat as my cheeks reddened. "He's done nothing but protect you, support you, and feed you from the moment we took you into our group! How can you take the word of some strangers over him?"

She shrugged her shoulders and looked defeated. Then she picked up her chin, visibly setting herself for the discussion. "Emma, you may not want to hear this, but Arthur's not . . . completely sane."

"I see no evidence of that!" I said, as softly as I could to avoid disturbing the baby again.

"Yes, you do, you must." She sighed and shifted her bow sling off her neck and onto her shoulder, then combed her fingers through her blonde hair. "Emma, I *have* to go to France. It's about the mists. I have to find a girl there. I think you know her."

"This is all very confusing, Susie. You won't give me a full story, just bits and pieces. You wanted to stay away from Winnipeg, so I made that happen, but now you're telling me to take you away from the group and take you to France by myself so you can meet some girl. Who, and what does this have to do with the mists?"

"She's a pretty girl about my age, maybe a little older. She has brown skin and speaks several languages. I think she had the same experience I did, with raiders—you know, all that . . . bad stuff. Her name's, like, Karen or Carrie or something." Susie raised her eyebrows in a quizzical expression.

Of course I knew who she meant. I knew exactly who she meant. "Caris," I murmured breathlessly, almost in shock. It didn't make sense. *How does Susie know about Caris, one of the children in the original band of orphans I shepherded around Europe in the first few months of The After? How is this possible? Has she developed a mist-driven psychic cognition? Is she going mad?*

"I'm not going crazy," Susie stated in a matter-of-fact tone. She smiled at the expression of consternation on my face. "No, I'm not reading your mind like Donny does. I just know how you think, Emma. I've pretty much got you figured out."

Fair enough, I thought, for we were a tightly knit band, a tribe, a family. "How do you know about Caris?"

She nodded slowly. "We are like . . . two halves of a whole. Our abilities let us complete one another, if that makes any sense."

"Psychic abilities?"

She kept nodding. "Ours is special. We can control the mists, confine them. We can bring them all together and destroy them."

"*All* the mists?" I clarified. "You can gather the mists together from everywhere on the planet?" My heart began pounding an excited staccato in my throat as I took in the ramifications of her statements: *Earth could be free of the ravaging, murdering mists, safe for humanity again, after all the travail of the last few years.* I had stopped believing it was possible.

"Yes, but we have to do it together. Neither one of us can do it alone."

"My God," I said. "Oh God. For the world to be free of mists, once and for all . . . ."

"Yes." Her face lightened, and her posture straightened, as if she'd set down a heavy load. "Now you know why I must get to France. I have to find Caris."

"But what about Arthur?" I asked. "He should know. He has the ability to control mists also. Maybe his ability can complete yours, and we won't even have to haul you across the ocean. Maybe the two of you can do it together, even right here, right now. There'd be no more deaths, and—"

"Emma," Susie said, gripping my forearm, "stop. I can't do it with Arthur. It's not him. I need Caris. She's waiting for me. We've got to do this together."

"We have to at least tell Arthur," I declared. "He has to know immediately. This changes everything!"

"You can't!" she hissed. "Promise me you won't, not yet."

"But, Susie, he must know this."

"He can't know, Emma. He's not . . . He can't be trusted. I know you're close to him, but you have to believe me on this." She leaned so close to me that I could see the sweat beading up on the fine, poreless skin of her face, which had blanched to the color of milk. "Promise me you won't say anything yet!"

"Susie, I have to——"

"Not yet," she insisted. "Emma, please? If you say a word, I'll never trust you again. I mean it." She took a breath. "Give me a chance to prove it to you, what I'm saying about him. You owe me that, don't you? Just give me one chance to prove it. Will you?"

I nodded grudgingly.

3 LUNCH, WHICH WAS REALLY AN EARLY DIN-
ner, started out as a raucous affair in the parking
lot of Jeni's Food and Hardware. We fired up an
outdoor grill with real charcoal and lighter fluid,
then barbecued a bison that Theo shot only a few kilometers
away from the store. Laurette stirred the canned peas into a
big pot on a portable camp stove, and I opened the peaches.
The peppermint schnapps was passed around, and we all par-
took, despite knowing we'd be riding again after the meal.

"This is good," Jeannie said, speaking through a mouthful
of bison steak. "Rich but tender." She ate as fast as she could,
tearing off chunks of meat and swallowing them almost whole.
She'd lost so much weight from being sick while she was
pregnant, and now she was nursing and looked like a stick, so
much so that Robert called her his "African Olive Oil." Traveling as we were, she had a hard time taking in enough calories
every day.

"It's a little sweeter than beef," Arthur agreed. He passed
his arm across his mouth, smearing grease on his chin. He
caught me watching him. "What? Have I offended your lofty
standards of personal hygiene?"

I moved around to stand in front of him. I licked my thumb
and swiped it at the streak on his chin. "We don't have to turn
into barbarians."

He smiled up at me, and his gray eyes darkened to plum. He put his hand on my hip. "You like when I'm a barbarian."

I rolled my eyes and seated myself.

"I estimate two to three months to reach Quebec, traveling at this rate," said Nwokocha. "It'll be an enjoyable trip if we continue to eat this well."

"Big 'if,'" Gaff said. "Pass me another can of them peaches, Susie."

Susie picked up an unopened can and hurled it at him.

Gaff ducked just in time. "Too bad those weird kids didn't improve your personality when they took you."

"At least I *have* a personality, which is more than you can say for yourself," Susie retorted. "All you do is scrounge for things. You're, like, an anteater or something."

"Guys . . ." I said.

"Susie, will you please retrieve the can?" Laurette said crisply. She gave Susie a glance with about as much sympathy as battery acid. It should have dissolved Susie where she stood, but somehow, it had the opposite effect and lightened the girl, who sprang up out of her seat. "Do not even think of throwing that can again!" Laurette called.

"We can make it to Niverville and find lodging there," Donny said. "It's about forty kilometers away."

"There's a great deal of farmland between here and there, if I recall correctly from our journey west," said Nwokocha, who always recalled everything correctly.

"The east part of the town was good, but the mists had taken a section west of the park. What was the name?" Laurette asked.

"Hespeler Park," Nwokocha supplied. "Niverville survivors were quite friendly."

"Wasn't that the place with the, uh . . . the church that made pizza?" Marco asked, bolting upright.

Robert laughed. "You aren't thinking of pizza, lad. You've set your mind's eye on that curvy little redhead."

Marco blushed furiously. "No. They were trying to make real Italian food."

"She was a silky minx, all right, and she had her eye set on you too," Jeannie said, in a dry tone.

"They'll have news," Arthur said. "They'll have heard of Alexei. They'll know what he's up to. In fact, if they're still friendly, we can wait there, till Alexei comes to us."

"I wish we weren't counting on that crazy Russian for help with the mists," Robert said, his tone uneasy. "Do we really need him? He's been nothing but trouble for any of us."

"Alexei's insane, but his powers must be joined with mine if my assault on the mists is going to have any chance of success," Arthur said.

"Maybe not," Nwokocha said. "Maybe once we return to France and our camp, you will find other people to join with you in a biomind field, create the right resonance, and support your efforts against the mists."

"No, I need him," Arthur insisted, "and he needs me. Somehow, somewhere in his sociopathic, unbalanced brain, he knows that."

"Arthur, maybe he stopped tracking you," I said. I couldn't sense Alexei in my dreams, which was how he communicated with me when he wanted something from me. "He vowed that he will not help you. Maybe he's really done with you."

"He will come to me. He's pursued me this far, and he won't give up so easily." Arthur stood and paced around the circle of chairs, stools, and milk crates we'd brought out to sit on. "I think about it all the time, the mists. When we created them, our goal was simple and pure. We wanted to eradicate war by destroying the weapons of war. My premise, ours, was that ridding the world of missiles, artillery, firearms, guns, cannons, torpedoes, rockets, missile launchers—you name it . . . We were sure if those were gone, war would dwindle and die. Hence, the mists were created to dissolve metals, to loosen their molecular bonds so they change state."

"That explains the yellow sand we see after the mists have passed through," Gaff observed.

"Noble aims with the worst consequences," Nwokocha said, releasing a sigh. He stretched his arms overhead, as if his shoulders were sore, then placed his empty plate on the ground beside him. He rested his elbows on his knees and his head in his hands in a gesture of profound weariness; we were all tired of the apocalypse.

"Boss, you didn't take into account the will to war," Robert said. For once, his merry Irish voice was subdued. "When people don't have guns, they'll shoot arrows. If they don't have arrows, they'll throw rocks. If they have nothing else, they'll spit. Man was made to wage war."

Arthur clenched his hands into fists. "That's the thing. We *did* factor that in."

"Oh. So that's why the mists affect people's minds," Donny said. A sick look of understanding crossed his face. Like Nwokocha, he set his plate aside, as if food just wasn't palatable any longer, despite the hunger that dogged us in The After.

"Yes. We engineered the mists to affect the human biomind," Arthur said.

"What's that, the 'biomind,'" Susie spoke up, a little too loudly, keeping her eyes fixed on Arthur. "You use the word a lot, but I've never really understood it."

"The biomind is our faculty for extrasensory perception—clairvoyance, telepathy, telekinesis, and other inherent faculties of our species which transcend time, matter, energy, and space, in terms of consciousness and subtle phenomena," Arthur said in his professorial voice.

"It's not that hard to understand, Susie," Gaff said with a sneer. "You know all those weird psychic abilities the mists have given people? The way Kangee can walk miles and miles with one step and how Emma heals with her hands and Donny can read thoughts and sometimes influence people? That stuff is all from the biomind. Arthur and his crew created the mists specifically to attack the biomind."

"Not attack. Influence," Arthur corrected in a rare tone of unease. He took a few breaths to master himself. "But that was very well said, Gaff."

"Seems like an attack to me, since people never asked for these new abilities and often go mad when they get them," Robert pointed out.

Arthur shook his head vehemently and resumed pacing. "No! It wasn't meant as an attack."

"Sure it was, Arthur. You meant to control enemy soldiers. You've admitted that before," I objected.

"That's what we told those who were higher up in the food chain," Arthur muttered. "We told them that because it was what they wanted to hear, what they lusted for. They wouldn't have funded us otherwise. We offered them a way to control the enemy, so it was irresistible to them. They were like sharks going after a wounded baby seal."

"If the intention wasn't for the mists to control the minds of enemy combatants, then what was the intention?" asked Nwokocha.

"It was meant to influence and to awaken. We thought, or at least assumed . . ." "What? What did you assume, Arthur?" Laurette coaxed, leaning forward and listening intently, her gamine face completely entrained on Arthur.

Arthur shrugged. "This has never been said outside our lab, but we assumed stimulating the biomind would awaken people to enlightenment. We thought it would mimic the effects of decades of meditating. We thought we'd have millions of Buddhas in the world. We thought those awakened people would help us shift the paradigm on Earth from a competition-based global culture to a cooperation-based one. We thought the mists would usher in a new golden age for humanity, free of war, with everyone collaborating to eradicate poverty and disease."

We were all silent for a few beats, taking in the magnitude of his words.

"A golden age?" Robert said, shaking his head. "My God, man! You thought you'd save the world. You dreamt of being the fucking Messiah. What balls."

"Not *me*." Arthur turned away and looked out into the distance. "The mists."

"*Your* creation, *your* brainchild," Susie said, then stared at me pointedly. "You thought you were God the Father."

I looked down at my hands, which were trembling.

"I meant to improve the lot of everyone on the planet," Arthur said sadly. "Big goals require big sacrifices. I never could have predicted what would follow."

None of us quite to knew what to say in light of the destruction that the mists, Arthur's creation, had unleashed on the world.

Arthur wasn't finished speaking though, in spite of our stunned silence. "Then the mists evolved, even while they were in containment. I went to Alexei to obtain a weapon capable of destroying them, but it was too late. The mists had escaped our facility. A few months later, they . . . well, destroyed everything."

"Including Alexei's wife, hence his vengefulness," Nwokocha said.

"Yes, and that will bring him back around to me. Revenge has him in its teeth like a terrier grips a rat," Arthur said. "When he comes again, I'll reason with him. Alexei has a son. He'll want the mists gone for his son's sake. He'll want Mikhail to grow up in a world without that kind of terror and danger. He hates me, but he'll understand that we have to work together."

"Yeah, reason has worked so well with that guy already," Susie said, her voice chilly with sarcasm. "That's why he kidnapped Emma's daughter and beat the crap out of her husband, then nearly tortured you to death, Arthur. You'd be a

one-armed dead man if it wasn't for Emma's healing touch."
She stood and kicked her plate across the parking lot, then
stormed off to her horse and put on his saddle pad.

The rest of us put away the schnapps and picked up after
ourselves, then silently mounted our horses and rode out in
formation.

WE ENDED UP on old Route 305 and crossed the Red River
in Ste. Agathe, where no houses stood; all had been razed by
the mists. The land was denuded of trees and bushes too. In
the murky dusk, we could see that the bridge still stood, so
we crossed two at a time. In The After, we couldn't be sure
of any bridge's support structure, so we minimized risk as a
matter of routine.

I rode abreast of Theo, who glanced around at the bare
landscape, out of which rose only a few metal poles for streetlights. The lights didn't work, of course.

"Emmy, not look like mists," he said, his broad face pursed
with thought.

"Does to me. Lately, the mists have been eating trees.
They're evolving." I wondered how long it would take us to
reach Niverville, how long we'd ride in the dark, and if we
would find a hot meal and a soft bed there.

"No, not mists. Something else." He frowned and rode his
horse close to the rusty guardrail, then took his foot from the
stirrup and kicked the topmost rail, emitting a clang. "Metal
was left. No mists come through here," he repeated.

When we reached the other side, Theo posted to a trot to
reach Robert, who rode ahead with Jeannie. "Robert, you see
what I see?" he called.

Susie and Laurette trotted up on either side of me.

Laurette asked, "What is Theo on about?"

"I don't know, just something about how it wasn't the
mists that destroyed these buildings," I said, shaking my head.

"When we came this way several months ago, there was a little grouping of buildings over there, just north of here, where the bridge begins." Laurette pointed to an area that was just as vacant as everywhere else.

"Must be the mists," Susie said.

"Theo doesn't think so," I answered.

"Oh, well, if *he* does not think so, then . . ." Laurette shrugged expressively.

Susie laughed.

"What?" I said. "So I listen to Theo. He's incredibly perceptive."

Susie said, "You and Theo are tight."

"Tight? I should say." Laurette laughed.

"Theo's family now, ever since that thing with his brother in France," I muttered defensively. "We've been through a lot together."

"Yeah, yeah. He says you're his sister," Susie said. "You're just lucky Arthur isn't jealous of Theo. He usually won't stand for any guy talking to you."

"He sees you with a baby in your arms and gets choked up," Laurette said. She gave me a stern look across the withers of our horses.

I said defensively, "I'm taking precautions."

"Avoiding him will not work forever," Laurette said. "He is wearing that hard-up look that men get. I estimate two days at most before he throws you up against a tree and makes short work of your knickers."

"Too much information," Susie grumbled.

"No trees in sight. Which reminds me, Laurette, I need more of your special herbal tea," I said. I sighed. "No more babies for me, at least not until everything is resolved with Haywood."

Laurette made a face full of scorn, something the French were good at. "What is left to be resolved? He begged you to stay, yet you walked out of his home. Your marriage is over, Emma. It is time you faced that. We will be in Quebec and then cross the Atlantic. You must not go to the new camp still pining away for your old life, the life you threw away."

"I didn't throw it away," I retorted, feeling the color rise in my cheeks. "I just couldn't stand by and do nothing while Jeannie sickened and died with a baby in her belly and Arthur was tortured to death by Alexei. I had to do something, had to answer the call. After everything we've all been to each other, we're family. I didn't have a choice."

"You *always* have a choice," Laurette said. "You just did not like your options."

Arthur and Nwokocha cantered up alongside, then passed us. Arthur turned in his saddle and gave me a half-grin and a wave as he passed.

"See?" Laurette sniffed. "Hard up."

"Just friendly," I argued.

"Ugh," Susie said, gathering her reins. "I'm gonna go listen to Theo and Arthur, find out what's going on. Arthur's got a bee in his bonnet about something, probably the same thing Theo's worked up about." She rollicked off at a canter.

"Do you know what is bothering Susie?" Laurette asked.

"Somewhat," I admitted. "She won't tell me everything, just bits and pieces."

"Anything of concern?" Laurette probed.

"Yes and no. I've got to suss it all out before I make any judgments."

Donny trotted up alongside us. "That's everyone. We take a left up here at Provincial Road, go north for five or six kilometers before turning east on 311."

"How far till we reach Niverville?" I asked.

"Another five or six kilometers after that, on 311," Donny estimated. "We'll be in the dark for the last part, but it's straightaway, so we'll be okay."

"Unless raiders are watching for an opportunity and ambush us as we ride in, and slaughter us to a person in our saddles," Laurette said sharply.

"That's what I like, optimism," Donny said. He touched his hand to his head and trotted faster, pulling ahead of us.

"Everyone's a little off today," I observed.

"Not me. I am always tranquil," Laurette assured me. "You should emulate me, Emma. You are much too emotional. I am an oasis of serenity in the desert of The After."

This, of course, cracked me up, even though it wasn't her intention to be funny.

4 PINE TREES AND CLAPBOARD BUILDINGS PEPpered the view as we rode north along Provincial Road, which ran mostly parallel to the Red River. Provincial Road crossed a stream winding off the Red River. It was a relief to see the landscape looking less razed, though I suspected that the night sky had always been as intimidatingly vast and clear as the cosmos. It was as if we stood in the heart of the Milky Way out here in the prairies of Manitoba. We turned east on 311, as Donny advised, and we continued at a fast trot, until Arthur and Nwokocha drew up sharply in the lead and hollered back at us to hold up.

Even with my eyes adapted to the dark, I strained in the inky night to make out the problem. A swath of yellow light flicked on and played on something lying athwart the road. Whatever it was, it had motivated the use of one of our precious flashlights. I put my heels to Count's sides and urged him foreword at a steady gait.

"Ashlar masonry," Arthur said to Nwokocha.

Nwokocha nodded sagely. "Inset into opus caementicium, with an overlay of opus incertum."

"I think we must consider it opus reticulatum," Arthur said.

"Only if you're being technical about it," Nwokocha rejoined mildly.

The two men chuckled.

"Are you guys talking about the wall?" I asked. "Was it here when you came west?"

Arthur shook his head and moved the light beam across it. Robert, Theo, and Laurette had their flashlights out also and used them to take a look.

"Damnedest wall I've ever seen," Robert remarked.

It was about six feet high and made of "stuff," as I described it to myself. There were rocks and logs and crudely baked bricks, of course, but there were also milk crates and concrete pylons, boom boxes and computer monitors, benches, and other pieces of furniture, like dressers and desks—anything hard that fit together like a three-dimensional jigsaw puzzle. The surface of the wall reflected the light back slightly, as if it was coated with a hard, shiny substance that also served to bind together the wall elements and fill in gaps.

"A defensive fortification," Arthur said. "I wonder who they were protecting themselves from."

"Raiders, no?" Laurette asked.

Gaff dismounted and walked next to the wall. He reached both hands out and felt it. "It's hard and slippery, like glass."

"Fascinating," Nwokocha said. "I wonder how they accomplished the surface."

"I think I can scale the wall." Gaff stepped back with his hands on his hips. "I think so, but if I was any shorter—"

"You're a midget, all right," Susie chimed in.

"So I'm not a giraffe like you. Listen up, okay?" Gaff snarled. "If I was shorter, I wouldn't be able to reach the first handholds. As it is, I have to jump." He jumped once and slid back down. He squatted deep down on his haunches, then exploded up as if on a spring and managed to cling to the wall.

"Can you see the other side?" asked Arthur.

"I help," Theo said. He climbed down from his horse and went to stand under Gaff so Gaff could step on his shoulders. He then passed his flashlight up to Gaff.

"Thanks," Gaff said, panting as he reached down to take

the flashlight. He placed it between his teeth, then raised himself up and threw one arm over the wall. He shined the flashlight down on the other side with his free arm. He grunted, a sound of dismay.

"What is it?" Arthur asked.

Gaff pushed back and jumped down off Theo. "We can't climb or jump over. There are sharpened sticks in the ground, and they'll impale us or our horses."

"I have to see," said Arthur. He dismounted and climbed nimbly up the wall. He hoisted himself up and balanced, sure-footed as a cat, atop the wall.

Shimmying up the wall also were Theo, Robert, Marco, and Susie, but only athletic Susie got all the way up. She poised herself next to Arthur like a tightrope walker on her wire.

"Yep," Arthur drawled, "sharpened stakes. A nice, wide swathe of them, set close together and extending almost three meters back. Niverville is serious about keeping someone out. Looks impassable."

"Maybe," Susie murmured, crouching.

"No, Susie!" Arthur commanded, flinging his arm to block her.

But it was too late. Susie sprang upward and outward, leaping as gracefully as a ballet dancer in a grand jeté. She must have cleared the stakes, because she called, "Emma, bring my horse, okay? I'll meet you guys at the gate, wherever that is."

"Susie!" Arthur barked. He shined his flashlight into the dark on the other side of the wall. "Susie!"

She didn't answer.

The light from Arthur's flashlight sliced through the inky night as he watched Susie go. He climbed down. "We'll ride around and find the gate." His face was set and hard, like a granite sculpture; he was quietly seething. It wasn't often anyone disobeyed his direct commands. He had a way of issuing them that naturally inspired people to fall into line.

"Don't worry. She's good at fending for herself," I said.

He gave me a scathing glance. "She's set herself against me," he said in a measured tone, "for some reason I don't understand."

WE RODE SOUTH under a yellow half-moon, into flat, over-grown fields, following the curve in the wall. The horses were knee deep in some kind of low-growing crop that wasn't being tended. The night was quiet and starry, and a faint glow came from within the wall. We didn't talk, we just rode, shadow riders in the dark. The air cooled and dampened slightly, and I wished for citronella or even heavy-duty carcinogenic DEET spray, because a cloud of mosquitos buzzed around my head and shoulders.

I shrugged on a jacket and worried about Susie. *What was she thinking, risking herself that way, jumping off the wall into a field of sharpened stakes? Is she truly going mad? Can I even trust what she says about Arthur? Is she just being delusional, or can she and Caris really destroy the mists?*

It wasn't long before we reached a gate at Krahn Road and St. Andrews Way. A cluster of broad-shouldered shadows indicated buildings behind a gate lit by a dozen torches set in sconces on the wall.

The gate opened. A rangy, bearded guy with a shotgun on his shoulder came toward us. "State your business, eh?"

Arthur held up both hands in a gesture of peace. "We passed through here several months ago, at least some of us."

"Arthur?" called a voice, a woman. "Arthur!" A willowy form with a sleek cap of blonde hair shrieked and ran out the gate toward his horse. She clutched Arthur and practically pulled him down off his horse.

"Lydia!" Arthur laughed as he embraced the woman.

She took his head in both her hands, but he rested his hand on her shoulder, keeping her at bay.

"Lydia," he said, "I'm here with my group and with Emma."

"All right, laa, Lydia," called Jeannie. "It's me, Jeannie, with my babies!"

Lydia didn't seem to want to let go of Arthur, but she did smile. "Jeannie, you had . . . Wait. Did you say 'babies'? You gave birth to more than one?"

Jeannie dismounted and went to stand beside the woman, showing her the baby at her bosom. Robert climbed down from his horse and joined them.

Lydia, still hanging on to Arthur's shirt sleeve, made all the appropriate admiring noises and coos.

Arthur watched for a moment, then lifted his head. His eyes swept around. He was looking for me.

I dismounted and led Count over to join them.

"Lydia, this is Emma. Emma, Lydia," Arthur said.

Lydia cocked her head. She had a sculpted, patrician face and the demeanor of one who was used to being heard and appreciated. Few of us in The After could carry off that attitude, but she wore it well. "So you're the woman Arthur traveled across the ocean for."

"And who are you?" I asked baldly, not at all caring that it didn't sound polite.

"A friend of Arthur's," she said coolly, looking at him and not at me.

"Always nice to meet friends of his," I said, openly sarcastic.

Arthur winced a little, and his gray eyes flicked across mine in a split second of dismay. He said evenly, "We need a place to stay for a while. I also have some questions about the wall."

"Of course, Arthur. You can come into Niverville anytime," Lydia crooned. She snuggled his arm against her side and pulled him toward the gate, ushering Jeannie and Robert along with them. She paused without looking back to wave a hand overhead. "Barry, bring them in. They're friends. We'll stable their horses and put them up. Emma, see to the horses, won't you?" she asked, but it wasn't really a question.

"So I'm the stable girl now?" I said, collecting the reins of Arthur's horse. That meant I was leading two horses, which, considering how incompetent I was with even one, struck me as hazardous. We also had Susie's horse to manage, along with Robert's, Jeannie's, and the horse we kept for Kangee.

"Let me, Emmy," Theo said, grinning. "Not want to see horses bite or kick, each other or you." He took the reins of Arthur's horse from me. "Arthur's horse big brute, not like to listen to anyone but Arthur." He shrugged. "Go in. I get horses."

The rangy fellow lowered his shotgun. "If Lydia knows you folks, you're okay." He gestured for us to enter the gate through which Arthur and the blonde had already disappeared.

"Lydia is a sweetheart," Laurette announced. "Emma, you will just love her."

"Clearly," I muttered under my breath.

But Laurette was already through the gate.

Only Nwokocha heard me, and his handsome, dark face broke open in a rare, wide smile. He didn't say anything to me but smirked to himself.

INSIDE, TORCHES WERE set into sconces that had been affixed to the poles of electric street lamps. St. Andrews Way curved through a housing development. A crude but large barn had been built on an empty lot, and that was where Barry led us. There were several other horses stabled there, but we found ample stalls for ours. Barry chatted amiably with Laurette, Nwokocha, and Marco.

"The wall around the town of Niverville is new," Nwokocha observed.

"Yeah." Barry nodded. "Took a lotta work to build it, but it's been a godsend."

"What, exactly, is the purpose of the wall?" Nwokocha asked.

"Better let someone from the council talk to all of you at once," Barry said, pouring feed from a bag into a trough for the horses Theo led. "We're keeping the crazies out," he said, lowering his voice.

"Which crazy ones?" asked Laurette.

Barry grimaced and walked toward my stall with the feed sack. "Like I said, the council can talk to you folks . . . but I've never seen anything like 'em."

"Mist crazies?" inquired Nwokocha.

Barry was smiling at me and appraised me with curious blue eyes. "So you're Arthur's gal, eh?"

"Me or Lydia," I said dryly.

Barry chuckled. "She's just that way, thinks highly of herself. Don't let her get to you. In The Before, she was head of our Chamber of Commerce. Now she's the mayor." He turned and called, "Well, folks, let me take you to the intake building. I'm sure the others are there."

The intake building was another timbered structure that looked like it had been hastily erected in The After on an empty lot. It was a broad hall, a long rectangle under a roof of beams. It didn't appear to be insulated, so I couldn't imagine what they did in the winter, but it was well lit with torches and hurricane lamps and even a few floodlights hooked up to what looked like car batteries. Long, rough-hewn tables with benches were set around the room at neat intervals, and a counter ran across one end. Arthur, Lydia, and Robert stood by it, and Jeannie sat up on the counter, swinging her long legs and nursing one of the babies.

I went at once to them. "So? Do we have lodging or what?"

"Of course," Lydia said sweetly, her gaze fixed on Arthur. "You can stay in Niverville as long as you like, Arthur."

Arthur blinked once. "Lydia was just telling us there have been strange happenings around here."

"Emma, would you please go to the kitchen and get some fruit juice? There's an icebox hooked up to a generator back there, stocked with excellent fresh berry juice. I'm sure Jeannie would love some," said Lydia. She waved one soft white hand in the direction of the counter, though it was clear she meant the area behind it.

"Aye, Em, some juice would be a godsend," Jeannie called. She licked her lips, reminding me how thirsty a business nursing a baby was, even when one hadn't been riding a horse all day.

"Coming right up," I said. I followed the counter, a well-sanded, well-varnished but unstained affair, to a latched opening. I undid the latch and noticed just how tanned and callused my hand was, unlike Lydia's. My hair was a ragged, shoulder-length mop, not a coiffeur that could have come out of some fancy salon. Only Laurette with her perfect bob managed to look chic on the road. We were traveling hard and fast, and I considered it an accomplishment to brush my teeth twice a day. "If I was safe and comfy behind the walls of a protected town, I'd look all feminine and elegant like Lydia too," or at least that's what I grumbled to myself.

The truth was that elegance had never been my forte. In The Before, my hair was a thick blonde mass that fell to my waist, and my hands had been stained with paint splatters, the same paint that adorned the smock I usually wore, even when I wasn't painting. I had always loved the smell of paint and the bright daubs of color; they reminded me that I'd soon be creating again. I couldn't really blame Lydia for her pristine appearance, nor could I pin my messiness on the apocalypse. I sighed.

I went behind the counter and spied a door in the wall. I walked through the door into a simple, utilitarian kitchen that held a fireplace, a wood stove, long tables, and plenty of cabinets and shelves. I yelped, "Susie!"

Tall and slim, her long blonde hair hanging straight down in a neat plait, she stood in the center of the kitchen with her back to me.

She waved me away. "Shh!"

But I was rushing toward her. "Susie, I was worried about you!"

"Emma, stay back," Susie hissed.

I had to skirt a center island chopping table to reach her, and I turned the corner so I could see her from the side.

She stood there, as unmoving as a sculpture. A meter in front of her quivered a white mass, about the size of a bed pillow, hovering at her chest. I had never seen the mists take that form, but that's the white mass had to be, some new and probably even more lethal evolution of the mists. A second later, the smell met my nose, the particular scent of death brought by the mists: honeysuckle and sulfur, sickly sweet and pungent all at once. The thing was small but deadly. If the mist wrapped itself around Susie's face and she breathed it in, it would kill her, dissolve her from the inside out, metamorphosing her into a pile of yellow sand.

"Susie, don't move. I'll get Arthur," I said, my voice rasping with fear.

The end of the mist bent toward me, revealing a face imprinted in the white fluff—a perfectly formed, inquisitive, inhuman face.

I shrieked. "Arthur!"

"No, Emma!" Susie said.

It was too late, for I was already running and screaming.

Arthur barreled in, as fast and powerful as a saber-toothed tiger, before I even reached the door. "Emma, what is it?"

"Susie . . . and a mist with a face," I cried, pointing.

"Go away," Susie said coolly. "I can handle this."

Arthur vaulted over the center table and screeched to a halt beside her and the lethal mist. He drew a sharp, quick breath. "I've never seen the mists take so compact a form. My God. Look at the face! It's perfect mimeses of human form. That's a recent development."

"It's one of those new mists if it has a face," Lydia said, running in to stand beside me. "How old is the girl?"

"How old? What does that matter?" I demanded. "Arthur, can you do something?"

"Those ones, small and bearing faces . . . We call them scout mists. They target children and adolescents, up to about age sixteen or seventeen," Lydia answered.

"Susie is sixteen." My heart beat in my throat, and my eyes burned as I stared at Arthur and Susie. "Arthur, can you do something?"

Arthur held up his hands.

"No need," Susie said in a calm, soft voice. "I got this." She made a tiny flick of her fingers.

The white ball of mist vanished. It was simply no longer floating in front of her.

Lydia and I cried out.

"Susie," Arthur said in a soft voice, "when did you realize you could dissolve the mists?"

WE SAT AROUND a table in the long hall, eating salt-cured beef and applesauce and washing it down with berry juice.

"We first saw them right after you passed through here all those months ago, Arthur," Lydia said, "little balls of mists that float down from the sky and zoom through our living spaces, both indoors and out. They move like the drones in The Before, with purpose, as if they're gathering information. They have well-developed faces, sometimes on both ends. Usually, adults can get away from the scouts, but kids seem to get mesmerized by them, frozen in place. Sometimes the scout mists engulf the child, and the child dies. They usually leave them alive, but the kids go crazy, really aggressive and deranged."

"The mists have come a long way," Donny murmured. "Faces? Christ."

"I've seen faces in the mists before, but it was different," I murmured. "That was in a mist bank above ground, just hovering, and the faces were unformed, vestigial, sort of like impressions. Only the eyes were well formed."

"Do these new mists have anything to do with the wall you've put up and with the razed land by the Red River?" Arthur asked. He was pushing the chips of dried beef around with his fork, studying his plate as if the patterns on it held a clue to the mystery of the mists' evolution.

Lydia nodded and sipped from a glass of water. "We didn't realize at first how deeply the children were affected by them. Then a large band of children traveled down from Winnipeg, following the Red River and setting fire to everything in their path."

"Fire!" Theo said with satisfaction. "I knew mists not destroy buildings by river. I knew."

I squeezed Theo's arm, then looked sideways to study Susie's face. She sat next to me in sullen silence; she'd refused to speak after dissolving the mist in the kitchen. It was becoming her habit to maintain radio silence after some unexpected event of which she was at the center, and that frustrated Arthur to no end. He snarled at Susie until Lydia stepped in and ushered us all to the tables and Barry brought out food for us.

"I suppose those kids we saw in Starbuck were the same group. I was always uneasy about their mental state. But what happened to the adults in Winnipeg?" Donny asked.

Lydia looked up into the eaves of the building and drummed her fingers on the table. "Many were slaughtered. We figured that when mist-affected children started murdering their parents here."

"So you built the wall to keep the affected children out?" Nwokocha asked, in his usual mild voice. The furrows on his face reflected his grave concern, and he and Arthur exchanged a troubled glance.

Lydia nodded. "Yes, and whenever the mists are found by a child, we immediately put the child out the gate, with food, a horse, and a weapon." She ran her eyes over Susie. "I don't know what to say about the girl. She made the scout mist vanish. That was a first." Then she smiled a little and leaned against Arthur's shoulder. "Other than you, of course, Arthur."

"I've never seen anyone else dissolve mists," Arthur said in a measured tone. His gray eyes narrowed as he gazed thoughtfully at Susie.

"The girl has a name," I said crisply. "It's Susie."

"Well, was Susie affected by the mists before she got rid of them?" asked Lydia. "We have to know."

"Indeed, Susie has some explaining to do," Laurette spoke up for the first time. "We must know how this has come about."

"First, we have to know if she's still sane," Lydia insisted. "So far, she hasn't struck at anyone, but it happens rather suddenly. Children just lash out, using whatever is at hand to attack the closest adult, be it a knife or fork, a garden hoe, or even a shoe. One twelve-year-old beat his mother to death with a book. He knocked her out, then kept smashing her head until it was mush."

Jeannie and I both recoiled, making primal sounds of horror and pity.

"The saddest part was that until the mist took hold of him, he was the most loving and devoted son," Lydia said somberly. She rested her blonde head in her long-fingered white hands. "If he ever wakes up out of this madness, I don't know how he'll live with himself. He was his mama's boy his whole life."

"I'm not a child," Susie said suddenly, speaking too loudly again. "I'm perfectly sane. I'm more sane than he is." She pointed at Arthur.

Arthur's symmetrical face registered blank surprise. After a few beats, he asked, "Susie, what's going on here? Why have you set yourself against me?"

"*You're* the crazy one," Susie answered, her brow lowering, "not me. I just have a gift. It came to me recently. I started seeing things in my dreams. Then I figured out what I can do." She fell quiet again and set her jaw. She stared at me fiercely, and I knew she was willing me not to speak, not to reveal what I knew about her gift.

"If you can dissolve the mists, maybe you can connect with me psychically, via the enhanced biomind," Arthur said in a tight voice. "Your gift and mine can reinforce one another, and we can dissolve the mists—all of them. We can set the world free, you and me, and I won't have to chase Alexei down to help me do so. Have you explored your gift? Do you know what you can really do with it?"

She gave him an obdurate look and didn't respond.

"Do you know if you can do more than dissolve them?" Arthur persisted. He leaned toward her. "Can you control them? Can you shape them and direct their movement?"

She broke eye contact with him.

Arthur leapt up. "You can! You can control them!"

"Arthur, maybe you'd better let her speak," I offered uneasily.

"That's what you're afraid of, isn't it, Susie? It's not me you're afraid of. You're terrified of what you can do with your power, with the responsibility of it." He walked around the table, pulled her chair out, and knelt to look into her eyes. "Susie, don't you see? This is a tremendous opportunity!"

She flinched.

"Don't worry," Arthur said soothingly. "I understand how you feel. Trust me, I do. You can do something, something awesome that other people desperately wish they could do. It makes you an outsider. You don't know the extent of your power or the limits of it, and you're afraid to test it too much because you don't know if the power will suddenly fail— maybe right when a mist is hovering in front of you or in front of someone you love."

Susie looked at me and paled visibly.

"Arthur, maybe Susie talk," Theo suggested.

"I get it. I understand. I know what you're going through." Arthur was speaking intently to Susie from within her personal space. "But don't you see, Susie? We need to know everything about this ability you have to dissolve the mists. Can you call the mists to you? Have you tried? Was that how the scout mists found you in the kitchen?"

"Not necessarily. The scout mists come into our buildings," Lydia said. "We don't usually see them coming, so we don't get to our sound system fast enough." She looked at Nwokocha. "You remember helping us mount a system of speakers on generators so we can play recordings of horses galloping, right? That's usually very effective, if we see the mists in time."

"Yes." Nwokocha pushed his glasses up his nose. "The particular rhythm of horse hooves on the earth is effective at dispersing mists."

"Susie—" Arthur started.

"Ta, Arthur, leave the girl be," Jeannie said in a sharp tone of reproof. "Our girl doesn't want to talk right now. Give her some space."

"We still have to figure out if she's—"

"Don't," I said sharply. "Susie's fine. When she's ready to talk, she will. She's been with us for long enough that we can trust her. Arthur," I leaned over and tugged at his arm, "give her some breathing room, for Christ's sake. You're crowding her, and we all know she hates that."

"But we have to find out about her ability," Arthur said.

"Arthur!" Laurette and I chorused.

Reluctantly Arthur rose and stepped back.

Susie took a shuddering inhalation.

"This conversation isn't finished," Arthur stated.

"What have I missed?" called a cheerful voice. A tall, skinny beanpole of a man wearing gold, wire-framed glasses marched up and stood behind Lydia. He was youngish and awkward, and he put his hands on her shoulders affectionately, then pushed her shoulders to insert more space between her and Arthur. He tilted his head at me with birdlike inquisitiveness. "Who are you people? I'm Asher."

I liked him immediately and offered him a wide grin. "Good to meet you, Asher, I'm Emma, and that's Arthur, and these are our friends. I haven't been to Niverville before, but Arthur and some of the others have."

"You're Arthur? I heard about you. Pleasure to meet you," Asher enthused. He reached one hand between Arthur and Lydia to pump Arthur's hand up and down.

Arthur rose and gripped the man's hand in return. "Are you new to Niverville?"

"Asher arrived shortly after you left," Lydia said, rising to pat Asher's arm. "He's been tremendously helpful to us. He's an inventor."

"An inventor? Really?" Arthur brightened.

"My background is in industrial design, chemistry, and engineering," Asher said, nodding. "It's useful, I suppose, now that we have to keep adapting to new circumstances."

Nwokocha jumped up and reached for Asher's hand. "Charles Nwokocha, would you have anything to do with that extraordinary wall that encircles Niverville, sir?"

"Why, yes! I created the vitreous substance that coats the wall," Asher said, looking pleased. "It works very well, binds the components and also coats the wall. It's much like glass but can withstand tremendous pressure without shattering."

"I'd love to hear more about that," Arthur said.

"So would I," Susie said suddenly. She rose suddenly and stared into Asher's face. "What else do you invent?"

"Oh, all kinds of things, whatever we need," Asher said, as if in preamble and as if he was about to launch into a lengthy recitation.

Someone else had the same expectation of an impending monologue. "Tomorrow would be a lovely time to hear about it all," Jeannie said in a businesslike tone. "I've eaten and fed the babies, and right now I need to lie down on a nice clean bed and rest."

"Me lady's right," Robert said. He rose with a baby cuddled against his chest. His freckled face looked hollow-eyed. "It's been a long day, and we're in desperate need of sleep. Breakfast is the time for a good chat with Asher. Lydia, sweetheart, we stayed in a different part of town when we came through here last. I hope we don't have to ride back there at this hour. Is there a guesthouse nearby?"

5

LYDIA WAS STILL STANDING IN THE HALLWAY when Arthur closed the door in her face.

We stood in a small room with a double-bed, a second-floor bedroom in a dormitory-style guesthouse near the intake building. I set the glass pillar hurricane lamp on an end table by the bed so its soft yellow light spilled through the room.

"Do you think she'll go away, or will she stand outside our bedroom all night so she can listen in on us?" I asked in a false, saccharine tone.

"Emma."

"Right. She probably has to get a manicure and pedicure. How else will she maintain those aristocratic hands?" I shook my head. "Really, Arthur? I mean, not that she's not a peach and all, but seriously. Her?"

"Well, darling, I've told you before, it's been a lonely apocalypse."

I made a face. "It still can be."

His grin fell away. "You left me in France, traveled off with Alexei, then flew away over the ocean with your husband. I didn't know if I'd ever see you again. I took comfort where I found it." Arthur came up behind me and wrapped his arms around my middle, squeezing me into him, pressing my back into his warm front. "Finally, we're alone," he breathed into my ear. He kissed my neck, the sweet spot behind my ear that always triggered weakness in my knees.

I turned in his arms and poured myself into him, my mouth into his mouth, my body into his body, my desire into his.

"Emma . . ." he murmured as he fumbled with the snap and zipper of my jeans.

I unbuttoned his shirt, because to run my hands along Arthur's chest gave me the keenest delight. His flesh was simply delectable to the touch. For all these weeks of riding, we'd been mindful of our fellow travelers, and we never indulged in the carnal pleasure that came so joyfully to us. Having this time alone in a room of our own was bliss. I worked his shirt down over his shoulders.

Arthur lifted his head. His gray eyes were liquid plums. "You know what I think?"

"You're *thinking*? Now?" My voice was tremulous with hunger for him, and I wanted him to hear it.

He released me to tear off his shirt and jerk my jeans down to my ankles. I kicked off my pants and kind of hopped up into his arms, wrapping my bare legs around him as he held me from under my bottom. Arthur lowered me to the bed. He laid me on my back and ran his hand down my belly, over my silky white panties. I moaned, reared up, and unbuttoned his pants, then tugged at them urgently.

"About Susie," he said.

I froze. "Wh-what?"

"Susie. I think her powers are immense. I think she can control the mists even more than I can." Arthur stroked the rise of my pudenda, then moved back to step out of his pants.

I sat up and leaned back against the headboard of the bed. "You're thinking about Susie and the mists right *now*? This minute?"

"I think about the mists all the time. You know that." His voice was scalding and intense, like a fever. "I can never *not* think about the mists. You understand that. Getting rid of

the mists is my reason for being. That's why I've been willing to meet with Alexei. I'd rather kill him, but I believe that
together, he and I can make a stand against the mists. I realized
that when I was able to bring Marco back out of madness."

"Arthur, um, we were about to—"

"I know," he said. He sat on the bed beside me and rested
his head in his hands. "You know how much I want you. It's
been too long, but I sense . . . I can tell that Susie's powers are
amazing, the key to everything."

"Everything? You mean to destroying all the mists?"

"Not just destroying them. Controlling them. Even if
Alexei joined with me, we couldn't do that, but Susie and I
could. Our psi gifts working in unison would be amazing."

"Arthur, what are you talking about?"

He turned toward me with excitement rising off him like
waves of steam. "Susie's gift is the completion of my work.
Don't you see?"

I was utterly confused. "See what?"

He rose up on his knees on the bed. "Emma, with Susie's
gift linked to mine, we can destroy the mists . . . *if* we want
to."

"What do you mean by that?" I cried. "Of course we want
to! That's what we all want, what every sane surviving human
being wants, to destroy the mists!"

"There's more," he said. "Don't you understand? I believe
Susie can control the mists with great precision. I am sure
she can call them to her from wherever they are, that she can
send them wherever she wants, then dispose of them as she
desires."

"There's no evidence of that!"

"Not yet. It's only an intuition, but . . ." His eyes were shin-
ing and oversized, gray saucers filled with liquid narcotic. "If
I'm right—and I bet I am—don't you see? This will give us a
whole new set of opportunities. It's not just about eradicating
the mists anymore. The possibilities are vast!"

My heart beat unsteadily. "Arthur, what opportunities?"

"Don't you see, Emma?" he grabbed my forearms. "We can use the mists as they were originally intended, to destroy the weapons of war, as I've always wanted them to do. Susie and I can deploy the mists to our ends. There are still people shooting people out there, in The After, but that can end. We can finally purge the Earth of all weaponry, as I intended before it all went wrong, so terribly, terribly wrong."

"Arthur . . ."

"I can use the mists, Susie and I can, to reverse the mist madness on a global scale, using mist resonance, similar to the way I did with Marco, except we won't have to endanger anyone by letting the mists get so close. We can harness the mists' power and use it, just as I always wanted to, in The Before."

"Use the mists?"

He nodded. "It's wonderful. After everything, my goals may finally be within reach. I can finally accomplish what I set out to do years ago. I know we've paid a steep price, and this won't redeem everything that has happened, all those lives lost, all the destruction and suffering, but Emma, here it is! It's finally within my grasp, the end of war through the end of weaponry!" He pulled me to his chest and kissed me with his usual searing passion for me.

For the first time since the day I'd met him, I was unresponsive. A bitter bewilderment niggled at the periphery of my mind. *Is Arthur mad? Has he always been?* Not mad like Alexei or the mist-crazy children who didn't recognize their own mothers. But mad with his own hubris, his desire to use the mists for humanity's betterment.

Arthur was kissing me, biting my neck, tonguing my collarbone and the swell of my breasts. Then he slid his hands inside my panties and pressed his fingers inside me, into the warmth that wasn't damp. He was ragingly erect and didn't seem to notice that I wasn't aroused. He jerked my panties off me, then thrust his knee between my legs and made a way for himself.

Just for a moment, I had to will myself to allow him. Then my body took over and responded on its own. Once I let go of my shock and perplexity, it was easy and natural with him, just as it always had been. Arthur still smelled like himself, like the man I loved, like cedar and wind and salt and horses. His flesh was still warm and strong atop me, as always. He still rocked into me with a rhythm that obliterated conscious thought.

When the moaning stopped, he rolled off me. Half of his mouth lifted in a smile. "I love you, Emma." Then his head lolled off to the side, and he was fast asleep.

I MUST HAVE fallen asleep, too, but I didn't realize it, because I was worrying about Susie and Arthur. I was starting to wonder if Susie was perceiving something about Arthur that I should pay attention to.

Then I jerked awake. The hurricane lamp still glowed soft yellow, but I was alone in bed. Where was Arthur? Had he gone to see Lydia?

Or—worse—had he gone to talk to Susie?

I retrieved my underwear, slipped on my pants and shirt, pulled on my shoes, and hoisted on my backpack, then went looking for Arthur.

The halls of the guesthouse were quiet and dark, a deep purplish black relieved only by the diffuse yellow pointillism of a candle set in a wall sconce. I tiptoed along, quietly pressing open doors and surreptitiously peering in. From inside the nearest room came the faint mewl of a hungry baby; Robert and Jeannie slept there. Inside the next door was the ragged growl of a loud snorer, probably Theo and maybe Laurette; over the course of our travels, I had slept beside Laurette enough times to know that she snored like a drunken soldier.

Across the hall, Gaff and Marco chatted in animated voices; I didn't bother to open that door.

The next room was quiet. I pushed it open and found an empty room, but it felt as if someone had been in there quite recently. Something about the warmth or the scent of the room told me so. Diagonally from here, Marco and Gaff could be heard talking. This must have been Susie's room. I felt it to be so. Gaff and Marco's room rang with hilarity, and I didn't want to be discovered by them, so I set off down the hallway.

I passed quietly through the guesthouse and made it downstairs and out the door without being observed. I walked quietly down the street, toward the stable. I was a shadow figure moving in the midnight gloom, almost unnoticeable.

At a small stand of trees, I encountered them, two forms squared off in the dark. They weren't speaking.

"What'd I miss?" I asked softly. I stepped toward them and nearly stumbled over a body. I yelped. "What's this?"

"Emma, will you please tell Susie to be reasonable? She listens to you," Arthur said, through clenched teeth, breathing heavily.

I knelt to check the unconscious person. By the wan light of stars and moon, I made out a long, narrow form, a man, with glasses on his face. *Asher*. I felt around for the welt I was sure to find; it stretched across the side of his head, oozing warm and sticky blood onto my fingers. I bent my head close to his mouth and heard him breathing. He'd been whacked over the head but was still alive. "Susie, did *you* do this?"

"I'm getting out of here," Susie said in a low, firm voice. Her arms were crossed over her chest, and she was glaring at Arthur. "I'm leaving."

"You're not going anywhere, young lady," Arthur said. "You're staying with the group, where you'll be safe."

"You just want to use me for my power over the mists!" Susie spat. "I won't allow it."

"Susie, you're young and idealistic," Arthur said sympathetically. "You're worried about the misuse of your gift. Believe me, I get it. After everything the world has suffered, after what all survivors have endured, you just want to see the mists gone for good."

"That's what any sane person wants!" she cried.

Arthur nodded. "I understand, truly, but don't you see? What you really want is to help humanity, and if we combine our gifts, we can do just that. We can use the mists to drive the madness out of everyone who's still crazy. If we destroy the mists before curing mist madness, those people may never be right again. We can control the mists and use them so that when humanity rises from the ruins, we will go down the right path. No more war, no—"

"Do either of you want to help me with this man who's lying here bleeding and unconscious?" I chimed in. "Sorry to interrupt your great philosophical debate, but Asher needs medical attention."

"He's not dead." Susie held up a sturdy stick, as thick as my wrist. "He's just unconscious."

I rose and gestured with both hands for her to give me the stick. It took her a few beats, but she finally laid it in my hands.

"This isn't a philosophical debate," Susie said.

"Susie's right. We're talking about the course of the future," Arthur said. Even in the dim light, I could see how rigidly his jaw was set. "How the next great civilization of man will be. Will it be a warlike civilization or a peaceful one? Because if we just rush out and destroy the mists without planning ahead, the outcome will be more wars, like the terrible ones that raged in The Before. World Wars I and II, Vietnam, Korea—all those many, many genocides of the twentieth century. That was why I went down this path in the first place. I lost family. My grandparents died in the ovens of Auschwitz, and my five-year-old father was dragged through Europe by his aunt. We have—humanity as a whole has—destroyed too many innocents."

I had never before heard Arthur speak of his family history. It made sense of some things, like his passion to create the mists. Now he wanted to preserve them, though, and that was a kind of madness. An insupportable madness.

"You'll never convince me, Arthur," Susie swore.

"Arthur, you know, I think Susie has a point," I interjected carefully. "We can't risk it. After what the mists have done, if we can destroy them, we have to do so immediately. We can't wait one more second."

Arthur shook his head and gripped my forearm. "Emma, don't you understand? The mists were engineered to help us, to improve life on Earth, to keep the world peaceful. Now, with Susie's gift and mine, they can finally do that. They can serve us."

"No," I said. "You've been there once already. You had your shot at using the mists for humanity's betterment. Look how that turned out."

Arthur recoiled, and his hands released me.

"That's right," I said, steeling myself for the confrontation. "The mists escaped containment. They devastated Earth, leaving billions dead. You didn't mean for that to happen, but it did. Worse than what the Nazis did, even. And you want to take another chance with the mists?"

Arthur started, "But now——"

"They did that under your watch, Arthur," I pointed out. Those words would hurt him, I knew. But they might also wake him up.

A few moments of absolute quiet passed, relieved only by the small flickering of fireflies in the dark.

When he finally spoke, Arthur's voice was gravelly. "I didn't have all the tools then that I do now. I know so much more now than I used to. I understand them, I've been inside them, and now Susie can join her psi ability to mine, and we can control them. Things have changed. What happened before . . . It won't be repeated."

"Too risky," Susie said. "Emma's right. You had your shot."

"I have to insist," Arthur said, his body tensing. "Susie, Emma, I insist that we stay together. Susie, you must sit down and listen to reason, to potential. I won't give up. I'm going to keep you right at my side until—" He crumpled into a heap on the ground.

I had swung Susie's stick and knocked him in the head.

Susie jumped back, giggling. "Wow! Emma, good for you! I didn't know you had it in you."

I sipped in a few panicked breaths, feeling too scattered and shocked at myself to think cogently.

"Emma, you know what you have to do," Susie said.

I didn't answer. I stood there in a haze of incomprehension. There were two unconscious men lying at my feet, one of whom I loved. *Did I really just knock Arthur out with a stick?*

"Emma, you have to help me," Susie said. "I'll do this on my own if I have to. You know I will. I'll find a way to get to Europe and meet up with Caris. I'll do whatever I have to. I want to end the mists, completely and forever, as soon as possible. I'd have a much better chance of success if you come with me."

Was she right?

"Emma, look at me," Susie said softly. "Emma, please."

"You can't say for sure that you and Caris will eradicate the mists," I said numbly.

"No, not for sure, but isn't it worth a try? Think about what's at stake. You have to help me. Please, Emma. I need you."

I looked into her eyes, and something inside me broke, right then and there. It wasn't a surrendering; it was a shattering. After everything we'd been through together and everything we meant to each other, after everything I'd sacrificed to be with him, I was going to leave Arthur behind. I was going to help Susie instead of him. I was going to take her from his grasp, which would hurt him as deeply as any betrayal could.

I was going to risk my life to get her to Europe. I didn't have any other choice. Susie was right: Too much was at stake.

Susie knelt and grabbed Arthur under his armpits. "You get his legs. We have to put him somewhere he won't be found right away and tie him up before he wakes up."

I knelt and gripped a knee under each arm, wrapping my arm firmly around his leg. "What about Asher?"

"We'll need him," she said. "I'll come back later, after we deal with Larry."

"Barry," I corrected. "How are we gonna get past him?" I was working to get Arthur's lower extremities in a proper hold, and I felt Susie smile, a lightening of her affect. Only one thing made her smile like that. I said, sternly, "You're not going to shoot him with an arrow."

"Spoilsport."

"There'll be plenty of opportunities for you to kill raiders while we're trying to get to France. You're not going to kill good people who are just doing what they're supposed to."

"Then how do you suggest we get past Larry?"

"Barry."

"And, Emma, after we get out of Niverville, how are you going to get me to France?" Susie asked.

"That's my problem now? I thought you had a plan."

"My plan was to get you to help me, you know, somehow," Susie said, a bit cheekily under the circumstances.

Again, I could feel her smiling. I shook my head, as I hadn't figured out the answers to her questions. I hadn't figured out anything. I couldn't even believe I was doing this, setting out apart from Arthur. Tying him up and leaving him somewhere hard to find was an incomprehensible turn of events. Nor was it going to keep him from pursuing us, when he was released. It was just going to make him mad.

"Where do we take him?" Susie asked.

"The stable?" I said, more of a question than an answer.

Susie approved, and Arthur swayed in our grip as we carried him. He was deeply unconscious, and I worried suddenly that I'd hit him hard enough to leave a serious injury.

My brain skittered like a small, crazed animal along all the avenues now open to us. I had to get us out of the compound, and Barry or someone else was on duty in the guard shack by the gate. As for ferrying Susie across the ocean to France, I hadn't a clue. I understood that I had to get her there and connect her with Caris, and I accepted that I had to keep Susie out of Arthur's grasp, but how to accomplish those goals was a mystery.

"Emma, are you listening to me?" Susie asked in an impatient tone. "You're kind of spacing out on me. Could you pay attention?"

"What were you saying?"

Susie sighed, then grunted as she stumbled over something. She almost dropped Arthur's head but quickly righted herself. "What's your plan?"

"Do what I always do when confronted with an impossible situation," I said, sighing. "Set out, take one step after another, and trust that each step allows the following one to reveal itself."

"Lame," Susie said. "You'll have to do better than that if you're gonna help me save the world."

WE ARRIVED AT the stable. It was warm and smelly and inky dark inside, filled with that good, lush stable scent of horse manure and hay and warm-blooded creatures and the sounds of breathing, chuffing, sleeping animals. A barn cat ran underfoot, purring, and we both jumped. Arthur fell to the ground with a thud.

Susie pulled out her flashlight, but I laid my hand on her arm; it was better not to alert anyone to our presence inside the stable. She shrugged, and I felt around the walls until I found some reins. We tied Arthur's feet, then bound his hands behind his back and dragged him into an empty stall.

I knelt beside him and probed around his head, felt the wet, ragged tissue of the lump above his ear. That was going to hurt. I let the healing tingles flow out of my palm into the wound, until I knew that he would be fine but before he woke. I kissed his forehead gently. "I'm sorry, Arthur," I whispered, which brought a snort from Susie.

"You better gag him," she said. When I refused to, she did it herself.

We fumbled with our tack in the dark, found our horses, and saddled them as best we could. We led the animals out along St. Andrews Way, and I paused to tighten Count's girth again. Arthur would have been proud of my horsemanship, except that I was sneaking away from him in the middle of the night. We went back to the gate through which we'd entered Niverville a few hours ago.

"Emma, take this," Susie said, laying her reins in my free hand.

"What? Why?"

"Don't worry. I'm not going to kill Larry!" she said before melting into the dark.

"Whoa there! Hold up!" Barry called a few seconds later. He trotted out of the guardhouse and shined his flashlight in my face. "Emma? Where do you think you're going? And with two horses?"

"Oh, you know, running an errand," I said in as breezy a voice as possible under the circumstances.

"You need *two* saddled horses to run an errand?"

"There's no law against that in Niverville, is there?"

Barry directed his flashlight into my eyes.

I winced and turned my face away. "That's really bright, Barry."

"Right. Sorry." He dropped the flashlight to his side. "You

shouldn't go out there right now, Emma. There's no law against it, but it's not safe, eh? Whatever you need to do can wait till first light. Don't you—"Then he sprawled over onto the ground.

"Susie!" I jumped back.

"I know, right? It was a big shock when you did that to Arthur," she said, giggling. "It wakes you right up, like a double shot of espresso. I'll drag him back into the guardhouse and tie and gag him so he doesn't send anyone after us when he wakes up."

"I guess you'd better." I bent over and felt Barry's head; of course there was a wet gash. "He's bleeding. Wipe him up, will you?"

"Nah, he'll be fine. I didn't hit him that hard," she said. "We don't have to baby him." She looped her arms under his armpits and dragged him back inside the guardhouse.

I had to have a discussion with her about the value of compassion. Not that she'd listen to me after seeing me knock Arthur out.

"I'm going back to get Asher," Susie whispered upon her return. "Wait here with the horses."

"Asher," I muttered, having forgotten about him. "Let him be."

"No way! We need him," she said.

"We can't kidnap him!" I snapped, but softly. Now was not the time to rouse any onlookers. But Susie was already gone. It gave me a few minutes to argue with myself. *Why am I doing this? To save the world from the mists, right? Right.What the hell have I gotten myself into?*

Susie returned, dragging Asher by his feet. "Whew. He weighs a lot less than Arthur."

"We're not kidnapping him," I said.

"Emma, are you going to stand here and argue with me now, when you've trusted me this far?" Susie asked. "We need to get out of here with him."

I faced her. "I agree that it's important for you to meet
Caris in France, crucial and maybe our best chance of sav-
ing the world from the mists, even if it's a small chance. I'm
willing to do my best for you. I proved that when I, ah . . .
disarmed Arthur."

"Disarmed him?" Susie chortled, covering her mouth with
her hand to keep herself quiet. "You knocked him out cold!"

"Regardless, we are not going to abduct innocent strangers. No."

"We need him," she insisted. "He's important to what we
have to do over there. I won't leave here without him." She
took a challenging pose, crossing her arms over her chest and
throwing back her shoulders.

I stared at her and shook my head.

"C'mon, Emma," she pleaded. "You've come this far for
me. Trust me just a little more. We're not gonna kill him or
anything. We're just bringing him with us."

"His life is here."

"He has skills that we'll need at the other camp."

"If we take him, we'll have the people of Niverville on our
butts, right along with Arthur. More people on our tail means
a greater likelihood that we'll be caught before I can get you
across the ocean to do whatever it is you need to do with Caris
to save the world."

"Emma, I know that. If he wasn't so vital, I wouldn't have
grabbed him."

"Do you even know why he's vital?" I demanded.

She shook her head.

We squared off for a few more beats.

"Emma, please! We have to go now."

"It's wrong, Susie, just wrong. He has to choose to come
with us. Otherwise, we're no better than the raiders who
abused you against your will."

Susie drew back sharply. "Okay. Fair enough. When we
stop, we'll explain to him what we're doing, tell him you're

taking me to France to end the mists forever and that we need his help. I'm sure he'll agree to come with us. If he doesn't, we'll let him go, set him free, but he will. He'll choose to come with us when he understands how important it is, after we tell him what we're doing."

"Not 'we,' young lady. You . . . and if he wants out, we're giving him your horse." I hated myself for capitulating. "People say *I'm* a pain in the ass."

"Pack his glasses in your backpack, will you? And grab his feet," she said. "He'll ride with me."

6 WITH ASHER LYING UNCONSCIOUS ACROSS the horse in front of Susie's saddle post, we headed north toward St. Adolphe, where there was another bridge over the Red River. We rode at a fast trot. Young Count was superbly conditioned and could go for hours at that pace; Susie, who was a fine rider, had ended up with a strong hackney who wouldn't tire soon. I felt bad for Asher, who was tossed around like a ragdoll and would surely wake up with some aching bruises.

We got to the crossing and I noted that here, as around Ste. Agathe, the land was treeless and bare. The mist-affected children must have set fires here. I called, "Do we need to worry about the crazy kids?"

"No," she yelled. "You're with me, and they want me to do what I'm supposed to. They told me that when they took me for dinner."

"Did they tell you why they burned everything down here?"

"They don't know why. They don't know they're crazy," she yelled.

Right. We kept riding. Asher was still limp. I hoped Susie hadn't knocked him into a coma.

Talk about people not knowing they're crazy.

WE DIDN'T STOP until noon, at the remains of a complex of industrial buildings that had been partly burned and partly eaten by the mists. It was impossible to tell what the buildings had once been, there between Lord Selkirk Highway and Red River Drive, but one big, aluminum-sided warehouse structure still stood amidst the piles of yellow grit and the charred ruins. Susie jimmied the lock with her hunting knife, and she and I worked together to roll the garage-type door up its rusty hinges. We walked the horses in and rolled the groaning door back down behind us.

We stood on a concrete floor in a cavernous space. Grimy windows filtered in sunlight from fifteen or twenty feet up. Susie pulled a boneless Asher off her saddle and gripped him around his torso to drag him with us; his feet scraped furrows on the dirty floor. The air swirled with old dust as we made our way past corrugated steel shipping containers, to a spot near the back wall. Susie propped Asher up, and we sat down to eat and rest.

We had dried meat in our backpacks, and I had an old protein bar with a wrapper that was getting ratty. Considering that it was manufactured of all-natural, non-biodegradable petrochemicals in The Before, I figured it was still serviceable. I tore it in half and gave her the bigger piece. "We'll have to do something about food after this."

Susie tilted her head. "Want me to take something down if I see it? There's plenty of game."

"Not yet," I said through a mouthful of rubbery protein mush. "Tomorrow or the next day maybe. I'm sure Arthur's up and about, on his way after us. If we're going to elude him, we shouldn't slow down just yet. We have to keep moving until we're clear."

"Okay." She chewed in silence for a few moments. It was slow going with the leathery bar. "What do you think is in these containers?"

"No idea, but we should have a look. Maybe there's something useful."

She nodded agreement, chewed hard, then finally swallowed. "Emma, where are we going?"

"Hell if I know."

"Bullshit. You've been thinking like crazy. I've been watching your face while we ride. You know what you're doing."

I sighed. "We're going to Carstairs."

"You're going to ask your husband to fly us back to Europe?"

"It's a long shot," I warned. "He warned me never to come back to his home. He said he doesn't ever want to see me again."

"But he's your husband."

I gave her a look.

"Arthur," she spat, then made a scornful face. "Tell Haywood you're sorry, that you were, uh . . . deluded by the mists. Tell him you want to be with him again and that you're over Arthur. Tell him you knocked Arthur out with a big stick to get away from him. He'll like that."

"I'm not going to lie to Haywood about being over Arthur."

"What's more important?" She leaned toward me with a serious look on her pretty young face. "Taking me to Caris so we can get rid of the mists forever or pissing off the only man who can get us there quickly? You have to choose what's important, Emma."

"It's not that black and white," I retorted. Susie had a problem seeing nuance in situations.

"You're the one who's being black or white, refusing to tell your husband what he wants to hear, even when that will serve our needs. In case you have forgotten, we're trying to save the world."

"Here's black or white for you. I hope you haven't seriously hurt Asher. He should have woken up by now."

I crawled over to the man and examined him briefly. His

head was rolled down onto one shoulder, his eyes were closed, and the welt had crusted over with reddish-black, dried blood, but he was still breathing. After I rested a bit, I'd lay hands on him and let the healing gift wreak its magic.

"It's a bump on the head. He'll wake up eventually," Susie said, frowning. Suddenly she dropped the butt of her bar and grabbed up her bow.

There was a crunching of footsteps on the pavement outside the door, and a hand rapped on the inset glass window. A deep voice yelled, "Emma, are you in there?"

"Donny?" I leapt up and snaked my way through the shipping containers.

"Is he with Arthur?" Susie asked tightly, following me. She nocked an arrow into her bow and took aim.

I held up my hand, cautioning Susie to wait as we stepped into the area in front of the door. "Donny?"

"Yeah, it's me."

"*Just* you?"

"I with Donny," yelled Theo.

"Just us two, but I think Kangee will join us," Donny added. "You gonna let us in or what?"

Susie maintained her stance, but I raised the door. As soon as I strained to raise it, Donny and Theo helped from the other side. The door screeched along its rusty hinges but went all the way up, revealing Donny and Theo, standing there with their horses, gawking at me.

"Girl, put your guns down. We're not here to drag you back to Arthur," Donny said, his baritone voice both kindly and humorous.

"How'd you find us?" I asked. I turned to see if Susie had lowered her weapon. When I saw she hadn't, I made a face at her and made a curt hand gesture. "Susie!"

Susie tightened her grip on her bow. "We're not going back to Arthur."

"We know," Theo said, giving me a reproachful look. "Why

you not ask us for help? Emmy, you are sister. We are family."

"Arthur's crazy," Susie insisted, drawing the string of her bow.

I slapped her hand, not caring that she flinched. "Susie, stop. Theo, I'm sorry. I didn't know who we could trust. And I didn't think things out, I just acted. Spontaneously. It all just erupted in the moment. Suddenly I knew I had to get Susie away from Arthur."

"Arthur is . . . unbalanced," Donny said sadly. He rubbed his chin and sighed, eying Susie with a look of both introspection and curiosity. "The question is, are you a little addled, too, Susie?"

"No!" Susie shouted. "I know what I'm doing!"

Theo walked in and grabbed me in a big hug. "Emmy, you save Pyotr. I say you then, my life is yours. You think I choose Arthur over you?"

"Yes," I said simply. I laid my head on Theo's sturdy shoulder for a moment. It felt good to have Theo with us. He was a good man to have at my back in a fight, and I had no doubt that I was now fighting: fighting time and Arthur to get Susie over the ocean to Caris. Somehow, the two young women were supposed to confront mankind's destiny together. It all depended on them. I knew this not just from what Susie had told me but also from my own intuition.

"No, Emmy. I am for you," Theo said.

"How did you find us?" Susie snarled.

"Donny's telepathy, of course," I said. I squeezed Theo one last time, and then we stepped apart.

Donny shrugged. "I felt you two leave. I meant to come alone, but Theo said he'd raise a fuss if I didn't bring him."

"Did you tell anyone? Do they know where we're going?" Susie asked.

Donny shook his head. "We must have left not long after you did. You went along paved roads, and there weren't visible signs of your passing. I was following Emma's thoughts, but they won't track you so easily."

"Next time, think more quietly!" Susie said to me in her usual surly tone of voice.

"What the holy hades is going on?" called a voice behind us. Asher came around from behind a large shipping container. He rubbed the knot on his skull and peered owlishly at the four of us. "Where am I?"

7

SUSIE WAS YELLING AT ASHER. "YOU HAVE TO come with us. Don't you see that what we're doing is important?"

Asher glared at her and shook his head so ferociously he almost dislodged his glasses, which I had returned to him.

"Susie, take a walk," Donny suggested in a deep, rolling voice that left no room for argument.

Susie gargled a few expletives, then grabbed up her bow and strode out of the warehouse.

We sat just in front of the back wall. Theo had given Asher water and some buffalo jerky. I wiped the crown of his head, his face, and his neck, mopping up the blood, making clucking noises to try to soothe him.

"That girl is dangerous . . . and nuts," Asher said, frowning. He leaned into me so I could keep cleaning him. "My head hurts."

"She very good archer," Theo said, chewing on jerky. "Lucky she hit you and not shoot you."

"I try to keep her from killing random people," I said.

Donny sighed and made a frustrated gesture with his hands. "Susie has some issues, but she's the real thing when it comes to dissolving the mists. For the last month, I've sensed that she's connected to another mind. That must be the girl from the old camp. They have a unique, powerful connection, and they are definitely linked to the mists."

"Caris is at the women's camp," I murmured. "She's not at Arthur's old camp, which has been relocated further south from where it was when I was there."

"Well, if Susie says she and Caris can work together to end the mists, I believe her," Donny finished. "It's a long shot, but it's worth trying."

"Caris sweet girl. Won't hit you," Theo confided to Asher.

"I'm not going!" Asher exclaimed with a shiver. "There's no telling what Susie will do to me. She might kill me in my sleep. I swear, one minute I was sleeping in my bed, and the next, I was waking up here, no man's land. I never even heard her come into my room and didn't even feel her bonk me on the head." He reached up and searched his scalp with tentative fingers. "And the mouth on her! Somebody ought to leash and muzzle her."

"She's not so bad once you get used to her," I said, rubbing at the last smear of blood on the back of Asher's scrawny neck. His shirt was stained, but he'd eventually get another shirt. "Drink more water."

"Are my pupils equal in size?" Asher asked. He stuck his head in my face, his eyes only an inch away from mine.

"Yes. I already told you so."

"Check again."

"Asher, really," I said, trying not to be cross.

"You'll be fine," Donny said. "You can ride with me or Theo until we obtain a horse for you. Emma, what have we got to trade?"

"No. Uh-uh. No way," Asher said, shaking his head vigorously. "I'm going back to Niverville!"

"Asher, I understand. Really, I do," Donny said, in a soothing tone of voice, "but surely *you* understand that we're talking about an attempt to save the human race—or what's left of it anyway. Susie's the key to the most important mission human-ity has ever undertaken, and she's chosen you to accompany her. You're a vital part of this, with an integral role to play."

"Well, geez, don't make it like the stakes are high or any-thing, so there's not too much pressure on me." Asher made a face. "I've got a giant knot here."

"Head hurt for two days, maybe three. Not as bad as arrow wound," Theo said, shrugging.

"What if I have intracranial bleeding?" Asher said. He wrapped his arms around his skinny abdomen. "I feel nauseous."

"If you have bleeding in your brain, you'll start seizing, and we'll let Susie take an arrow to your skull so we can drain the blood," I said sweetly.

Asher shuddered.

"Asher, we need you," Donny said, sighing again. "Susie's right about that. You're some kind of genius, and my intuition matches hers. Somehow, you're a necessary part of this mis-sion. I trust my gut. You should come with us, son."

"But I don't want to," Asher objected. "I want to go back to Niverville. Lydia and I—"

"You and Lydia? No way in hell!" Theo laughed.

"Sometimes she, you know . . . hangs out with me," Asher said indignantly. "Is that so hard to believe?"

"Yes, too hard to believe," Theo said dryly.

"Women like smart men," Asher said, with a pout.

I bit the inside of my lip to keep from laughing. After a few breaths, I said, "Asher, think how impressed she'll be with you when you play a part in getting rid of the mists. She'll do a lot more than hang out with you. You'll be a hero."

Theo nodded vigorously. "Lydia give you action if you save world."

Asher lit up. "You really think so? Hmm. In that case, I'm in!"

"Good man!" Theo grinned and clapped Asher on his shoulder.

Asher toppled over sideways, and his glasses clattered on the floor.

I helped Asher up and handed his glasses back to him. I stood and walked away a few paces, working hard to contain my mirth and despair. So this was my crew for what Donny had called "humanity's most important mission ever": a bloodthirsty girl with PTSD, an ex-cop who read minds, a Serbian who spoke tortured English, and a nerd. Kangee, the Sioux woman with a gift for instantaneous travel, would probably show up too. Then we'd be all set, six of us to elude Arthur, an armed and trained soldier riding with other experienced warriors.

I pressed my fist into my mouth, wanting to laugh, even though I knew it wasn't funny. It was overwhelming. It was scary. I still didn't understand what I'd done or why. We had to keep from getting caught by the lover for whom I'd left my husband, the lover I'd knocked out and left bound and gagged in a horse stall. We had to make our way across the ocean to Europe, where we'd likely face gangs of rogue fighters, some of whom were cannibals, before we'd even reach the women's camp. *And then what?* I didn't know. I only knew I had to deliver Susie to Caris.

I'd had less and still managed to do what was necessary. Not even a year earlier, I'd left on foot and alone in the snows of Alberta to save my daughter Beth when she was kidnapped by raiders. Just a few months ago, I'd ridden with a mangled and dying Arthur, almost 1,000 kilometers before I was finally able to heal him. I could handle a big challenge. That would have to be my mantra.

Arthur. My mind went back to him, and I felt a stab of yearning for him. *He'll be so hurt, feel like I've betrayed him.* After everything we'd shared and everything we'd endured to be together, he would be stunned that I had rendered him unconscious and then absconded with Susie. I was still stunned. It was incomprehensible.

"Emmy, you good?" Theo called.

No, I'm torn up by a million conflicting feelings. "Yeah. I'm just thinking we should search the cargo bins before we ride out, in case there's some kind of food or other valuable goods," I called back. "Donny's right. We'll need to trade for a horse for Asher." I took a deep breath. "We should be quick about it though. I'm sure Arthur is coming after us."

"He is," Donny said, "and he's mad as a hornet."

THE BINS YIELDED electronics: cell phones, speakers, and computer components. We opened the last container and found sneakers.

"Damn," I said. "I was really hoping we'd find food or something valuable enough to trade. Asher needs a horse."

"Wait a minute," Asher said, holding up a pair of high-tech running shoes. "These are valuable."

"Sneakers?" I asked with some skepticism in my voice.

"Asher right," Theo said. He dug around the bin and threw several pairs out onto the floor. "No one making sneakers now."

"I'm going to snag a pair for myself," Donny said. "They're not great for riding because they don't have heels, but they're good to have. Shoes wear out on the road. I've had blisters on top of blisters, giving birth to blisters and their grandchildren."

"Really? Donny, I'm so sorry. Maybe I could have helped you." I held up my hands with their healing gift. "You never complained."

"Laurette complains enough for me," Donny said with a grin.

I grinned back at him.

"Laurette complain enough for us all," Theo said. "Emma, these your size? They look nice for you." He tossed me a pair of blue and green women's shoes.

Susie sauntered back in from outside and watched us root through the container.

"What size are you, Susie?" I asked. I gave her a sidelong glance. There was blood on her arm and hip, but I didn't want to ask about it. She'd probably shot a bird for the practice. Or we'd find a body lying somewhere outside and we'd pause to burn it, so pestilence didn't come to these parts.

"Nine in a sneaker." She moved over to stand behind me.

I tossed her a pair.

"Pink? Are you kidding? What if I have to sneak up on someone in the dark and kill them? These shoes will announce me a mile away." She threw the shoes back at me. "Get me some dark ones."

"Keep that crazy chick away from me," Asher muttered.

WE RODE OUT with a few dozen pairs of sneakers bundled up in rotting canvas tarp we'd found in one of the bins. Theo had used sneaker laces to attach our bounty to our saddles.

"We get you horse soon," Theo promised Asher, who was riding on the back of his horse.

"It'll have to be a gentle one," Asher said as he clung to Theo. "I'm not a very good rider."

"Emma terrible rider," Theo replied.

"Horrible," Donny affirmed.

"Hey! I'm improving!" I said.

That made Susie giggle, such an unexpected sound that Donny and I exchanged a glance. Susie had been even more sullen than usual over the past few weeks. It had been a while since we'd heard her laugh.

"I got to Niverville on a bicycle," Asher offered.

"One with training wheels?" Susie asked wryly.

Asher made a nasal, whuffling sound. "People who kidnap other people and intend to use them shouldn't make fun of them. No, it was a real bike, a Pinarello. I used to bike all the time, in The Before."

"Pinarello nice bike," Theo exclaimed.

"We should pick up the pace," Donny said. "I feel Arthur's intention to find us, and it's beyond powerful."

"Can you mislead him, send him away from us?" I asked. "You did that with Alexei, when I escaped after I traded myself for Arthur and Alexei was hunting me."

Donny shook his head. "Arthur's not telepathic the same way. I just hope he doesn't figure out where we're going. Which is . . .?"

"Carstairs. He'll figure it out." I knew that the same way that I knew my own name. Arthur had pursued me across an ocean and a continent to find me once already, and he would do it again. Eventually, there'd be a reckoning. I only hoped it would be on the other side of the Atlantic Ocean.

"How far is Carstairs from here?" Asher called.

"It's 1,000 kilometers plus," Theo estimated, "maybe 1,200 or 1,300."

"That's so far!" Asher said, with a small whimper.

"We'll go into the outskirts of Winnipeg to find a horse for Asher," Donny said. "Yah!" He moved ahead.

I pressed my heels into Count's sides, and he sprang forward.

Theo and Susie urged their horses on, too, and we were on our way.

WE RODE THROUGH the afternoon and into the evening without stopping. We looped west, along the perimeter of Winnipeg, and came to a rural municipality called St. Francis Xavier. We then made our way to a well-lit Roman Catholic church, where a group of families were cleaning up after dinner in the community hall. They invited us to sit and served us their leftover buffalo meat and early peas; every bite was fresh and delicious.

The priest, a small, lithe Spanish man wearing a thread-bare broadcloth clerical shirt, sat and chatted with Donny while the rest of us ate quietly. The priest looked Susie and me over carefully with his piercing but not unkind eyes, then rose from the table to speak with a parishioner and her toddler.

I looked at the little boy, then at the other children play-ing or rolling on the floor or hanging onto their parents. The kids here seemed happy and sane. I wondered if this munic-ipality had suffered through scout mists, as Niverville had. I wondered if they'd lost children to madness and parents to murder.

Donny reached across the table to touch my arm. "There's a family that keeps horses about twenty kilometers northwest of here, outside a town called St. Eustache. Father Juan thinks they'll trade for sneakers. He asked us to donate a pair."

"Of course he wants something from us," Susie said, with a very teenaged rolling of her eyeballs.

"We can donate a pair, and we should. We ate their food. We'll still have enough to trade," I said.

Donny nodded. "It's the right thing to do."

"Those sneakers are like money was in the old days," Susie said. "We will need them to buy stuff. We have to hang on to them."

"We will, girl, but we can do right along the way," Donny said. "We can't forget who we are."

"Nothing matters but getting me to Caris," Susie said.

Father Juan bustled back, carrying a tray with small pots de crème bowls. He set one in front of each of us, and I saw they were filled with a yellow and white pudding. He took the last bowl for himself and sat down to eat it. "So you're headed west now?"

"East," I said brightly. I lifted the spoon to my mouth and

nearly swooned with rapture. "Oh! This is amazing! What is it, honey and clotted cream?"

Father Juan smiled. "One of our parishioners is a chef, and he's become an expert at making delicious meals with what we have on hand. He's got a particular talent for sweets."

"Fresh honey," Theo groaned in delight. "Mmm . . ."

"We keep bees," Father Juan said proudly. "I was under the impression that you're headed west, after visiting the Allen's horse farm."

"East," I corrected.

"East," Theo repeated.

"East," Susie said firmly.

"That's right, east," Donny agreed, in his usual affable tone.

"We're going to get a boat in Quebec," I added.

"Boat in Quebec," Theo stated solemnly.

Father Juan shrugged. He looked skeptical but didn't pursue the matter.

We all focused on the pots de crème honey-and-cream dessert, which was insanely delicious, soft in the mouth like a custard, with rivulets of golden honey running into the tangy cream. Spoons clattered, and we all sighed. Theo licked his index finger and ran it around the inside of the little bowl, gathering the last sweet slicks onto his fingertip.

"Theo, manners," I chided.

"Too good, Emmy," Theo said apologetically. "Best honey. Too good."

"I think we can spare a jar for you, especially if you're donating a pair of sneakers," Father Juan offered.

"We need our sneakers. If we give them away, we'll have nothing left to trade!" Susie snapped. "Who do you think you are, hitting us up for our goods?"

I trod on her toes. "We'd be delighted to accept a jar of honey, and we'll leave you two pairs, one for women and one for men."

Father Juan smiled. "Five pairs and I won't mention you

were here when whoever you're running from comes looking."

"Father, that's highway robbery!" Susie shouted. "You're mugging us."

Father Juan spread out his hands without a whiff of shame. "Just taking care of my parish. Sneakers are hard to come by, and my people need shoes."

"Emma, you can't do this!" Susie said hotly.

"Four pairs," I countered, placing a warning hand on Susie's arm.

"Deal!" Father Juan reached across the table and shook my hand.

Susie tossed her head and emitted a sound of disgust.

The priest avoided looking at her.

Asher broke the awkward silence. "Any chance you have a doctor in your parish, someone who could look at my head?"

"Sure, son," exclaimed Father Juan. "I noticed that big lump. Are you okay?"

"He's fine," I said in the take-no-prisoners voice I'd perfected for dealing with naughty children. "He doesn't need a doctor. We'll leave you the shoes, take our honey, and be on our way."

"It's late. You're free to spend the night if you wish," Father Juan offered.

"How many pairs of sneakers will that cost us?" Susie snapped.

Father Juan grinned and shook his head. "Putting you up for the night would be the Christian thing to do."

"No, we have to go," I insisted. "We want to get to Quebec quickly. We just need directions to the horse farm."

THE EVENING WAS cool and pleasant, embroidered with the chirping of insects. My stomach was full, which was always a good thing in such precarious days. I situated the big thermos of honey in my backpack, then mounted Count and trotted out from the church parking lot to Route 26. I looked behind and saw that Donny was still taking leave of the priest. In the torch-lit lot, a few parishioners waved and smiled and called out good wishes.

Nice folks, living outside a Safe Zone. They hadn't been scourged by the mists yet, but the mists could come at any time. I thought how much happier they'd be when they didn't have to fear the mists' incursion. I imagined them safely living ordinary lives, whatever "ordinary" could possibly mean in The After. It boosted my energy and eased some of the second-guessing that had bedeviled me since we'd left Arthur behind. Donny had said we were on "the most important mission humanity has ever taken," and if we succeeded, it would be worth all the hardships. I sat up straighter in my saddle.

Susie rode up next to me. "Do you think the priest bought it, that we're going east?"

I shrugged. "He's a canny one."

"Greedy too. Four pairs of our sneakers!" Susie grumbled. "I don't like him."

"He's good at his job."

"I still don't like him."

"You don't have to, but you can respect what he's doing for his people."

"Emma, you're such a Pollyanna." Susie grunted and pressed her horse to a faster trot, moving ahead of me.

Donny joined me. "Should only take us a few hours to reach the horse farm, if we keep this pace."

"Susie's getting harder to handle," I murmured. "She's more stubborn and recalcitrant every day."

"Yes, I've been wondering what you plan to do about that."

"I don't know how much longer I can keep her in check," I said. "I cannot imagine what she'll be like if she gets beyond my reach. I hope she doesn't decide we're hampering her and shoot us in the back."

"We'll get her to the other girl across the Atlantic," Donny reassured me. "Your husband will agree to help us."

"He was pretty adamant that I should never come back."

"If I was Laurette, I'd tell you that's your own damn fault," Donny said, wearing a smile I couldn't see in the fresh purple air of night but could certainly hear. "Since I'm not Laurette, I'll tell you to hang in there and do your best. Things will work out."

They have to, I thought; I didn't speak aloud because it wasn't necessary. He understood the import of what we were doing.

"It'll all be worth it. You'll see," Donny continued. "Someday soon, this world will be free of the mists, and we'll have played a role in that."

"I wish you had precognition instead of telepathy."

That elicited a snort of laughter. "You and me both, woman."

Theo, with Asher riding behind him, trotted up to join us. "What joke I miss?"

"The joke that Donny can read minds instead of seeing the future," I said in a light tone.

Theo made a sympathetic face. "Emmy, you worry too much. Don't worry."

"I think she should worry," Asher said in a glum tone. "I'm worried. Worry is for sane people who are riding in unknown territory outside the Safe Zones in the dark, following a crazy chick to who-knows-where and who-knows-what."

Theo turned around and smacked Asher on his head.

Asher squealed. "Hey! I've got a head injury here! You could give me a concussion."

"Do not make Emmy feel worse!" Theo scolded. "Bad Asher!"

But Bad Asher was only voicing aloud the refrain in my head.

8 WE DIDN'T REST FOR ALMOST TWENTY-
four more hours. We found the horse farm near
St. Eustache and woke the family, left twenty-two pairs of brand-new, high-tech sneakers
with them, and rode off with Asher sitting atop a gentle bay
gelding who was only a little long in the tooth.

We rode east when we left the family because we said we
would and we wanted them to see us doing it. We kept riding
until the first pink and orange puffs of dawn wafted up on the
horizon. We approached a town called Rosser, and only then
did we loop around and head northwest.

We rode through the day and stopped briefly at an abandoned farmhouse for water and a few bites of beef jerky. We
let the horses graze and drink water from a trough filled with
rain water, then rode out again.

We finally reached Portage la Prairie, a town that had
been mostly devoured by the mists. Yellow grit coated great
swathes of ground; it wasn't in piles anymore, it had settled
into swirling kilometer-wide fractal patterns. Nothing had
been burned. A very few structures still stood: some houses, a
few garages, some office buildings, a school, a florist shop. We
saw no people or domesticated animals. We all needed food
and rest, so we rode up to an abandoned brick house near the
serpentine Assiniboine River.

The door to the house had been locked. Theo took

a screwdriver to the lock plate and the door gave way. He entered first, with his gun drawn—because this was The After, so there could be a crazy person inside. Anything was possible.

I stepped in behind Theo and breathed in moist, stale air. Dust sueded the furniture and the lights had long since gone dark because of the failed electricity. Otherwise, the house was just as it was the day its hapless owners had left it. They had probably fled the mists.

Theo and Susie settled the horses while Donny and I went through the house. Asher stretched out on the living room sofa, rubbing his bottom and complaining about saddle sores.

"He doesn't have saddle sores," I told Donny. We stood in the kitchen checking cabinets. "I've had saddle sores. They're unbelievably painful. You literally can't sit."

"Asher likes to bellyache, it's what makes him charming," Donny said. He held up a can of tomato sauce. "Lotta canned goods. We can feast tonight."

"Good, because we've barely eaten since the church," I said. "Any protein?"

"Ha, yes!" Donny crowed. "Looky here!" He held up cans of tuna in each fist.

"Whoa!" I crowded in behind him to see into the pantry. "And pork and beans, and chili, and rice, and my, oh, my, is that spam?"

"Yes, and we should pack it for when we can't hunt. I prefer the game that Susie or Theo shoots," Donny said. He was rummaging through the cans. "Carrots, peas, beans, pears, corn, fruit cocktail, tomato sauce, lots of soup . . . ."

"I don't think we should hunt tonight, just heat up what we've got here," I said. "We'll pack up the rest and take it with us."

"Did I hear someone say soup?" asked Susie. For once, her pretty face wore a bright smile. She came over and stood behind me, peering over my shoulder.

"You sure did," I told her.

"I'd kill for some tomato soup," she said. She rested her chin lightly on my shoulder, a rare affectionate gesture.

"Don't kill anyone before dinner, sweetie, it's not polite," I responded, in a dry tone.

"Sheesh, Emma, you're so literal." Susie giggled. "I'll see if I can get the grill outside going so we can start cooking."

"I'll help," Donny said.

I continued looking through the kitchen. I'd become an expert at scavenging, as we all had. You never knew what you would find or when it might suddenly become essential. Food wasn't the only valuable resource. Knives, can openers, silverware, tools, matches, batteries, flashlights . . . all those items had a utility in The After that I couldn't have imagined in The Before. Though recently the batteries we'd found had been dead, even the ones still factory-wrapped in new packages. Some canned goods weren't good anymore. Sooner or later the expiration date would come due for all old comestibles, of course.

I just hoped the mists would finally be gone, completely vanquished, when that day came. I hoped this mission that we were on would have led to that outcome.

After a feast of canned goods, Theo and I pushed the sofa in front of the door so no one could enter without waking us. Then we all slept ten hours. Susie and I had bunk beds in a girl's room upstairs. Donny took the master bedroom, Theo slept in a third bedroom whose school awards and soccer trophies identified it as an older boy's room, and Asher curled up his long, skinny form onto a futon behind a pool table in the finished basement.

It was late morning when Susie and I went downstairs. Donny was up and handed us each a mug of steaming hot tea.

"Earl Grey, with sugar," he said, gesturing with a flourish.

"Oh, wow," I said, inhaling the beautiful, crisp scent of the tea. My body kind of wilted in anticipation. I loved caffeine in The Before, seldom got it now. Tea was a treat.

"SpaghettiOs for breakfast," he said.

"My favorite!" Susie said. She took her mug to the kitchen table and seated herself. A big cast-iron skillet sat on a trivet on the table, and she ladled SpaghettiOs into a bowl. "This is yummy, it's like, a real breakfast!"

Her cheerfulness was so unexpected that Donny and I exchanged a glance.

"Susie, are you okay?" I ventured. I went to sit beside her and serve myself some food.

"You're upset when I'm cranky and you're upset when I'm happy," Susie said, around a mouthful of pasta. "Make up your mind, will you?"

"The mood swings aren't so easy for us," I said, but gently, so as not to trigger one.

She shrugged and kept eating.

Theo came in and sat with us. "Horses good, are grazing."

Donny set a cup of tea in front of him. "I'll go pick out their hooves. Emma's horse's gait was off last night."

"Already done," Theo told him. He looked at me with a crooked grin. "Emmy horse walk good today."

"Thank you, Theo." I patted his arm.

He bobbed his head. "Man of house too tall for me, too short for Donny. Not many clothes here for us. Maybe Asher."

"I saw that," Donny said. "We won't be able to scrounge much here. But Emma, the woman of the house must have been about your size. You should look through the closet in the master bedroom." He set another cup of tea onto the table at an empty place, and on cue, Asher stumbled in.

"What'd I miss?" Asher asked.

"You're just in time for breakfast," Susie answered, with a lilt. "Chow down!"

Asher took the seat with the extra mug, scrunching his face at Susie. "What's wrong with Susie?"

"Susie in good mood," Theo said, shaking his head. "Very

dangerous, Susie in good mood. Maybe some dead raiders outside front door?"

"Yeah, Susie, let me check your quill, are you missing some arrows?" Donny teased.

"Ha-ha, you guys." Susie made a face of mock-disgust. "Emma, there's a really nice down coat in the front hall closet. It would be perfect for you. It looks new—the tags are still on it. You should take it for next winter."

"I'll pack it," I said.

"From here to Carstairs?" Asher asked. He sipped his tea. "Is that the plan?"

"It'll be a month of riding hard," Donny rumbled. He seated himself, finally, having attended to the rest of us.

"Maybe we really should go east," I said, uneasily. "If Haywood refuses to help us, we'll have wasted that month."

"If he doesn't agree to help us, we'll threaten to shoot him," Susie offered, with complete equanimity.

We all looked at her.

"She's back," Asher said, in a disgruntled tone. He was heaping SpaghettiOs onto a plate but he paused to give her a sour look.

"That's what you guys expect me to say," Susie observed.

"We're not shooting my husband," I said, a little wearily.

"Arthur thank us if we do," Theo noted.

"Do you have a plan for approaching Haywood, Emma?" Donny asked, changing the subject. He unscrewed the lid on a jar of maraschino cherries, perfectly preserved for all these apocalyptic years by carcinogenic Red Dye No. 67, plopped several onto his plate, and passed the jar to Susie on his left.

"Well, yes. I'll appeal to his reason and his better self. We're on a mission to save the world after all. That's what you said, Donny, and it's true. That ought to mean something."

Donny sighed. "You left the man for your lover, you really think he's going to listen to reason? He's got some pride."

Asher pushed his glasses up the bridge of his nose and

squinted at me from behind the thick lenses. "I think you should have a backup plan."

I said, "I do. I'm going to grovel and plead."

Asher said, "How about seducing him? See if there's any hot lingerie here and bring it with you."

"We were married a long time. I don't think he'll be susceptible to that," I said doubtfully.

Asher leaned over to grab my arm. He actually winked at me. "He's a man, he'll be susceptible. I can imagine you in hot lingerie. You'd be very convincing."

Susie wrinkled her nose. "Ick, Asher."

"Don't imagine me that way, Asher," I said. "It gives me the creeps."

"We'll shoot him, that's the backup plan," Susie said.

"We're not shooting Emma's husband, the father of her children," Donny said sternly. "No more of that talk, young lady."

Susie shrugged.

"Begging might work," I said. "It might."

AN HOUR LATER, we left with our horses laden with objects, clothes, and food scavenged from the house. We packed every single viable foodstuff, and we'd found backpacks and canvas sacks to attach behind our saddles.

The weather was mild, sunny, and warm. The next several days of riding passed uneventfully. There was no sign of mists or raiders or Arthur. We rode from early morning until dusk. We looked for abandoned homes to sleep in, and only once had to camp outdoors. That night we didn't build a fire because we didn't want to alert anyone to our presence; we ate the canned tuna we'd found in Portage La Prairie. There was no sign of anyone pursuing us, but smoke traveled, so we didn't take the risk.

Sleeping out under the stars, I dreamt as I hadn't in a

while. First I was walking along a river bank with cherry blossoms arching overhead. It smelled wonderful, and I was aware of the sweetness of the flowers permeating my breath. A cloud of blue butterflies rose up out of the water. Suddenly, as a swarm, they fluttered back down to the quickly undulating surface of the river. I watched them in confusion as their wings stilled and they were pulled under. I was worried but then I realized that I wasn't alone.

A man was sitting under a tree, looking out onto the river. It was a Rastafarian man with glossy dark skin, long black dreadlocks, and a saintly, beatific expression on his face. He glanced up and his smile of welcome and compassion grew larger. He waved at me.

I went over and sat beside him.

"What's it to you?" he asked. "What is it to *you?*" He moved his hand through the air, and then he opened his hand, and he was scattering crystalline beams of light everywhere.

"I've seen you before," I said.

He laughed as the Buddha might laugh, with peace and understanding beyond human comprehension.

"You come here and talk to me but I don't know what you mean," I said. In the dream I tried to grasp his arm, but it slipped away, like time or certainty. "What are you saying? What does it mean? Why did the butterflies fall into the river?"

"It's your dream, my girl," he said, laughing still.

The dream evaporated and I was left with an inchoate feeling of loss. I woke still sad and tossed about on my bedroll. I watched the stars for a while and then must have drifted off again.

I was walking up a set of stairs and I paused on the landing, remembering this place, this building, these stairs. *Oh, yes, I'm in Outpost City, in a guesthouse where I once went with Arthur*, I thought. That thought was pursued by another: *Is Arthur here?*

That thought hadn't fully evanesced from my head when a crunching sounded on the stairs below me. I turned, and it was Arthur, treading up after me, lifting his head to meet my gaze.

"Arthur!" I thrilled to look into his gray eyes.

"Emma, finally," he said, with a sound that was part dismay and part laughter. Roughly he pulled me by my shirt front into his body. He was tall and warm and strong and his desire emanated from him in palpable waves.

I put my hands on his chest. I wanted to surrender to his mouth and hands, I yearned to touch him and receive him, but I had to talk to him. "Arthur."

"No," he breathed. He captured my wrists and held them together with one hand. "You won't knock me out and leave me tied up and gagged in a stable." He jerked my arms up and wrapped his other arm around my waist. He bent his head to kiss my neck, and his tongue left a thin, exquisite line of fire where it traced along my collarbones.

"Arthur, I had to take Susie. I had to go." My voice trembled. I was hungry all over for him.

"You could have stayed and talked to me. We're together, you and me. You could have chosen to trust me. To work it out with me. I deserve that of you." Arthur pushed me back down onto the stairs. He gripped my wrists tightly above my head and used his other hand to unbutton my shirt. "But I will find you."

Unless I sent him in the wrong direction. "Arthur, we're going east. East. Meet me in Quebec."

"Wait for me," he whispered against my throat. "Stop traveling and wait."

"I will."

"East, fine. We'll meet you." He ran his mouth over the lace of my bra. His hand unzipped my pants and moved them down over my thighs. "No more talking, Emma. I want you."

I didn't argue with him because my tongue was tasting his, and my hips were rising to meet his, and deep waves of pleasure held me in thrall.

When the pleasure subsided, he was absent as if he'd never been with me. Only the marks of his teeth on my neck and belly, and the soft padding of his skin in my fingernails, remained.

Now I was walking through a stone canyon, like the Grand Canyon, only larger, much larger, so large that I was a tiny speck of dust drifting in the granite basin, staring up at red and yellow and gray stone walls that loomed higher than the sky.

A figure waved in the distance.

I felt relief. I ran to join the other person. The walls shifted around me like a living labyrinth, cutting me off and redirecting me over and over again.

"I can't find you!" I was shouting.

"I found you," said the person.

I turned and there he stood, as warm and imposing as life, a big blond man, tall and muscled, wearing the calm expression of the innocent and the deranged. I said, "Alexei."

"It is me," he said, in his throaty Russian accent. He stared around at the canyon walls. "What a sad dream you create for yourself."

"What are you doing here, Alexei? What do you want?" I asked.

He gave me a bitter smile. "What do I want? What do I always want? To help you, Emma. To be with you and to help you."

"That's not what you always want."

"Have I not help you many times before?"

I said, "You kidnapped my daughter and beat my husband almost to death."

"I hurt your husband in body. You hurt him much worse, in heart," he parried. He narrowed his eyes, as if in concern. "Why do you not make a happy dream for yourself? This is, how do you say, oppressive."

"My dreams just come to me," I murmured.

Alexei laughed. "No. We choose our dreams with our life's choices."

"You've been silent for a while, Alexei. You've left me in peace. Why are you here, now?"

"You need me, Emma. Arthur comes to you." He shouldered closer to me so I could feel the warm outline of his body against mine.

"Arthur thinks we're heading east, that's what we told the priest and the family at the horse farm." I tried to step away but in the dream, my feet were rooted to the spot, as if they were stuck in thick molasses. I couldn't leave Alexei's side.

"That's what you told him when he made love to you just a few minutes ago," Alexei noted.

"He believed me. He said he did."

"No, Emma. You did not fool Arthur. Arthur is smart. I do not like the man, but I never underestimate him." Alexei clucked his tongue, admonishing me.

"Arthur said he would meet me in Quebec, he believed me!"

"Arthur pretended to believe you. He is coming toward you right now. He is man possessed, driving his people and horses past exhaustion. I never treat my men and animals so bad." He put his hand on my shoulder and pressed down. "Wake, beautiful Emma, wake and ride. Ride south and west. North there are raiders, and Arthur your dream lover is coming for you. Your dream lover whose head you hit with a stick."

"No, Alexei, you're wrong," I shouted, but in the dream the words froze in my throat.

"Wake. Come to me, Emma, I will help you. Not Arthur, but I will help you. And the girl with the power!" His hand became a giant stone on my shoulder.

I sat up with a cry in the dawn. I was clutching at my shoulder, which tingled as if it had received an electric shock. The mauve light of early morning wrapped me in a cool breeze like a mantle.

"Emmy, you okay?" Theo crawled over and wrapped his arms around me, embracing me snugly.

I was shaking and my teeth were chattering.

"Bad dream, Emma?" Donny asked. He, too, clambered over to sit by me. He took my hands and rubbed them briskly between his, as if my hands had suffered extreme cold and frostbite.

Susie stood on her knees behind me and rubbed my shoulders over Theo's arms. "Emma, what are these marks on your neck? They look like hickeys."

Arthur had left marks. How real was the dreamtime? Were the boundaries between worlds effacing more, as the mists evolved? "Bug bites," I finally managed. Then, "Alexei showed up in my dreams. He says that Arthur is on our tail."

"We left a red herring for him back at the church and at the horse farm, he'll think we're heading east," Donny said.

I shook my head and gulped in air as if the alveoli of my lungs were dehydrated. Maybe they were, because of the dreamtime experiences, which had such a palpable effect on me. "Alexei says Arthur wasn't fooled, and that he's riding hard after us, driving his people and animals to exhaustion."

Donny released my hands and sat back on his haunches. "That sounds like Arthur."

"It sure does," Susie said fiercely. From behind me, she jumped to her feet and went to roll up her blanket. She called, "Saddle up. Let's go!"

I leaned forward to whisper, "Alexei knows about her. I think he wants her."

"Trouble," Donny muttered. He started rubbing his chin, chafing at it the way he did when he was upset. "If he wants her, he may come after us."

"Big trouble," Theo whispered. "Arthur and Alexei both want Susie."

"Tell her?" I wondered.

Both men shook their heads.

"Susie, she's . . ." Donny scrubbed at his chin ferociously. Abruptly he dropped his hands. "She's stretched too taut already, like a rubber band about to break. I think we need to minimize stressors."

"Agree," Theo said. "You can ride, Emmy?"

I nodded and we roused Asher and rode off, headed south and west.

9 ONE MOMENT IT WAS QUIET. IT WAS A WARM day and we were riding west along route 257, south of a deserted town called Virden. The mists had been through but many buildings remained. Donny was debating with himself the merits of veering off to scavenge. The rest of us rode quietly, not really listening to him, each absorbed in our own thoughts.

The next moment, horses raced out of a side street that joined 257 at a narrow oblique angle, so the trees hid it from view.

We heard the heavy thudding of fast hooves and suddenly Susie's horse reared straight up.

Susie screamed, "Raiders!"

At least a dozen raiders burst out, surrounding us, shooting arrows and throwing spears. One of them had a gun and was firing. They weren't speaking but simply worked together in tight, experienced battle mode.

Still mounted, Susie was nocking arrows and aiming with almost inhuman speed. Theo and Donny had leapt down and were firing their guns from behind their horses. I struggled to get my gun from my backpack.

Then Count went down onto his knees and I saw a thick wooden shaft and a gush of scarlet blood rising from the meat of his shoulder. I knew he'd been hit and I jumped off before he could roll atop me.

The leap probably saved my life, because an arrow whistled past Count right where I'd been just a second ago, and then another arrow slammed into my poor young horse's chest. He went down on his side and I knew he was done.

I had my gun in hand and was aiming. There were only a few bullets so I had to make them mean something. When the gun was empty, I had a knife. I was buzzed with the smell of fresh blood and pumped up with adrenalin and terrified by the loud banging of the gun and unnerved by the silence of the raiders. It was hard to focus.

I looked one of them in his eyes, which were blank like granite, and nailed him in his throat. The gun's recoil went through my whole body. The raider tumbled off his horse, but his foot caught in the stirrup and he was dragged a few meters, spraying blood.

All of a sudden it was over. Rider-less horses pranced around, flaring their nostrils; Donny's horse and some of the raiders' horses were down, whinnying with pain. Theo, Donny, Susie, and I stood panting and looking around in shock, our weapons drawn. Asher had, wisely, taken cover behind Count. We'd have to get Asher a gun or a bow, maybe off one of the dead raiders, I thought, a reflexive assessment.

Theo called, exulting, "We got 'em! Were they Alexei's men?"

"No, Alexei's men have one sleeve differentiated, to commemorate when Alexei's arm was gone," I said.

"They're just run of the mill savages," Susie said, sneering.

"Run of the mill, down and dead!" Theo said, pumping his fist in the air.

I turned to hug Theo but at that moment, a second wave of silent riders stormed out from behind the trees. There were more of them this time, fifty maybe, coordinated and throwing spears and shooting arrows. All we heard was galloping hooves. Then the sky darkened with projectiles. They were on us.

Susie never faltered. She was amazing, shooting arrows smoothly as if she'd never paused. Each one hit a bull's eye in a raider's chest, neck, or head.

Theo and Donny were laying down covering gunfire, trying to shoot raiders and at the same time keep her clear so she could keep shooting.

I had to choose my targets carefully. I had maybe two bullets left. I got one guy in his belly and another guy in his thigh. The thigh shot wasn't optimal but the raider slumped over his horse, seemingly disabled. People were grunting and some of the fallen raiders were moaning and cursing. Arrows were still raining down. I ducked and dodged and crawled on the ground to reach one of the fallen raiders, so I could take his bow and shoot his friends.

I had the fury of battle running through my veins like liquid fire, but the part of my brain that could record and evaluate was telling me that we were done for. There were too many of them and too few of us. We would run out of firepower. Susie's quill would empty and the guns carried only a few shots anyway. There had been other, prior battles that cost us the ammunition.

Theo dropped his gun and grabbed up a bow.

"Emma, remember your promise to me," Susie yelled. She had come to the same conclusion I had: that we were doomed.

I fought down a swell of nausea. Long ago, when she first joined our group, I had solemnly promised Susie, on the lives of my children, that I would never allow her to be taken again by raiders. She had suffered too much the first time. I had promised her that I would end her first, through whatever means I had.

"Emma, remember!" Susie yelled again. "Emma, get a bow, keep your promise!"

Donny grunted and went down with an arrow sticking out of his leg. I couldn't see how bad it was.

I scrabbled toward a dead guy and rolled him onto his side.

I took up his bow and then grabbed his quiver off his shoulder. I wasn't nearly as accurate an archer as Susie, but then who was? I aimed carefully, the way Arthur had taught me to, and an oncoming rider took the arrow in his gut.

One down, dozens to go.

"Emma, now!" Susie howled. "Come on!"

I turned to see that she knelt on the ground surrounded by three raiders whose arrows were trained on her.

Her quiver was empty and her bow was dropped. Her hands were raised above her head. Her plum dark eyes met mine. She yelled, "Now!"

Another wave of nausea shook me. Hand shaking, I aimed at Susie.

Without warning, the world split open again. Dozens of forms materialized among us. They were howling and flinging slingshots and wielding knives even as their bodies took corporeal form. But these were not silent, mounted warriors. These people were too small. They were children, and they ran at the raiders' horses and slashed at the raiders' legs. Some of them simply threw themselves at the horses so the horse reared or stumbled, and woe betide the raider who was unseated, because the shrieking children fell to dismembering him.

The remaining raiders quickly drew back in tight formation to fire at the children. The children kept running at them, and the mounted raiders simply aimed their arrows and let loose. It was a slaughter.

Susie was unencumbered again and she was crawling on the ground, knife in hand. I knew she must be looking for a dead raider with a quiver full of arrows.

A little brunette girl no more than six or seven years old went down in a spray of blood, an arrow sticking out of her eye socket, and I felt her death in my own body—the shocking absence of gravity, the intense complete immersion of light.

I couldn't move. I was frozen in place, watching the massacre. Still the children emerged onto the street from some mysterious fold in space. As they solidified, they ran toward the raiders. When those in front fell, the children in the rear clambered over their fallen comrades. I saw a tall Asian boy, a teenager, leap from behind two of his friends who had taken spears to their chests. He literally threw himself up a horse, and one of his hands jerked the raider off his saddle and the other hand slit the raider's throat.

"No, Emmy!" Theo screamed. He jumped in front of me and took an arrow in his solar plexus. He fell and rolled, groaning.

That arrow had been meant for me.

I dropped the bow and fell to my knees to pull Theo face-up. "Theo!"

"Oh, no, Emmy," he whispered. "Fight now, heal later." Blood leaked out around his mouth.

"Emma!" yelled Donny. A quiver of arrows landed near me.

"I have to heal Theo," I yelled.

"Not this second," he hollered back. He was dragging himself along the ground, leaving a trail of blood.

"Theo, don't die, wait for me," I begged. I wanted to weep but I grabbed an arrow from the quiver and started shooting. My first arrow went wild but the next one got a raider's horse in its quarters, and when the horse stumbled, a group of children tore the raider down. A confetti of flesh and blood exploded.

The Asian boy was lethal and wreaking havoc. He had killed another raider with his leaping technique, and he got the guy's bow and arrows and ran them to Susie. Then he stood with his back to hers as she fired. He moved slightly from side to side behind her and he slung stones from a slingshot. His stones took down raiders.

I saw that he was protecting Susie so I tried to protect

him. I looked for raiders with him in their sights and I aimed
at them. I got one just as he was launching a spear at the boy;
the spear went wild and the raider fell.

The boy met my eyes: Thanks. Then he was back to sling-
ing stones. His aim with that small weapon was just as deadly
accurate as Susie's with her bow.

Donny had dragged himself to my fallen horse. He struggled up to stand on his knees. Asher ducked down and came
around behind him and clasped him around his barrel chest in
support. Now Donny could hold a bow and draw the string.
Donny was sweating and shooting back at the raiders while
scrawny Asher held him up.

Theo lay at my feet, gurgling and bleeding. His rasping
breath told me that he was suffering.

I used up the arrows in the quiver and looked about for
some more.

The Asian boy grunted and dropped, an arrow in his hip.

Then there was stillness.

The raiders were all down. Children were hacking at them
with knives, and there were limbs and body parts strewn
everywhere.

I knelt by Theo. "Theo! Talk to me!"

He couldn't speak and just looked at me from out of glazed
eyes. His face was smeared with blood and creased in agony.

"No, Theo, don't die on me, please, Theo, I need you," I
said. I held out my hands and they answered, filling with the
tingles and warmth of the healing current that had magically
come into them in The After. I laid my hands on Theo and the
soft flow of energy ran off into him.

"Emma, we need you over here, Tae-yul needs you!" Susie
called, urgently.

"Not now," I yelled. I stayed focused on Theo. The healing
current was draining out of my hands into him, but his own
inner current, the thrum of his personal energy, was terribly debilitated. It wasn't vibrating anymore and the resonance

was fading. I could feel him weakening. The healing current wasn't healing him.

Susie came over and dropped to her knees beside us. "Oh, Theo," she said in a low voice. She took one of his hands in her own and kneaded it pleadingly. "Don't go. Emma needs you."

Theo tried to smile. Then his body shuddered.

"No!" I cried. I intensified the healing current and forced it into his body. I perspired both from the exertion and from the heat of the powerful current. My hands had never poured forth this much energy, not even when Alexei held a gun to my head and promised to kill me if I didn't heal his son, not even when I had finally regenerated Arthur's amputated arm and brought him back to life. This was it, the moment of maximum healing power, the very peak of all that I had experienced.

A foul odor leaked out as Theo's body shuddered and expelled its waste.

"No, no!" I gasped. I amped up the current one more time.

"Emma." Susie laid her hands on my arm. "He's gone."

"I can bring him back," I cried. One more time, I intensified the strength of the healing current.

A gust of wind carried to me the faintest whisper of my name. It was a sound I almost heard but couldn't swear that I did for sure. It made me look up and there stood Theo, beside his body, whole and perfect and decades younger. Just for a split second our eyes met. Then he was gone.

"No!" I said, weeping.

Susie gathered me into her arms. "Emma, I know you want to grieve. But we need you right now. Right now!" She squeezed me fiercely and then nearly dragged me over to the Asian boy. "Help him. Help Tae-yul!"

The healing current was still gushing through my hands, shaking me with its power. I was glad to have a recipient who would complete the connection and ground the current.

Susie and Asher dragged a groaning Donny over beside

Tae-yul, and then they went looking for other children I could help.

I worked from one body to the next. My body pulsated with the intensity of the healing current, which worked miraculously, without my conscious direction, because I was sobbing. Wounds closed up in front of my eyes. Exsanguinated bodies plumped and reddened and filled with blood. As long as the person was still breathing, the healing current wrought a marvelous restoration.

When Donny's leg was whole, he stood and kissed my cheek.

"It's not me, it's not my energy," I muttered as I bent over a ten year old boy with an arrow pinning his arm to his side. "It's just using me to do its work."

"Thank the Good Lord you're allowing that," Donny said. He touched his thigh. "I am grateful and awed." Then he joined Susie and Asher in triaging the fallen children.

At a certain point, the uninjured children gathered behind me in a semi-circle, watching. As I healed one child and then the next, snatching some of them from their last gasps and restoring them to wholeness, the children made little noises of appreciation, the way children do when they get a birthday present or a surprise treat.

Then a group of them murmured my name. I was crouched down beside a seven year old with a spear in his ankle, but I looked to see what they wanted.

The children waggled their fingers at me and called my name over and over. "Emma, Emma!"

"That's their way of applauding," Susie said, somberly.

Then that group of children moved inward to cling together. They took a step forward as one and a bright but dark opening extruded, and they vanished into it.

I went back to the injured boy.

He beamed up at me as the hole in his ankle closed. He waggled his fingers at me. "Emma."

I swiveled around to the next body. A girl with long braids, a teen, almost Susie's age, lying face down. She had an arrow sticking into her knee from behind. I said, "Donny."

"I hate this part," Donny muttered, kneeling on the girl's other side. "Deep breath, girl!" Then he yanked the arrow out.

She screamed, but I was already pouring healing energy into her, directly into the wound. She fell silent and her body went limp. There was a quiet but audible wet gurgle as the flesh sewed itself together and grew whole.

"That's, thank you!" the girl cried. She rolled over onto her back and drew her knee up almost to touch her nose. "I was ready to die here, and after the arrow hit me, I thought I'd never be able to walk the right way. This is amazing. Thank you!" She twisted around like a cat on its back and then rose to standing. She went to join a dozen other children, who all waggled their fingers at me and called my name.

Another mysterious opening happened, and the children stepped through and vanished. Where were they going? How had they known we were in trouble?

But other children waited on the ground for me to work on them.

THE LAST GROUP of children departed into the ethers and Tae-yul remained.

"He's with us now," Susie informed us, in a quiet, firm voice.

I flopped down onto my back beside Theo's body. What did I care who joined us? Theo, my adopted brother in The After, was dead. How was I ever going to explain this to Arthur and the others, when I saw them again?

Donny sat down beside me and stroked my hair back off my face. "We'll bury him, Emma. Then we'll find you a place to bathe. You're covered in blood."

"And vomit," Asher said. "Some of those kids barfed on

you. It was amazing what you did for them. I never saw anything like it."

"How many died?" I asked.

"I counted seventeen dead children," Donny answered.

"Not bad, considering," Susie said. "You saved a lot of
them, Emma. Good work."

"One dead kid is too many," I said.

"This is The After," Susie said sharply. "We can't afford to
be sentimental like that. And we've got to get moving. Arthur's
still on our tail."

"Twenty-two horses," Tae-yul spoke up suddenly. He stood
at Susie's shoulder. "That's what we have. Twenty-two completely unharmed horses. Twelve more that are hurt bad and
dying. And ten that we probably should put down because
they're injured and they'll die eventually without the right
care."

"Come on, Emma, see if you can help the horses," Asher
crawled over to nudge me up to sitting. "You helped all those
people. Maybe you can help the horses. It's terrible to see
them suffer. Horses are valuable. And when you're done with
that, would you please put your hands on my head? I've still
got a painful lump from where Susie bashed me."

So I went to help the horses while Donny, Asher, and Tae-
Yul dug a grave for Theo. Susie scavenged the raiders, taking
everything of value off them. She cut throats of the injured
raiders who were still alive and then she retrieved arrows
from bodies, wiping off the meat and blood and replacing
them in her quiver.

I saved all but two of the injured horses that were still
alive. Count was not one of them.

Donny and Asher laid Theo in a shallow grave, and we held
a brief, heart-wrenching ceremony for him that consisted
mostly of me crying and Donny praying. Asher rocked back
and forth, davening and chanting the Hebrew Kaddish. Susie
and Tae-yul stood shoulder to shoulder, watching impassively.

Since Count was gone, I chose a compact, well-shaped black gelding that looked at least part-Morgan horse. Rather, he chose me. He kept nuzzling me while I worked on the wounded animals. I finally turned to pat his muzzle, and he gave me a deep look of appropriation and sentience, as if claiming me. *Finally*, I thought dully, *a horse of my own.*

Susie's and Donny's horses had survived. Asher took a shine to a mild-mannered bay mare who didn't seem too spooked by the battle, and Tae-yul chose a lively pinto horse who seemed perfectly suited to the boy's athletic style.

We rode out leading several horses, with others in tow. Theo's backpack was tied onto my saddle. The black Morgan trotted in a calm but lively fashion, responding flawlessly to such a light rein that, after so many years on horseback, I began to understand what all the fuss was about riding. I named him Dory, after the last syllable of "Theodore." It was a tribute to my fallen comrade.

10 We rode fifteen, sixteen hour days, taking advantage of the stretched out summer days to cover the kilometers as quickly as possible. I rode in a kind of numb daze. I couldn't stop thinking about Theo, about the adventures we had shared on two continents, about watching him fall. Over and over in my head I replayed that scene: Theo yelling "No" and leaping, the hiss of the arrow and the wet thud as it slammed into him, Theo rolling on the ground with the arrow meant for me in his gut. It was like a clip from a film that I couldn't stop watching because it had branded itself onto my brain. When we made camp at night, whether in an abandoned building or outdoors, it was an hour or more of reliving the scene before I could fall into a troubled, tentative sleep.

We were riding along Highway 40 west of the abandoned town of Cut Knife when Kangee joined us. The old Pound-maker trail cut straight across flat farmland. We were exposed, but on the other hand, no one could approach us without us seeing them. And the pavement was still good, only lightly pockmarked and damaged by the snow, so our horses made good time.

Suddenly a tiny black-haired figure stood in the distance, directly in our path. Donny rode alongside me but he whooped with delight and pressed his horse into a canter. Susie and Tae-yul joined him. I stayed behind with Asher, who was still getting the hang of the saddle. The pack of horses with us raced around Asher and me to follow Donny.

When we joined them, Donny had dismounted, and he stood with his arm around his wife, who wore a maroon Juicy Couture track suit.

"Kangee," I called, trying to sound lighthearted, "you're a sight for sore eyes. It's been a month of Sundays, etc. and so on. How are you?"

"Sorry about your friend, Emma," she said, making a sorrowful face.

Me, too, I thought. But I slid down Dory and exchanged a hug with Kangee. I was pleased to note that she felt real and solid in my arms. "You're really here!"

"Where else would I be? You know, Arthur's not far behind, only a day's ride." She glanced over my shoulder. "Who's the geek?"

"Kangee, Asher; Asher, Kangee." I made the introductions.

Asher gave a half-hearted wave. "Pleased to meet you. I'm not really a geek, I'm an inventor. Susie kidnapped me and now I'm along for the ride."

Kangee nodded back at him.

"Kangee, any suggestions for how to throw off Arthur and the others?"

"Ride faster than them," she said, with her usual small, quirky smile.

It was the smile that did me in. I didn't mean to but suddenly I was crying like a toddler and hanging on to her shoulders.

"Emma, this is a new outfit, try not to wipe your snot on it," Kangee said, but in a kindly tone. She stood very still, accepting my grief, giving it space to breathe.

After a while I wasn't crying anymore, and Donny led the horse he'd chosen for Kangee to her. She approved and we all mounted up. We picked up the pace.

AT THE OUTSKIRTS to Carstairs, I called everyone to a halt. "Hide your guns, the folks in Carstairs are friendly but they don't particularly want armed strangers riding around in their town," I warned. "It's possible they'll confiscate our weapons if they see them."

"So we're going to ride up to the husband you abandoned and ask him nicely to fly us across the ocean to France, to the camp and Susie's friend?" Asher asked. "Are there even any planes left, or fuel for them?"

"She's not my friend, I've never met her," Susie corrected him. "Not in person."

"I always wanted to see the Eiffel tower," Kangee offered.

"Only part of the Eiffel tower still stands," I said, with a sigh. "Paris was pretty well demolished on The Day." On The Day of the mists' first catastrophic incursion, the mists had spread across the globe and devoured buildings, cars, trains, planes, bicycles, and people—anything with a certain balance of metallic elements in their chemical composition. I had been in Paris with my younger daughter Mandy. We had made it out of the city alive only by an inexplicable freak of good fortune.

"Emma, seriously?" Asher persisted, in strained tones. "What is the plan here?"

"I told you back in Portage la Prairie, Asher. First I'll use reason and try to connect with him through our shared past. Then I intend to beg and plead so pitifully that Haywood relents and does what we need him to do. I'm hoping that part of him still loves me, and that he'll see how important our mission is."

"There are still planes and fuel, if you know where to look," Donny said, in a brooding voice.

"Good luck with that," Asher said.

I wasn't sure who he was speaking to. I cleared my throat. "We'll stop by the town offices first, so everyone knows who we are."

"Polite and reasonable," Donny said. "That way they won't try to detain us as soon as we arrive in town."

"They will, but we'll say we're friends of Carl's. He's the deputy mayor." I hoped Carl would be sympathetic to our cause. He was present when Haywood had given me the ultimatum: stay with him and leave my beloved friends to their fates, or go to help Jeannie and Arthur, but never see him or our daughters again. Carl had known Haywood even in The Before. He was bound to feel for Haywood. But he had also liked me from the time of our first meeting.

Kangee said, "Only one way to find out."

WE RODE TO the town offices in quiet, orderly formation, waving peaceably to folks as we went through town. A compact, olive-skinned man with jet black hair came out to greet us. Carl himself.

"That can't be Emma," he said with a smile.

I clambered down from Dory and hugged Carl. "In the flesh. Good to see you, Carl."

"I sense you've weathered a storm." He stepped back to eye me quizzically. "You must have come to visit me."

I shook my head. "Haywood."

Carl frowned and his sharp blue eyes focused even more sharply. "Now, Emma, you know he doesn't want to see you anymore."

"It's important. Or I wouldn't be here."

"He specifically asked me to keep you away, if you returned to town. The man's been hurt enough, don't you think?"

"Mandy and Beth are my daughters, too," I said, with more energy than I had intended. I inhaled through braced ribs and forced my tone to soften. "I have rights. And this is important, Carl. It's urgent that we see him."

Carl's mouth puckered and his gaze skimmed over Kangee, Donny, Susie, and Tae-yul, and then the pack of horses trailing us. "Where'd you get the horses?"

"Raiders." I didn't have to say more; Carl would understand. He frowned. "How was it?"

My eyes got watery of their own volition and my voice was hoarse when I answered. "We lost one. Theo, you met him before, when he came to get me."

Carl flinched. "I suppose you have a story to tell me. Why don't you friends come in and sit for a bite to eat?"

"Because we don't have time," Susie said, too loudly. She jumped down from her horse in her graceful athletic way and stomped over to stand between Carl and me. "Mister, we have a mission."

Carl laid an easy hand on her shoulder, but Tae-yul almost magically appeared at his elbow, open switchblade in hand. "Whoa!" Carl gasped. "Back off, young fella!"

"She doesn't like to be touched," Tae-yul said in a soft and menacing voice.

Susie gestured at Tae-yul, who stepped back. Susie squared her shoulders. "Mister, what Emma didn't tell you is that we're on the most important mission ever. We're going to save the world from the mists. We're going to try. I'm going to try. But I can't do it alone. I have to be with a girl who's across the ocean in Emma's old camp. She's, like, the other half of the equation. So we need Haywood to fly us over there, like he flew Emma here. Do you get it? This is everything!"

Carl stroked his face for a few beats. Then he smiled crookedly and shrugged. "Let's go talk to Haywood."

THE HOUSE WAS the same as I'd left it, except that the grass around it was tall and the rose bushes and marigolds were blooming, yellow and pink and orange, and bees buzzed heavily from one blossom to the next. I could smell the sweet and sour flowers as we approached.

Haywood's mother Renee stood on the patio, sweeping. She picked up her head at the sound of the horses. She stiffened. "Emma, no."

I dismounted and walked to the patio. The others stopped and kept their distance. My heart was thumping so loudly in my chest that I was sure she could hear it. It must have been audible to Dory, because the horse trotted after me, following me up the driveway with his muzzle practically leaning on my shoulder. I stopped to push him back to a more courteous distance. Arthur always told me to exert my dominance with horses. And why was I thinking of Arthur just at the moment I had to make a connection with Haywood? I said, "I've got to talk to him, Renee."

Renee's mouth set itself into a hard straight line. "You can't keep hurting him, Emma."

"It's important," I said. "I have to speak with him. Truly, really, the most important thing you can imagine."

The screen door burst open and Mandy hurtled out toward me. "Mommy!" She threw her body into my arms, my delicious younger daughter, all knees and elbows and the unbridled enthusiasm of a puppy.

"Mandy, Mandykins!" I clutched her to me and said her name over and over again.

"Mama," said a soft, tearful voice at my side. It was Beth, my big daughter with the long blond tresses. When did she get so tall? I reached my arm out and dragged her into me, and the three of us held each other so fiercely that our edges softened and smudged into one another, we were almost as one person.

"I love you, I love you," I was babbling. "I'm sorry, I love you."

Mandy pressed her soft nose into mine and snorted air against my cheek. "Take me with you."

"Take us with you," Beth said. She was trembling against my shoulder.

"I can't. I want to, but it's not safe," I said, aching all the way into my bones. Now that I was holding my children, I didn't know how I'd ever let go of them.

"Girls!" Haywood called. My tall husband stood on the patio beside his mother, his arms crossed over his chest. His face wore an expression of scorn that I'd never seen before. His auburn hair had stayed the white it had turned after his captivity in Alexei's camp. He stood very straight so I couldn't tell if he was still crippled from the beatings he'd received at Alexei's hands.

Mandy and Beth peered back at him but huddled deeper into my arms.

"We talked about this," Haywood said, his voice sharp and his eyes baleful. "Your mother abandoned us. She doesn't care about us. Come here to me."

The girls were clutching me, showing no signs of releasing me. But I needed Haywood, we needed him, I wanted him to be soft enough to hear my request. It hurt in every angstrom of my being, but gently I peeled the girls off me. I tried to send them to Haywood. They refused to go and stood a few feet from me, crying. Mandy threw herself on me. I turned her around by her shoulders and faced her toward her father.

"Emma, you know you're not welcome. Why did you come here?" Haywood demanded. "Just to upset everyone all over again?"

"Girls, go to your father," I said, in as stern a tone as I could manage, under the circumstances. What I really wanted to do was hold them, tightly and deeply. How had I ever not felt Beth's soft hand on mine or Mandy's warm cheek on my throat as she hugged me? How had I gone one single day without these deeply heartfelt sensations? How had I gone one single hour without seeing my beautiful daughters' faces and hearing their sweet voices and hugging them? How could I go one minute more without them close at hand?

Was any man worth the sacrifices I had made for Arthur? What hell had I wrought for myself?

"You should leave," Renee said.

"Haywood, I need you. We need you," I said. "We have a chance to put a stop to the mists, to finish them off for good. I can't do it without you."

Haywood shook his head. He held out his arms and Mandy and Beth finally ran to him. He bent low and squeezed them close to his chest.

"Susie has psi power over the mists." My voice trembled. "But she's only half the equation. She has to join with a girl from Europe, a girl I knew at the camp there, Caris. The two of them together can join their abilities. They can gather and terminate the mists. Eradicate them. For good. At least, we think so. That's what we're trying to do."

Haywood rose and opened the screen door. Physically he ushered the girls into the house and closed the door behind them. Then he came to the edge of the patio and looked down the steps at me. "You want me to fly you and Susie back across the ocean." It was a statement, not a question.

Tears leaked out of my eyes. I stepped forward. "Please, Haywood. I'm sorry, so sorry, about everything. I know you've suffered, but don't you see? I didn't have a choice? About any of it? I always did what I had to do. One thing just led to another . . .

"I'm sorry you got hurt along the way, I never meant for you to be hurt. I never stopped loving you. I don't know if I ever will. I know you felt like I abandoned you. But now none of that even matters. Something else has come along that makes everything else meaningless.

"Susie and Caris have this amazing, world-changing gift. They can get rid of the mists, once and for all, and we can all be safe again. The world can be a safe place for people, and we can rebuild, finally. The world can start over again. After all the billions of deaths. Please, can't you forgive me, at least for a little while, and help me do this? Help us? Because we were married for a long time, don't you think you can help us? You're the only pilot left in the world with the skill and courage to fly across the Atlantic Ocean. Please, Haywood, I need you, we need you. Please say you'll help us!"

Haywood stood tall and erect, with his chin lifted, as he surveyed me from eyes that had once loved me as much as a man can love a woman. "You say you never stopped loving me, but from the day you met him, you loved Arthur more than me. Even when I risked my life to fly to Europe in that small plane to bring you home, even when I went to help you free Beth and I was captured and beaten into blood and broken bones, you loved him more. Nothing I did ever made a difference. Nothing ever brought you back to me, your husband, the one who'd been there for you always. You chose him over me and the girls. You say you didn't have a choice, but Emma, you always had a choice."

"Haywood—"

A red flush stole up from his collarbones to inflame his face. "I have a choice now. If what you say is true, if the potential is what you say and the stakes really are as high as you say, then you'll find another pilot. There are still a few of them around. But I won't be your pilot. I won't let myself be hurt by you ever again." He backed up toward the door and reached his hand behind himself for the handle. "Don't come back, Emma. Never come back here. You made your choices, now you live with them. I had to." He opened the screen door and stepped backward into the house, then pulled the screen door closed and shut the heavy wooden door, also.

Renee resumed sweeping. "You have your answer. Go along, now."

I wrapped my arms around my middle and choked, "Renee, I love my children with all my being."

She didn't answer but kept sweeping.

I wept without inhibition. *Do they really expect me to live without my children forever?*

Dory nickered into my ear. He nudged and nuzzled me. He pushed his nose into my neck and shoulder.

Donny pulled me by my elbow. "Come on, Emma." He wiped my face with his shirt sleeve, and then took me by the hand to lead me to the end of the driveway, where the others waited. He steered me to Dory's left side and helped me up into my saddle.

I couldn't speak, but I didn't need to. They had seen and heard everything.

"We don't need him," Susie said, in a low, furious voice. "We'll find another way. Yah!" She kicked her horse forward into a fast trot.

Kangee leaned over and took my reins into her hands with her own.

Numb and wordless, I sat on the horse. I was unable to talk when we returned to the town offices, and I couldn't say good bye or even wave to Carl, who urged us to stay for a meal.

"Ordinarily we'd accept gratefully, sir," Donny said. "If you have any food that's packed to go, we'll take it gladly. But we've a journey to make." He arranged to leave most of the extra horses with Carl, so that we wouldn't be traveling in such a large, unwieldy pack. The town was welcome to use the horses but we'd like them back if any one of us ever came back alive this way. We each had our own mount and we brought two more for carrying packs.

I just let Dory move forward on his own.

"Emma, snap out of it, at least for a minute," Susie said sharply as we set out from Carstairs. "We still have to get me to Europe. What are we going to do? Where are we going?"

I didn't think, I just answered instinctively, I couldn't say how because I was too distraught to think coherently. If I'd

been rational, I'd have suggested someplace else, any place but
the town where I was wanted for a hanging offense, where
I had already stood on an execution platform with a noose
around my neck. "Outpost City."

"Of course!" Asher said jubilantly. "Outpost City! I should
have thought of it. That's the perfect place to find a pilot.
Everyone finds their way there, and all who go there are desperate. Everyone can be bought for the right price."

"Good thinking, Emma," Donny approved. "Well done.
That'll buy us some time with Arthur too. He won't expect
you to head to Outpost City. Second, if there's a pilot willing
to fly us to Europe—"

"Crazy enough," Asher interjected.

"Well, either way, if there is one, he'll be in Outpost City,
where everybody's selling something, and we'll get him for a
price," Donny finished.

"Or her," Susie said sharply. "It could be a woman."

The mission continued.

11 We followed Highway 581 east under a limitless mirroring sky. The prairie land was even and verdant and dotted with grain elevators and fir trees, gray stone cairns commemorating the dead, empty churches and lakes full of trout, and bears and moose and antelope, and coyotes grown large from feasting on ground squirrels and pets left behind when the mists swept through.

I was alternately numb and incoherent. The finality of Haywood's refusal pierced me. I knew now not only that he was done with me, but also that he would try to prevent me from ever seeing our children again. He was angry and embittered and he felt justified. Even though I'd gone months without my daughters, I had kept them close to my heart. I had always planned to be reunited somehow. For the first time, I wondered, was that possible?

I couldn't eat when we left Carstairs, couldn't sleep that night. Before dawn I got up and walked outside to sit on the stoop of the vacant farmhouse where we'd taken shelter. It was still inky and indigo, the moon and even the stars had set. I could not remember a darker night, ever.

I curled up into myself and rested my cheek on my knees. *What is the point? The point of the struggle, the loss, the effort, the hard choices, the sacrifices? Has any of it mattered in the face of so many dead, so much destruction, such a personal loss as the separa-*

tion from my children, after all I went through to protect them? Did Haywood really mean to keep me from my daughters? If I am even still alive at the end of this mission, will he really attempt to cut me off from them?

Since the day we had met, whenever I had reached an impasse, I could reach out to Arthur. No matter where I was, I could feel our connection, I could feel him. It was a living bond. It had sustained me. But now he stood on the other side of a chasm from me, the chasm of our different intentions toward Susie. When I peered into the chasm, my vision itself was a beam of light that disturbed a splendor of butterflies. They soared upward, away from me, revealing their implicate, enfolded passion as they departed.

They were beautiful but I was left, once again, alone and pervaded by despair.

What is the point?

"Emma, Emma," a whisper sounded.

I picked up my head. Wait, was that, could it be, Theo?

He stood faintly glowing, a specter on the street in front of the house, but clearly recognizable. Theo, my friend, my brother. He beckoned.

I rose with my first smile since Haywood had shut the door between me and my daughters. It was a smile of relief. I felt almost limp with gratitude. How good of Theo my brother to come for me. I'd go wherever he led me. The others could find their way to Outpost City and locate a pilot and a plane without me.

But when I reached the place where he stood, he had receded down the road. I walked after him. He sped up, so I did, too. Then I was running, running into the dark. Then there was a small figure running toward me, a dark form growing larger in the grainy night, was that finally him? I broke into a sprint and raced to meet the figure.

"Help," cried the figure. "Help me!"

I knew that voice! I shouted and ran faster than I'd ever run in my life—it was the greatest sprint of all my years. A second later I barreled into her, Beth my daughter, my beloved eldest child, and I wrapped myself around her and we fell shrieking to the earth.

"Mama, that's you? Is that really you?" Beth asked. She wept and stroked my face, wound her fingers into my hair.

"Beth, what are you doing here?" I cried. I pressed her into my heart and rocked back and forth. I shuddered with the primal thrill of holding my child in my arms after having lost her.

"Mama, we have to get up right now, right now!" she said urgently. She stood and dragged me up.

I managed to keep her enclosed tightly in my embrace. "Are raiders coming?"

"No, no, it's a giant cougar, it's been tailing me ever since I left Daddy's house," Beth said. She shook with fear and her voice was raw. "I was so terrified it was going to eat me that I just kept walking and running all night!"

"A cougar?" I turned to look behind Beth.

There it was, a sleek tan form painted pink and orange by the first glimmers of dawn. It stared at me from burning topaz eyes. A thick red scar twisted around one eye and curled around its nose, and another wide, jagged scar ran over its chest.

He was an old friend. When I'd walked out of Edmonton to rescue Beth from Alexei, the animal had followed me, protecting me, all the way to Alexei's camp. Alexei had hurt him grievously, but he lived still. The cougar sniffed the air and laid down on the road, his tail switching back and forth.

"Oh Beth, you don't have to worry about this cougar." I snuggled her close to my chest. "He's here to protect you."

"Are you sure?" Beth asked, tremulously.

"Sweetie, yes, don't worry," I reassured her and kissed her forehead about a thousand times. "What are you doing here? How did you find me?"

"Mandy and I talked. We decided we weren't going to let you be by yourself. One of us was going to go with you. She was with you in France before, so it was my turn. I wanted to go this time. She stayed home to take care of daddy." Beth lifted her head away from me to wrinkle her face at me. "Maybe you're right about the cougar helping me, though he is awfully big and scary. He kept cutting me off every time I went in a different direction."

I laughed and hugged her some more. I couldn't get enough of feeling her warm body in my arms. "Is Mandy okay?"

"Yes. She's good at making daddy laugh. She'll see us when we come back, when we've finished the mission. When the mists are gone for good."

"Oh, sweet Beth, do you think we'll succeed?" I wondered. "It feels like such an impossible task."

Beth wriggled out from my tight embrace. "We have to. We have to, so we will."

BREAKFAST WAS A happy occasion. We felt we had a small space of time to linger. Arthur wouldn't expect us to go to Outpost City, even if he knew how seriously we were looking for a pilot; Alexei seemed to be at a distance. Chickens who had grown feral lived at the farm house in and around a rickety wire coop, and Tae-yul rounded up more than a dozen eggs. He also beheaded and then plucked one of the hens. Donny made scrambled eggs and roast chicken on a wood burning stove that had been used for warmth in The Before, not for cooking. While waiting for the food to cook, Asher and Beth scavenged the upstairs and Susie and I went through the downstairs.

"I'm glad you're okay now, Emma," Susie said. "You were in a bad way. I was worried about you."

"You were worried about me?" I was rummaging through a bathroom cabinet, looking for medicines that weren't too long past their expiry. Any kind of antibiotic was useful to have on hand, and I now believed that most medications remained potent for a generous period of time after their suggested expiration date.

"Of course. Shall I do up my coiffeur today?" Susie waved a curling iron around and we both giggled.

"Worried you'd have to shoot me or abandon me?" I asked drily.

She snorted. "I like Beth. She's cute. And brave—setting out on foot by herself like that. I'm glad she found us." Susie tossed down the curling iron and held up some tampons. "Oh my God, am I glad I found some of these!"

"Me too." I was referring to Beth, not the feminine toiletry articles, though the latter were exceedingly useful. "Let's pack every one of those you can find. And the toothpaste."

"I know how you feel about toothpaste," Susie said with mirth in her voice. Then, wistfully, she said, "I miss my mom. I don't know what happened to her. She's probably dead. Beth is so lucky to have you. I know why she came after you. If I thought my mom was alive somewhere, anywhere, I'd go find her." Susie's heart-shaped face with its spattering of freckles lightened. "After, you know, Caris and I save the world."

"Of course, after you save the world," I responded. Slowly, so she could observe, I stretched out my arm and curled it around her slim, strong shoulders. "Minneapolis was where you were on The Day, yes? You got out. Maybe your mom did."

"She went to the grocery store, I was home by myself. My neighbor came to get me and said we had to leave. Everyone was in a panic, it was terrible, the mists were rolling all over the city, destroying everything. They came out of the lakes. I got separated from my neighbor and then some guys grabbed me, and they joined other guys who became raiders." Susie's face furrowed in on itself.

"She could have made it out. Plenty of people did." I

clasped my other arm around Susie and squeezed her close. "You may see her again, Susie. It's possible."

"I used to daydream about that all the time. Especially when the raiders were, you know, using me. And I'd look for her whenever I saw people. Sometimes I'd see a woman walking and maybe from behind she'd be the same size and shape as my mom, or just blonde like her, and my heart would pound and leap into my throat and for a minute, I'd think, *Mom!*" Susie shrugged. "But it was never her."

"I'm sorry, Susie," I said softly.

Susie gave me a half-smile. "I always think about this Emily Dickinson poem I had to memorize in ninth grade:

> "A loss of something ever felt I,
> the first that I could recollect.
> Bereft I was—of what I knew not,
> too young that any should suspect
> A mourner walked among the children
> I notwithstanding went about . . ."

I felt a lump in my throat. "You have me now, you know that. I'm not your mom but I am here for you."

Susie squirmed away. "Yeah, yeah. You're lucky to have me. Remember Alexei's soldier, the one who was trying to rape you? I shot him."

"I'm grateful every day for your aim, Susie!" I shook my head wryly. Indeed, Susie's expertise with a bow and arrow had stood us all in good stead.

"Isn't that Donny calling us?" Susie picked her head up attentively. "Breakfast must be ready. I'm hungry!" She pecked me on the cheek gingerly and then flounced from the bathroom.

I was left pondering the incomprehensible burden that rested on a person who was simultaneously fragile and strong. Then I hoped I wasn't thinking about myself.

"EMMA, I NEED to speak with you," Donny called. He rode up alongside me and his dark eyes swept over Beth, who rode next to me on a gentle packhorse we called Ned.

I suggested, "Beth, why don't you join Susie for a few minutes?"

Beth immediately rose in her saddle. "Look, mama, I'm posting to a trot!" She had been taking riding lessons in Carstairs and was eager to show me her skill. She guided her horse toward Susie and Tae-yul.

"You're a better rider than I am, Beth," I called.

"That's not saying much," Donny rumbled under his breath.

"I'm improving," I said tartly.

Donny smirked. "Well, okay, that might be true. That new horse of yours knows how to carry you for sure. But listen, we've got a problem. Alexei is sending me images. He's not waiting for you to come to him anymore. He's actively tracking us. He thinks you need his help."

"He's tracking us?" My heart dropped into my stomach, palpitating all the way. "Is he close?"

"He's coming, that's all I know. That's the image he's sending me." Donny rolled his head around on his burly shoulders and growled with frustration and dismay. "Emma, I don't know how much advance notice this is."

"How close is he? Can we outrun or outmaneuver him?"

"Unclear. He's got a lot of men. He's sending me images as a courtesy. That's what he telepaths me."

I couldn't prevent a wry smile. "Alexei can be very courteous that way, letting us know before he takes us all prisoner."

"Yeah, he's a real sweetheart."

"Maybe he's not that close. We couldn't find him when Arthur was looking for him."

"That's true," Donny admitted. "With Alexei, you never really know what's going on. He and his army could be thousands of kilometers from here and he could just be mind-gaming me for his own reasons."

I ruminated silently, listening to the birds and the hoof beats and the distant lowing of cattle. Dory lifted his head and perked his ears forward as if following my thoughts. I had to pat him, he was so adorable. Finally I said, "We'll ride faster and try to reach Outpost City before he finds us."

Donny frowned. "He knows exactly where we are. He's been tracking us through our minds. Yours and mine, I mean. He'll know we're in Outpost City."

"I hate making it easy for him," I grumbled. "Even if he and his men are nearby, they won't be able to take us prisoner in Outpost City."

"He could kidnap one or more of us."

"Easy to slip away in Outpost City. That place is all about not being found."

Donny shrugged. "As you said, he's in a courteous mood, maybe he doesn't intend to take us all prisoner. He didn't have to let me know he was coming. Maybe he really wants to help us get Susie to Caris."

I made a face. "Alexei always complicates everything, and he's always got his own agenda. Do we have a plan for dealing with him, if he catches up to us before Outpost City?"

"That's what I'm asking you." Donny grinned.

I considered. "If he finds us, we stay together, stay tight, and escape at the first opportunity. In the meantime, we'll pick up the pace and ride longer into the night. Our goal is to reach Outpost City before he finds us. We can hide there while we look for another pilot."

"Understood," Donny said. He stood up in his stirrups and his deep baritone voice rang out, "Gather together, folks! We're getting company and we've got a strategy."

That's when I realized how completely they were relying on me to lead them. I had a burst of empathy for, and also envy of, Arthur, who made decisions with seemingly effortless certainty. I was making it up as I went along. This tactic had served me well enough when I was on my own. But now other people depended on me—important people, including my precious daughter and irreplaceable Susie, the one girl on this continent who might just possess a viable way to end the mists. Somehow I had to grow into this greater role. Somehow I had to develop better insights and strategies.

WE CAMPED OUTDOORS that night because I didn't want us to get caught unawares indoors. We didn't stop until almost midnight and we were all exhausted, people and horses. I was patting down a blanket for Beth to sleep on when Tae-yul approached me.

"I'll take first watch, and I can get rid of that big cat who's following us," Tae-yul offered. He held up his slingshot, a faint blur of motion in the night.

"No!" Beth and I chorused.

"Let him be, he's a friend," I said.

"Are you sure?" Tae-yul asked doubtfully. "He could lie in wait and pounce on one of us while we're sleeping—and eat dinner."

"He won't do that," Beth assured him.

"Hmm," Tae-yul said.

"Really, Tae-yul," she said earnestly. "He'll help us. You'll see."

Tae-yul looked at me and I nodded. He shrugged and went off.

"Alexei will be here soon, if we don't reach Outpost City," Beth said. Her beautiful oval face wore a worried look.

"We're not far from Outpost City." Then I had a sudden intuition. "Can you feel Alexei or sense him somehow?"

She nodded. "Yes, ever since I was at his camp, I feel a connection to him. Like he's there at the very back of my mind, if

I want to go there. He was nice to me. He used to talk to me about his son Mikhail. But, Mama . . . Oh God! What he did to Daddy?" She closed her eyes and shuddered eloquently. She had witnessed Alexei brutalizing Haywood.

I remembered all too clearly the same moment she did at Alexei's camp. Haywood swayed, bleeding from a dozen cuts and bruises, both eyes blackened, lips and nose broken. Alexei was one-armed at the time, it was before my healing gift had restored his limb to him, and he had pummeled Haywood with his single fist almost faster than the eye could follow. "He hurt your dad back then," I said quietly. "But he says he wants to help us now."

"Help us or get Susie?" Beth wondered, in her quiet, serious way. She leaned close to me. "I think if he tries to take her away from us in any way, she'll kill herself. Then what will the world do? The world needs her. They don't know it, but she's the key to our salvation."

"We'll make sure he doesn't get her," I promised. "I've escaped from Alexei before. I'll do it again. Now you lie down and get some shut-eye. We'll be on the move again before dawn."

"Kangee was on the outside, back when we were at Alexei's camp, but now she's with us," Beth said, climbing onto her blanket.

"No, I'm leaving now," Kangee said.

Beth and I turned around to face her.

"I don't want to be here when Alexei arrives. I don't like feeling that man rummaging around inside my head," Kangee said, the tone of her voice souring with distaste. She seated herself beside Beth on the blanket and smoothed her hand over it. "Nice and soft. You'll sleep well tonight, Beth."

"Will you come back?" Beth asked.

Kangee nodded. "It's not that easy to get rid of me, don't worry." She looked up into the warm night air, her eyes large and luminous, as if she was seeing past the fireflies and bats into another realm, the secret miraculous realm through which she traveled to cover long distances in a few moments. "Emma, I wanted to tell you. Keep tight reins on Tae-yul around Alexei's men. If Tae-yul's a smart ass with them, they'll hurt him." She stood. "Bye, Beth. Don't worry." Then she vanished.

Beth gasped and sat straight up, reaching for Kangee.

"I know, it's disconcerting when she does that." I gently prodded Beth back down onto her blanket. "Rest now. I'll be right next to you, and Donny'll be on your other side. We'll get up with first light." I rose and went to find Tae-yul, to warn him to contain himself around Alexei's men, whenever we met them.

IT WAS EIGHT days ride from Carstairs to Outpost City, but we were swinging around it to the south to stop at Cypress Hills first. The corridor to Cypress Hills was studded with gray stone cairns. We had all seen them many times, of course, these conical piles of delicately balanced, tightly knit stones. But they seemed taller and fatter now, rising sometimes to three stories in height, some glowed faintly green, and a few emitted a low hum.

At a brief halt for lunch on our last day, Beth skipped over to examine one of the cairns. I chased after her to pull her back. I'd once had a peculiar experience with a cairn and remembering it left me uneasy. The cairns were more than they seemed to be, but what that more was, I couldn't quantify.

"Beth, honey, let's leave the cairns alone," I called. I took her arm so I could pull her back to the path.

"Mama, listen." She tilted her head.

Was the subterranean *basso profundo* hum getting louder? I said, "Let's get out of here. Come on, let's go back to the others."

"They're like the nuraghe, sort of," Tae-yul said. He and Susie trudged over to stand with us.

The hum increased.

"What are nuraghe?" Susie asked.

"They're like these beehive towers in Sardinia," Tae-yul said. "My family went there on vacation once. There were thousands of nuraghe."

"Look!" Beth cried, pointing, her eyes wide.

I followed her finger to a shadowy spot on the cairn, about as high as my shoulder, where a stone was extricating itself from the interlock. It was a fist-sized, oblong piece of quartzite. "Beth, whatever it's doing, we don't want to be a part of—"

The stone flew out and thwacked the ground with an explosive percussion like a cough or a sneeze. The hum that had been swelling receded, audible only as a vibration felt on my sternum.

"Cool!" Beth ran to the stone and picked up. "I think it's giving this to us!"

"No! Leave it alone," I murmured.

Beth said. "Isn't this cool? It's giving us part of itself."

"I don't think it's a good idea to play with it," I said. "Is there a name on it?" I had seen the names of the dead written on stones within the cairn. I had even seen the faces of those deceased people informing the stones.

"Nope, no name," Beth said, turning it over and over in her hand. "I like it and wanna keep it. I think it's good luck."

Tae-yul leaned over and examined the fractured piece in Beth's hand. "It's a nice rock. She'll be all right."

"It's for me. I can feel it," Beth said, holding the rock closer to her face.

As she gripped it, a hole opened in the face of the cairn. The stones shifted and writhed, then swirled outward in a vortex. The vortex swirled open larger and larger, making a kind of tunnel that extruded from the cairn. The humming noise intensified again, and within the tunnel, a tall figure began to materialize.

I was mesmerized and couldn't move or speak.

The figure buzzed gray in an outline that slowly filled in with color and detail.

Susie yelped and pointed, and Tae-yul whipped out his slingshot and made it ready.

The figure in the cairn tunnel turned toward me, and the head clarified into that of a familiar, rough-hewn blond man. His blue eyes looked directly into me.

Seeing his face, meeting his gaze, broke the spell for me. I cried, "Alexei! No!" I plucked the stone out of Beth's hands and threw it back at the cairn, into the tunnel where Alexei was taking shape.

The stone was sucked soundlessly inward, and the tunnel collapsed into a small vortex that instantly withered and shrank. In seemingly an instant, the cairn was as it had been before: a tall, rounded pile of stones.

"Mama," Beth whispered, "Was Alexei coming out of the stones?"

"He was trying to," I said. "Stay away from the cairns, Sweetheart."

"What does it mean that he tried to come here through the cairn?" Tae-yul asked.

"I means that he's keeping an eye on us," I said. I spoke in a neutral voice so as not to alarm them.

Susie said, "It looked like a rock in Beth's hand."

But nothing in The After was what it appeared to be.

I took Beth's hand and marched back to the horses.

WE VEERED DUE south and stopped on the last day in Cypress Hills Provincial Park, twenty kilometers south of Outpost City. Around Reesor Lake, a village had sprung up in The After. The folks there knew us and would stable our horses for a very reasonable fee while we were in Outpost

City, where the town government confiscated horses as a matter of law, eminent domain in The After.

We left the good people of Cypress Hills the rest of our sneakers, as payment for stabling our horses. We also bartered our thermos of honey for a ride to Outpost City. It would require twenty-four hours of travel to reach there on foot; we didn't want to encounter either Alexei or Arthur, so it was worth the extra payment to get a lift.

I wondered what Outpost City looked like now, as the mists had rolled through when Arthur and I and the others left it a few months ago. Arthur had dissolved the mists there, so they would never return to Outpost City. It was now a Safe Zone. But did its citizens know that?

En route, we found an abandoned strip mall. It had long since been thoroughly picked over and was littered with knee-deep piles of shrink wrap and empty boxes, but in a flotsam-covered aisle of the drug store I found a pristine package of hair dye mousse, color Chestnut Brown. I took it as an omen to quickly give myself a makeover.

Donny gathered water from a nearby stream in buckets and helped me apply the mousse to my head and then rinse out the chemicals. I was now a brunette and anyone who knew me casually as a blonde wouldn't recognize me immediately. I didn't want to be recognized in Outpost City, especially if Alexei and his men arrived there.

12

A COUPLE OF MONTHS HAD PASSED since I had literally fled Outpost City, running and gripping Arthur's hand as a giant wall of mists churned buildings—and people—into sand. At the time, Arthur had used the mists' proximity to set up a resonance pattern in Marco's mind and bring him back to sanity. We had merged with him in the space of the human biomind, me and Donny and Theo and Laurette and a red-haired young woman named Amy. We had lent him our psychic abilities, thereby strengthening his. It had allowed him to direct the mists' resonance into Marco in such a way that the insanity was disrupted. "Wave pattern interference," Arthur had called it. But it required the close physical proximity of the mists.

So Marco came back, but the mists had swarmed through Outpost City. Over half the city had been destroyed. The remnant was a shattered mess of buildings covered in fine yellow grit. Not that Outpost City had ever been anything but a grotty collection of hovels surrounded by high barbed wire and populated by the riffraff of the world and various barnyard animals, the latter being cleaner than the former.

It still was, and it still stank. We could smell the city almost as soon as we saw dark shapes rising above the prairie. Our friends from Cypress Hills let us dismount and retrieve our belongings from the pack horses, then they waved and turned around to ride as fast as possible back to their home.

"Oh God," Beth sputtered, waving her hand in front of her nose. "What is that disgusting smell?"

"Outpost City," Asher said. His face softened and his hazel eyes behind his thick glasses got misty.

"You're not saying you like that place, are you, Ash?" Susie asked, despite knowing that he hated having his name abbreviated that way.

But Asher didn't take the bait. He just smiled in a vague way at some private reminiscence.

"Norm said he was going to put plumbing in when he was rebuilding, but clearly he didn't," Donny grumbled.

"Duh," Susie said. "How long before we get used to the stink?"

"I know about that," Tae-yul said. "It's called olfactory adaptation. It's when the smell seems to fade."

"Olfactory sensory neurons adapt to the repetitive odorant stimuli by reducing their rate of firing," Asher said absently. His face still wore a dreamy expression.

"How friggin' long does it take?" Susie asked sharply.

"It takes as long as it takes," Donny said. He sighed. "Let's get this over with. Emma, which gate?"

"South gate, if it's still there. I got through last time without being questioned."

Donny frowned and rubbed his chin. "I wonder if there's still a bounty on your head."

"Mama, why would they question you, and what bounty is on your head?" Beth asked. "Is this why you dyed your hair?"

I shrugged my shoulders, affecting nonchalance for my daughter. "When the raiders captured you, I came through here and tried to steal a horse. That's a hanging offense in Outpost City."

"They better not try to hang you now!" Beth put her arms akimbo. "They'll have to go through me."

"Don't worry, Beth, Arthur and a bunch of us rescued your mama," Donny said. "Course, that made them a little more mad at her."

"It'll be okay," I said, from hope rather than certainty.

"Yeah, yeah. Norm's a big muckety-muck in Outpost City. He'll vouch for Emma," Donny said, but he kept scrubbing at his chin the way he did when he was worried.

I wished he wasn't doing that, because it alarmed me. As far as he and I knew, the bounty had never been lifted. It was possible, if I was recognized, that I'd be jailed and hanged in Outpost City.

A KILOMETER OUT, a line of people moved slowly toward the city. They were lean and ragged and they carried their belongings in bags or pushed carts or dragged wagons piled with the things that had survived and that still mattered. We joined the queue. Other folks streamed in behind us.

"Good thing we have food and water," Donny said to me, sotto voce. "We'll need them on this line."

"S'cuse me," Susie said to the group ahead of us. "Why is there this big long line to get into Outpost City?"

They were seven people, four adults and three children, closely enough resembling each other that they were probably a family. A woman with salt-and-pepper hair turned to face us and smiled. "Haven't you heard? Outpost City is now a Safe Zone. All of it and about twenty kilometers around it. The mists came through two months ago and will never come back."

That was true, that was what Arthur had said: once he dissolved the mists, an energetic residue was left behind that the mists avoid. But how did people know that? He hadn't told anyone but our group. I asked, "Excuse me, ma'am, how do you know that?"

"Everyone knows," she said with complete confidence.

I nodded and smiled back, thinking about the interconnectedness of the human biomind. It allowed for the spread of information without any overt channel of communication, even human-to-human conversation. I had never noticed it in The Before, when we had the distraction of electronic telecommunication, but now I saw it everywhere.

Susie said, "So now it's a Safe Zone and everyone wants to live here."

The woman nodded. A little one, her daughter, leaned into her side, and the woman stroked the girl's hair away from her face. "That's right. But they're overwhelmed, processing people as fast as they can and throwing up shelters for people to live in."

"They're funneling everyone through this gate?" I asked.

"And the East gate," she answered. "But they're pickier there. Here they're pretty relaxed about people coming in." She cupped her daughter's chin and turned her face toward me.

The girl's eyes were vacant and despoiled. She was mad.

I made a gesture of sympathy.

"Better watch that," Susie said, out of the side of her mouth. "Some crazy kids are killing their parents."

The woman's lips tightened. She took a breath, and grated, "I heard about that. But those kids were infected by one of the little mists that scout around. That's not what happened to Janine. Janine's been like this since the mists went through Tampa."

"You're from Tampa?" I asked. That was a long way from here.

She nodded and we exchanged a look that didn't require any words. I knew that she'd walked here from Florida, seek-

ing safety for her child. She understood that I knew. She turned
back to her family because, after all, there wasn't that much
to say. We were all waiting in line for a safe haven in Outpost
City. Safe haven was the great dream of The After.

Except that I was looking for something else, or rather
someone: a pilot. One willing to fly us across a mist-ridden
ocean on the hope, the slender but implacable hope, that we
had a way to rid the world of the mists, once and for all.

AS WE INCHED forward, we got a better look at the town
ahead. Through the gulag-like expanse of barbed wire encir-
cling it, Outpost City was visible in all its squalid splendor.
Prior to the mists incursion, it had been an unsightly sprawl
of lumpy structures; it was even uglier now. The mists had
razed half the city, and the half that was left was surrounded by
misshapen lumps and bumps that were shanties. Shanties were
constructed of odds and ends like canvas, dinner tables, milk
crates, and concrete blocks. Interspersed among the shanties
were half-built timber and stone buildings. One day they'd
be properly finished—maybe. Or maybe not. People were
already camped out in the partial structures.

The streets were a labyrinth of dirt paths cutting around
the buildings. The stench came from crude outhouses on the
periphery of town, just inside the fence. Evidently wooden
stalls had been thrown up over open pits.

As we neared the head of the line, we saw people moving
about inside the gate. As before, they came in all sizes and
shapes and colors. They were all armed, too, even the little
kids. Donny gave knives to Asher and Beth. I tied a makeshift
belt and sheath around Beth's waist and showed her a hor-
izontal scout carry, with the knife at the small of her back.
Arthur had taught me this carry because it allowed for access
in virtually any position with either hand, including if I was

on my back.

Asher approved so I fixed him up the same way. I showed them how Arthur had made me practice. Asher almost cut Tae-yul's arm with a wild swing, which elicited hoots of amusement from Susie. She took over the training.

After several hours, we arrived at the head of the line, at a long table twenty yards in front of the gate. Royal forces soldiers strolled around, keeping things peaceful. The intake table was manned by about a dozen civilians, both men and women. It was late in the afternoon and the shift was changing, with fresh intake clerks coming out of the gate to relieve those who'd been sitting all day. The newcomers were high-energy and cheery, laughing and slapping the backs of those who'd served a long stint and were glad to stand and stretch their legs.

It was our turn and a few clerks were open, largely because there was a lot of confused milling around at the tables and no one directing the queue forward. I peered at faces and wondered who'd be likely to let us through. I spied a thin, blondish guy with a pronounced widow's peak near the end. He was looking around for his replacement. He was blinking blearily, rubbing his neck and rotating his head to get the kinks out. He appeared generally disinclined to question anyone too closely. I trotted over to him with the others in tow.

"Hello, sir, we're a family group," I said with a smile.

His blood-shot eyes focused on me for a moment and then lost interest. He bent over the sheets of paper in front of him. "Why are you here?"

"Safe haven," I chirped. "Want to live in a Safe Zone."

He nodded. That was what he'd heard all day. "Name."

"Angie, er, Smith. This is Beth Smith. And Donny Smith, and Asher Smith and Susie Smith and Tae-yul Smith."

That got a snicker out of him, but he didn't contest it. He wrote it down. "Any of you Smiths crazy?"

I smothered a flippant response. *Yes, we're all crazy, under-*

taking a mission to save the world. Hopefully save the world. "No, sir. Just hungry and tired and scared of the mists."

He grunted. Then he picked his head up and tried to focus. "Any of you been here in Outpost City before?"

Before I could utter the lie I'd spent the last day concocting, someone behind him hollered out in a way that grabbed his attention. He swiveled all the way around to wave both arms at a woman coming toward him. Then he turned back to us. "Two rules: one, no freebies. Everybody trades or else works. And two, don't try to steal a gun or a horse. Those are capital crimes. We hang people for that."

He rose and slapped a paper in my hands. "Welcome to Outpost City. There are some new shanties over by the Badlands part of town that aren't too crowded. Try your luck there for a place to live." He turned away and greeted his replacement in a loud, jolly voice.

"Let's go!" I waved to the others. I was thinking, *Quick, before anyone recognizes me.* I showed the paper to the guard at the gate.

He was young, with reddish hair and a ruddy complexion, and his eyes slid over us in bored fashion, but then kindled when his gaze fell on Susie. He started to smile but Tae-yul shouldered in front of Susie, loosed his slingshot, and bared his teeth at the guard. The guard made a face and waved us in. "I should call for a sanity check on that one," he grumbled to me, pointing at Tae-yul.

"He's okay," I murmured in response. The others bunched up around me. As we walked into the town, I clasped Beth's hand in one hand and with the other, I gripped Tae-yul's elbow. "Knock it off," I whispered. "Don't do anything like that again. Don't draw attention to us. It jeopardizes our mission."

He jerked his arm from my grasp and didn't answer.

"Mama, look at all the animals," Beth said. She held out her hand for a young white goat to sniff. "They're everywhere!"

"Be careful of the poop, it's everywhere too. Watch where

you step," Susie advised her. She punched Tae-yul in his shoulder. "Mellow out, okay?"

He gave her an impassive look.

We moved forward on the wide dirt path leading into the city from the gate. Then the path branched into several smaller paths. Everyone turned to look at me.

I looked at Donny. "To Norm's?"

"If it still exists," Donny rumbled.

"Surely one of his bakeries is still going."

"I don't know who Norm is, but I'd love some Outpost ale," Asher said.

"What's that?" Beth asked.

"It's a very special beverage," Asher said. His narrow face softened and a treasured memory seemed to weave around him.

"If by 'special' you mean it tastes like lighter fluid only it's more toxic, and it's about four thousand proof alcohol and causes blindness just from its fumes, then that's an accurate description," I said. "Beth, you aren't going near that stuff. Asher, first things first. Norm is our friend and he ran some establishments here, including some bakeries. That's where he liked to work."

Tae-yul stepped forward and sniffed. He held up his finger as if testing the air, and then stuck his finger in his mouth and sucked it. "There's a bakery this way," he said, pointing. He fell back beside Susie and we went in the direction he had indicated. I wasn't sure if he really knew there was a bakery in that direction, but it seemed as good a start as any.

WALKING THROUGH THE city, I experienced afresh, as I'd done during the time I'd spent here before, how much larger it was than it appeared from outside the barbed wire. In fact, it had grown. Outpost City was oblong and had been roughly twelve kilometers east-west by six kilometers north-south;

now it was about double that. Some of the crop fields that surrounded the city had been reclaimed as the town spread. There was an immense amount of construction going on, all of it by hand, of course, using old fashioned barn-raising, stone masonry, and brick laying techniques.

It was impossible to tell how many people lived here now. Gaff had once told me that it was about 20,000 before the mists incursion. It was surely five times that many since. All the dirt paths were crowded, every building was stuffed to overflowing, and folks traveled in packs of a dozen or more, every person visibly armed.

I stopped worrying about being recognized. The city was so over-populated, with throngs of refugees around every bend in the dirt path, that no one single person was going to stand out without considerable effort. Even if Arthur or Alexei arrived and combed the city for me, it was going to be almost impossible for them to spot me, a task made more difficult by my brown hair. Only someone who knew me well would recognize me, and they'd have to be staring directly at my face through the teeming masses. I was safer here than I'd feared.

After an hour of forging slowly along one of the jammed pathways, we reached a four story clapboard structure that Donny and I recognized.

"This way!" he and I chorused, pointing at a smaller path that angled off into an even more densely inhabited area. We exchanged a smile. Tae-yul had been tracking something, all right. Norm's main bakery, if it still stood, was just 100 meters away.

The bakery was intact even to its windows, no small miracle. Despite the late hour, there was a line of people waiting at the door. A lithe gray-haired man tenderly rubbed the front window with a rag. Glass was precious these days. The people in Cypress Hills village had created a rudimentary glass-making facility using old glass-blowing techniques, but sheets of plate glass were probably still far in mankind's future. None of that really mattered, though, because I recognized the gray-haired man from behind, as did Donny, and the two of us ran over to greet him.

"Norman! It's me, Angie," I sang, just before throwing myself at him.

Norman spread his arms and hugged me first and then shook hands with Donny. He laughed. "Good to see you two! And Susie. Where are the others?"

He meant Arthur and Robert and Jeannie and Laurette and Marco and Gaff. He also meant Theo, who would never return. He knew us all intimately, as we'd stayed with him during our last visit to Outpost City. He was one of our own but had chosen to stay behind to rebuild Outpost City.

Donny and I froze. Finally I squeaked, "It's complicated."

Norman frowned, instantly guarded. "Tell me later, then," he said. "Amy's inside, why don't I bring you in to say hello?"

We let him usher us ahead of him, bypassing the line of waiting customers. He opened the door and the succulent, yeasty smell of baking things wafted out and hit me in my gut. Saliva gathered in my mouth.

"Mama, this smells awesomely yummy," Beth said, which drew some chuckles.

"Amy, look what the goats dragged in," Norman called.

A woman with a mass of curly red locks stood behind the counter. Her fine-boned face lit up. As she came out to greet us, she pointed to a roundness at her belly. It was small still, but she was definitely pregnant, definitely showing.

I squealed and hugged her. "Amy! This is wonderful. How far along are you?"

"About four months," she said proudly. She smoothed my hair away from my face with a merry expression. "This is some dye job, Em. Clearly you did this on the road."

"Call me Angie," I responded quietly. "And don't tell anyone it's not my real hair color."

Amy nodded as she turned to Beth. "I remember you. I'm glad you're all right. Your mother went to a lot of trouble to rescue you."

"I know, that's why I'm helping her now," Beth said, in her serious way. "We're trying to save the world."

Amy raised her eyebrows. "That's good news. I want to bring my baby up in a world that's been saved."

"Save the world, huh?" Norman said. "That's a tall order."

"Yes and yes." I nodded.

"This have something to do with why the others aren't with you?" Norman asked.

"Long story, rather tell you in private," I told him.

"I'm Asher," Asher said, sticking his hand out at Amy.

She shook it with a small grin. "Welcome to Outpost City, Asher. It's the armpit of the Earth, but now it's a Safe Zone, so people arrive every day."

"I've been here before," he confided. "I know my way around. It's not so bad."

"Really? Then you'll find that it's what it always was, but even more so, because there are so many more citizens now, triple or quadruple what it used to be." She turned and draped her arm around my shoulders. "You need someplace to stay?"

"Yes, please," Susie answered, with uncharacteristic politeness. "Can we possibly stay with you while we're here?"

I smiled approval at her. Then I noticed the calculating gleam in her eyes as she looked at Amy, and I wondered what she was planning. I'd have to be stern with Susie that she couldn't bash any pregnant persons over the head, it would be too dangerous.

"Of course you'll stay with us," Amy said. "You're family, Em, ah, Angie, you know that." She patted Beth's head lightly. "If it wasn't for your mom, I wouldn't have found my way back to Norman. He and I would never have gotten back together. Now we're having a family. We owe her."

"Mama does good stuff," Beth replied. "Wait until you hear about our mission. But first we need a pilot."

"Whoa, young lady, hold your horses," Norman laughed and handed her a sweet roll, round and yellow and glazed with honey. "A pilot, huh? This is a tale to be told at home, over some Outpost ale."

NORMAN AND AMY now lived in a four room cabin, two downstairs two upstairs, made of logs under a sod roof. "We're on the list for bricks to build a bigger home, but it's going to be a few months," Norman said in a regretful tone. He ushered us in, saying, "I'm sorry the accommodations aren't as nice as before." He was referring to the modular home that had been eaten by the mists.

I said, "Don't be silly, this is a mansion for us."

He smiled and showed us upstairs, to a room furnished with a few crude cots. "You women can stay here, the men downstairs in the living room." He then apologized for having to return to his bakery to close up and left us to get situated. "Help yourselves to any food you find!" he said on his way out.

An hour later, Amy and Norman returned. Amy carried a ceramic jug of liquid on her hip. She sat it on the dinner table and then rustled up several mugs. "Emma, I know you love this stuff."

I moaned. "Not Outpost ale. Please, no." I covered my face with my hands and backed away.

"Indeed it is," she said, her eyes dancing. "Tastier and stronger than ever. They're calling it 'second life ale,' because this is the second life for Outpost City." She poured a mug full to the brim and handed it to me.

I took a deep breath, fortifying myself against the

onslaught. Then I took a swig. I was immediately sure that Amy was playing a prank on me and that she'd given me a draught of battery acid slurry. It was thick and meaty and foul and smelly and burned my mouth. I choked and looked for a place to spit it out. My eyes teared up and I swallowed. "Are you trying to kill me?" I gasped.

The others burst into laughter. Donny and Asher each asked for a cup.

"Don't be stingy," Asher told Amy. "I've already acquired the taste for Outpost ale."

We all giggled when he gagged and gurgled, trying not to spill the ale out of his mouth.

OVER DINNER, WE had the opportunity to explain what was going on.

"So, you cracked Arthur over the head with a big stick and then tied him up and left him there to rot in a horse stall," Norman said. He leaned back on his stool.

"Technically, yes, but there's a lot more to it than that, because Susie's gift is so important," I said uneasily. "He wasn't going to rot, there were too many people around to find him. And you know, I really didn't have any other choice."

"Sure you did," Norman said, shaking his head. "You didn't have to swing that stick."

"I for one am glad she did," Susie spoke up.

"Sure you are," Norman said. "I get that. You have an ability that might just save us all. Maybe, you think. If you get with the other girl."

"Exactly, but Arthur didn't see it that way. He's kind of unbalanced," I said. "So you see, I didn't have any other choice but to, um, disarm him and get Susie away."

"'Disarm him', my, isn't that a pretty way to put it?" Norman asked. He raised his eyebrows at me. "Remind me never to get on your bad side, Emma."

I flushed. "We have a mission. An important mission. The most important. If we succeed . . ."

"The mists are gone. Yep, it's important. So you're looking for a pilot willing to fly you back to Europe so Susie can combine her psi gift with the other girl's." Norman chewed his lip for a moment. "And that crazy Russian Alexei is chasing after you."

"That about covers it." I stabbed at the last few green peas on my plate with my fork. They were tender and flavored with pork fat. "This is really good, Amy. What a treat."

"I can't dissolve all the mists by myself," Susie said. "I can handle a little mist here or there. But to really get them, all of them, I need to be with Caris. We're a team. We have to do it together. She's waiting for me." Susie sipped some fresh goat milk that was frothy, fatty, and delicious.

I was glad that she and Beth were getting generous portions of the milk.

"It's hard for me to imagine that Arthur is crazy," Amy murmured. "I mean, this is Arthur we're talking about!"

"He's not outright criminally mad, like so many of the people who are infected by the mists," I clarified. "It's different. It's like, oh, he's unbalanced."

"He's lost sight of what's really important, which is getting rid of the mists for good," Donny added. "Arthur still wants to control and use the mists. It's a delusion. It's like he's just blind on this issue. This one issue."

"This one all important issue. It's a delusion we can't risk him acting on," I said, sighing. At the periphery of my consciousness, I could feel Arthur feeling for me, and I missed him. I wondered if he had realized I was leading my group to Outpost City.

Norman nodded slightly. "I guess I understand. There's

been too much devastation and loss of human life for Arthur to risk keeping the mists around for one second longer than we have to."

Susie smacked the table. "That's right! You get it. You do! So do you know someone who can help us? Do you know any pilots?

Norman scratched his gray head. "There is one pilot I can think of."

"Not Franklin," Amy groaned. "You've got to be kidding."

Norman shrugged. "He's not ideal."

"Not ideal?" Amy rolled her eyes. "He's falling down drunk and indentured to that bitch Yeva. How's Emma going to get Yeva to release him?"

"Same way anyone gets anything out of Yeva," Norman said.

"Really? And if she succeeds at that, she's going to be able to sober him up?" Amy laughed.

"Susie can sober anyone up," Tae-yul said with total confidence. "She'll give him a choice: he can sober up or she'll slit his throat. He'll stop drinking."

"Can we please go an entire day without the threat of Susie killing anyone?" I snapped. "Just one day? Please?" I focused on Norman. "Is Franklin a good enough pilot to get us across the ocean? Who is Yeva, and what do I have to do to get him away from her?"

"He can fly for sure," Norman said. "Franklin was a test pilot in the Navy, then a commercial pilot for twenty-five years. He was flying a jumbo jet airplane on the polar route on the hour of The Day that the mists rose up. He figured out from air traffic reports that Edmonton was a Safe Zone and he flew the plane through the mist attacks to Edmonton. But Edmonton International Airport was getting a pile-up of planes, so he set the plane down in a field outside the city. Beautiful landing. Not one passenger lost."

"So he can fly." Donny narrowed his eyes. "What's this business with the woman?"

"Would we call Yeva a woman?" Amy wondered. She folded her arms over her chest and leaned back in contemplation. "Really, I don't know. It's sort of an insult to our gender."

"Could you just tell us her story?" I asked. "We need a good pilot, an expert pilot, and it sounds like your Franklin is one."

"She's the proprietor of a tavern and brothel, The Dark Horse." Norman scrunched up his face. "Do you play cards, Em? Do you know anything about poker?"

Now it was my turn to smile. Once upon a time, before mists rose up to devour the people and things of this Earth, I had been an artist and an illustrator. How had I made spending money for myself in art school? Playing poker. "Might know a little something about cards, Norman. Might play a little poker."

13

DEEP IN THE BADLANDS, THE WORST section of Outpost City, I leaned against a new, mostly completed brick building. I was watching The Dark Horse saloon across the dirt road. The saloon was a four story wooden structure that had clearly survived the mists incursion; possibly it had even stood here in The Before. Organ music spilled out, but the music wasn't coherent. Someone was practicing scales and arpeggios and a few measures of various songs. I guess the pre-lunch crowd didn't mind the dissonance.

This was recon. I wanted to see Franklin and Yeva in their natural environment before approaching them.

Boisterous groups of people swirled, ebbed, and flowed in front of me, all loud, dirty, and armed. Many were haggling over goods or services, in mostly English but a garble of other languages as well: Spanish, Navaho, French, German, something Slavic, and something Semitic. I wasn't sure what they were all saying; I only knew I had no desire to stand in front of the speakers who were spitting out all those guttural "ch's."

Two brawny men with knives, short spears, and bows stood guard at the door of the saloon—bouncers. They stepped back with alacrity when a tall, large-boned woman wearing a coiled crown of hair strode out of the bar. She wore a long dark skirt and a black leather vest and a nasty-looking, long, sharp dagger at her side. Her face was round and pale with large cheekbones and her blue eyes were slightly slanted. One might call her handsome despite the sneer of scorn she wore. One would want to make sure that word pleased her before uttering it in her hearing.

She dragged behind her a small, lean man who was shorter than her. She slung him around so that he ricocheted forward and stumbled into her ample torso, at which time she thrust a broom into his hands. She leaned down so she was only a few centimeters from his face and I could hear her yelling, though I couldn't distinguish her words. Her last word was more of a growl: "Franklin!" Her accent wasn't American. She stormed back into the saloon.

Yeva was big and ferocious. I didn't think I could take her in a fight, even with all the training in hand-to-hand combat I'd received from Arthur, Theo, Robert, and even Jeannie, who was a prize-fighting boxer before she got pregnant. In The Before, she'd won some matches in her hometown of Liverpool. Even postpartum, stalwart Jeannie could probably take Yeva, who looked formidable.

Franklin was another matter. Beth could sit on him and bring him to heel. He was pitiful, the world-class fighter pilot who was going to fly us to Europe in our effort to save the world. From the back he had a scraggly brown ponytail. He started sweeping, weaving on his feet as he wielded the broom. Not even noon yet and evidently he'd imbibed several too many glasses of Outpost ale. I guess they called it Second Life ale now, but in my mind it would always be Outpost ale.

Franklin turned as he swept, revealing his front. He wore dark aviator sunglasses that hid his eyes; gray tufts of eyebrow curled over the rims. He had a lean, lined face and a mustache that was white and brown and that sprawled all over his face in a completely haphazard, ungroomed manner. His mouth was sloppy lax in the manner of drunks.

That's what I had to work with. A pilot who could figure out that Edmonton was a Safe Zone, and then land a jumbo jet on a field outside of the city while the mists were ravaging the Earth, was a pilot who could get us across the ocean using whatever planes and fuel we could find. He'd need to be sobered up, of course. That was going to take some work.

I watched him sweep. *How has he managed to get himself indentured to Yeva? Neither Norman nor Amy volunteered that information. They alluded to poker and then quickly changed the subject both times I asked. Maybe I don't want to know. Does it really matter, as long as I can get Franklin to do what we need him to do?*

Arthur would tell me to do my homework, to gather the intel I needed to ensure success. Poker was as much a game of knowing your opponents as it was a game of strategy and chance. Arthur always insisted on thorough preparation; it was one of his strengths as a leader.

Arthur. No sooner had I smiled with sadness and love and longing and regret than a butterfly flew across my gaze. It had big yellow wings tipped with brown and it skimmed over the heads of a passing group of Chinese men.

Behind the Chinese men walked another group of men, and there was something about the brisk coordination of their movements, and the way they were scanning other pedestrians, that set off a warning bell in my head. I was invisible here because of the great throngs of people and my dyed hair, but I didn't think it wise to press my luck. Those men were looking for someone. They didn't look like Alexei's men so it probably wasn't me, but why find out? I melted back into the alley behind the brick house, resolving to return later.

THE NEXT DAY I spent several hours at the bakery, helping Amy sell loaves and rolls. She gave me a jaunty khaki linen hat with a visor to wear, to shadow my face and further hide my identity—in the unlikely event that someone who remembered me from when I was almost hanged came into the store.

Amy and I walked back to her place, where I greeted everyone and hugged Beth. Donny and I grabbed some thick slabs of sourdough and walked back out. I was returning to The Dark Horse for more observation. Donny was going to poke around a few other saloons.

"I'll buy drinks and see who knows where there are planes and fuel left," he said, between bites of the sourdough.

"You have credits or something to trade so you can lubricate your sources?" I asked.

He nodded and swallowed. "I have money. While you were out today, I went to a municipal bank and traded in some stuff to get it."

"Municipal bank?" I asked, with more than a little mirth. "Outpost City has such an establishment?"

Donny grinned. "You gotta to see it to believe it. It's a hole in the wall with soldiers stationed around it. They've instituted a kind of currency." He held up a round wooden disk with a hole through the middle. The inside lip of the hole was inscribed with a logo that combined the Royal Forces insignia with 'OC,' the initials for Outpost City. He laid the wooden disk in my hand. "These are one credit. Red ones are five credits and green ones are ten."

"I saw some at the bakery, though most people are still using the old record keeping system. Amy keeps a notebook along with a lockbox for the credits."

"What was your impression of the pilot?" Donny asked. He finished his chunk of bread and sighed and licked a crumb off his index finger.

"Good, right?" I smiled.

"Best bread I ever had," he stated. "Even better than before the mists came through. I can't wait for Kangee to get here and taste it. She's gonna love it."

"I'll be happy when Kangee arrives, and not just for the bread. But Franklin . . ." I shook my head.

"That bad?"

"Worse."

"I'll keep an ear out for other pilots," Donny said, frown-ing. "If I'm asking about planes, the conversation will go there naturally."

"Probably wise. I think we can work with Franklin, once we dry him out. But he may have the DT's and that will slow us down."

"Jesus," Donny muttered. "Guy sounds like a peach. I understand the desire to get sauced and stay sauced in The After, we've all lost so much and seen so much. But at a certain point, we all have a responsibility to suck it up and rebuild."

"Amen," I said. "That's my street." I pointed to the turnoff toward The Dark Horse.

He waved and ambled on.

I shouldered through the crowds passing in front of the saloon and made my way to the same brick wall I'd been lean-ing against the previous day. The light was still bright because it was summer, but there was a faint underlying hue of peri-winkle saturating everything. The afternoon would soon wane into dusk.

In The Before, when I was an artist, I had loved to paint en plein air at this time of day, to capture this specific, delectable quality of light, which felt so rich and multi-dimensional. Day was pregnant with night and the spectral nuances of shadow were alluring to an artist.

Indistinct yelling emanated from The Dark Horse and the bouncers stood at attention. Franklin stumbled out of the saloon with a rag in hand. Yeva followed him. She gave him an earful of what was colorful diction in several languages, from what I could discern.

A passerby happened to look askance at her, and when she noticed, she charged the man and slapped his chest with both hands. She cast derogatory aspersions on his manhood, par-entage, and sexual proclivities. He was a big guy, husky and carrying an axe at his belt, but he made pacifying gestures and backed away. She snapped her fingers in his face, snarled, and strode back inside the saloon.

Yeva didn't like to be questioned. Not by men, or not by anyone? I wondered.

Swaying drunkenly, Franklin rubbed at the front window. He leaned over and puked on the ground, then tried to scuff the vomitus away from the saloon. Fortunately for him a young white goat bounced over to sniff and then consume the mess.

I felt someone watching me and it sent a lush shiver down the sensitive vertebral peaks of my spine. Only one man made me tremble that way. I looked around and at an angle from me, peering out of a space between buildings, I saw him.

He stepped forward and my heart raced. Arthur. He had trailed me to Outpost City. He tilted his chin up at me. His expression softened when our eyes met and I thought he didn't look angry.

He must have been reading my mind because he smiled ruefully and shook his head. No, he wasn't angry. He just couldn't believe I'd knocked him out, tied him up, and left with Susie.

I kind of shrugged with empty palms, what was I supposed to do? I took him in anew.

He wore a navy blue tank top that showed the clean, rolling delineation of muscles on his arms and chest. He was so perfectly proportioned that you wouldn't know, at first glance, how tall he was, unless someone stood beside him. He didn't have the lanky, gorilla-armed look of so many tall men. There wasn't an ounce of anything but muscle on him, but he wasn't narrow, he was well-built front-to-back, hard flesh over a robust chassis. He had perfect posture and his torso tapered to a 'V' cinching in at a good, solid pelvic block—he had some power there.

I felt the old hunger for him simmer up.

He tilted his head as if he was still following my thoughts, and he might have been, because we were so tied to each other.

It wasn't a tie I could indulge at this moment. I had a mission to accomplish, a mission that I feared Arthur would derail utterly. I wanted to go to Arthur, though, I couldn't help longing to be with him, to be in his arms.

My heart felt ragged and I wondered, was it all worth it, everything I had done over the last few years, since The Day? Getting involved with Arthur in the first place, on that fateful day in the south of France, when he and his men thundered up on horses and rescued Mandy from certain death by a mist? Falling in love with him? Leaving Haywood and my children to rescue Arthur from Alexei? Swinging a stick into the side of Arthur's head and leaving him tied up in a horse stall so I could get away with Susie, on the ever-more-slender-seeming hope that she could eradicate the mists forever, if I helped her unite with Caris?

It was all unresolvable and chaotic and if I pursued it, it would unhinge me. I started to sidle over into the alley alongside the brick building, but Arthur held up a warning finger.

He pointed down the alley, and when I peeked around the corner of the building, I saw three men coming toward me. They wore bandanas tied around their heads and muddy leather pants and they carried themselves like raiders, with the swagger of their weapons and their aggression. Then I saw the dark sleeve on the right side of their shirts, and I knew they were Alexei's men.

They probably wouldn't recognize me but I wasn't going to hang around and test them.

Arthur receded from view.

I skipped out from my alcove and joined one of the endless crowds of people. This one was walking toward that angle in the adjoining street where Arthur had stood. I wove my way to the center of the group and threw glances back over my shoulder at Alexei's men, who came out and stood looking down the street. The group passed by Arthur's hiding spot and

I slipped from their midst and darted into it. I ran down the alley after him, knowing I shouldn't, not caring.

Where was he? There was no sign of him.

I let myself get very still. Then I sought him with my feelings. My feet started moving again. I ran down the alley onto the next street and turned left. My feet kept going and they led me down another street.

I stopped in front of a lodging house that looked like a dormitory from a school. I threw open the door and saw a young Asian woman behind a desk. Filipina, probably. On her desk, she had lit a hurricane lamp against the coming evening.

"A big dark-haired man just came in—"

"Second floor, Room 23," she said. She pointed toward a door just past the lobby area. I turned. "Wait a minute," she hollered.

I tossed the wooden disk from Donny at her.

She snapped it out of the air with two slim brown fingers and then motioned me forward.

Heart pounding, I raced up the stairs. I ran down the hall to Room 23. At the door I stopped and took a deep breath. This was wrong, I knew it. I turned the knob anyway. I entered a small candlelit room.

Arthur stood in the center of the room, waiting. His gray eyes were smudged with dark circles and thick stubble covered his chin and hollowed cheeks. For the first time, there were white whiskers dotting the black. He didn't move. He didn't scold me or question me or demand that I turn Susie over to him or anything I might have expected. He said, "Choose me."

I went to him and put my arms around him. I stood up on my tiptoes to kiss his mouth.

Arthur held my forearms gently in his hands and perused my face. "Emma."

"I shouldn't be here," I said.

"Why are you?"

I said, "I just have to be." I kissed him again.

Arthur responded but he didn't initiate anything more.

I kept kissing him and then pressed my tongue between his lips and touched it to his tongue and then probed his mouth.

A kind of primitive electricity surged between us. His breath caught and a tremor went through him but he didn't take hold of me as I expected. He was simply responding.

Then I was kissing and biting his neck and chest around the fabric of his shirt.

"Emma," he said hoarsely. "You can't just . . . Not after . . . Why are you here?"

"I want you."

"I don't understand. You left me. Like you left Haywood, I guess. But you didn't hit him with a stick and bind and gag him." He smiled bitterly and the pupils of his eyes shrank to tiny pinpoints.

"I'm sorry," I whispered. I pulled his tank top upward and he held his arms down, preventing me from pulling it over his head.

"You act like things just happen to you," he said. He shook his head. "God damn it, Emma. Choose me. Choose *me*. For real. Forever. Right now."

"I do choose you!" I cried. "But you . . . you don't get it about the mists. Maybe you can't because you created them and you're too invested and too close to the situation."

"You're not even giving us a chance to work it out?"

"Susie asked me to help her, and I said I would."

"So you're choosing Susie, instead of me. Like you chose Haywood before. Twice. You go with him and then you come back for me. Now you've gone with Susie, who's haunted by her own special kind of crazy. You choose someone else, over and over again. I'm supposed to be okay with that. How do you think I feel about it?"

I closed my eyes and leaned into him. "Just for now. Not forever. Just this minute. Please, Arthur. I miss you so much."

Arthur breathed raggedly, then raised his arms to let me slide off his shirt. It surprised me and then I was ravenous with hunger for him.

I ran my tongue down his belly. He wore loose drawstring trousers so I untied them and pulled them to his ankles. He wasn't wearing underwear, and I had some fun with my hands and mouth before I pulled his feet out of his pants. He was allowing me to lead and it excited me in a way I'd not expected.

He was naked and his breath was rasping all the way into his gut and he was hard so invitingly that it made me want to throw a leg over him and ride hard. So I did. I pushed him back onto the small cot and tore off my jeans. I was astride him when I yanked my shirt over my head and threw it off.

I knew it cost Arthur something to lie back and let me have my way, and that intensified the sensations for me. Usually Arthur was so forthright and proactive that I didn't get to do this. I loved the way he desired me, but it was delicious for my desire to have its own space to unfold. I was wet and thrilling as I moved up and down atop him, slowly, because that was the way I liked to start. Slowly at first.

Arthur gripped my buttocks and matched my tempo. One half of his mouth curved in a smile.

I gripped his shoulders and leaned forward to kiss him some more. I loved the feel of him beneath my hands, his warm taut body and the length and strength of it, the roundness of his deltoids and pectoralis, the flatness of his belly, the luscious power of his thighs. It drove away every other thought or feeling. My doubts and confusion and uncertainty evaporated. As always with Arthur, I was completely consumed by the smell of his flesh, his personal scent: cedar and pine and vanilla and horses and sweat and the wind and the sky.

Then the tempo took over with a will of its own. The ancient frenzy seized us both, and I was shuddering and crying out atop him, and his cry rang out just after mine.

I lay down beside him, curling into him. I stroked his chest and ran my fingers gently over the scratch marks I'd left. I thought about healing the marks and my hands paused, but Arthur lifted my hand to his mouth and kissed my palm. He wanted the scratches. It made me obscurely happy, because I wanted him to wear my marks.

A single rectangular window showed the violet light filling the streets as dusk fell. His handsome symmetrical face was turned toward mine and he rested his cheek against my forehead.

I sat up and put my hands on his chest. The familiar tingles of the healing current prickled in my palms.

"I hoped I'd find you at The Dark Horse," he said.

"How'd you know?"

"I just did. Same way I knew you'd follow me here. We're connected, Emma. In a way that can't be broken. Even if you won't believe me about the mists."

"I can't believe you about them," I whispered.

"Is this where you put me to sleep, instead of talking things out with me?" he asked, his voice thick and slow. "Fuck me and leave me. You've done that before."

I smiled tremulously.

"Stay and face me. Choose that. We can work it out about Susie. Trust me. Emma, trust me. I know what I'm talking about with the mists, precisely because I'm invested and close to them. Give me a chance. All of humanity deserves this chance."

My heart shivered. He still didn't get it—the mists could never be completely controlled. We were going to destroy them at the first opportunity. My despair returned as the tingles in my hands intensified.

His lids closed over his eyes and his head tilted away.

14

WHEN I RETURNED TO NORMAN'S place, Kangee was sitting at the dining room table. She gave me a sly look, raising her eyebrows. "There you are."

"Glad to see you, Kangee." I hugged her gently and seated myself on an empty stool between Beth and Asher. Susie and Tae-yul sat across the table. Norman sat at one end. I asked, "Donny's not back yet?"

"Soon." Kangee smiled crookedly. "It takes a strong man to let a woman run the show."

I blushed a little and Susie sat up straight in her chair. "You have that look. You're glowing! You've been with—"

"I've been gathering information." I took a draught of Outpost ale to cover my chagrin.

"What information did you gather?" Asher asked casually, but he was eying me quizzically and intently through his thick glasses.

"The information that Franklin's a drunk and Yeva's a nightmare," I said. "Really, she likes poker?"

"That's her thing," Norman said. "She won Franklin in a poker hand. She runs a game every night in the back of her tavern. Gambling isn't illegal in Outpost City."

"Only stealing a horse or a gun is," I said drily.

Amy set a plate of sautéed greens and roasted meat in front of me. "You ready to take her on?"

I was ravenous and ate a huge bite of greens before answering. "She's something. What, I don't know. But something."

Amy giggled. "That's one way to put it."

"She's good at poker," Norman said, solemnly. "The woman can play. Took dozens of loaves of bread from me in one game."

"Before I stopped letting him play," Amy said grimly.

"Skill or luck?" I asked. In my experience with cards, both mattered.

Norman gave me a wide-eyed look but didn't answer.

"I could kick her ass," Susie said. She leaned forward. "What's her deal?"

I was chewing a bite of meat which I figured was mutton. Hoped so, anyway. Goat was a bit exotic for my taste. Of course, in The After, I was lucky to have meat; I wasn't going to question its origins. I swallowed. "Her deal is that she's a very tall, big-boned woman and mean as a snake. Meaner. I saw her assault a guy just for looking at her funny. She's got some kind of hold on Franklin and she keeps him working for her. Plus she's got some tough-looking bouncers standing guard at the door."

"That's not all you found out," Kangee said with a lilt.

I colored, couldn't help it. "Arthur is here in Outpost city. The others must be, too. I didn't see them."

"I knew it!" Susie sprang up from her seat and paced around the table. "You—you," she glanced at Beth and then shook her finger at me, "*dallied* with him! Why would you do that? You know he wants to stop us from going to Europe so he can use me to control the mists."

"I had to know," I said softly and a little sadly.

Susie demanded, "Know what?"

"Know if he still feels that way or if maybe he changed his mind."

"He does, doesn't he?" she challenged. "He can't change his mind, Emma. Don't you get that? He's obsessed. It's his own personal mist madness. He thinks the mists are the key to humanity's future. He doesn't get it that we have to get rid of them permanently. You're lucky he didn't try to stop you from coming back here."

"He didn't."

"What if he had, what would you have done? What would have happened to us?" Susie pounded on the wall. "What were you thinking, Emma? You know Arthur can't be trusted. He wants to control the mists for his own purposes. He wants to use me to do that. He'll try to interfere. He'll try to take control of me. I won't let that happen. I'll kill him first."

"I got this," Tae-yul rose and stood beside Susie. His lethal little slingshot swung back and forth in his skilled fingers. "Where is this Arthur? What's he look like?"

"No one's killing Arthur!" I snapped. I pointed to their empty seats. "Susie, Tae-yul, sit down this minute. We're going to finesse the situation. We're not going to hurt Arthur. I mean it. Sit down. I've got a plan."

"Did he follow you?" Susie asked.

"No. He was asleep when I left him. He did not follow me."

"He'll find us." Reluctantly Susie sat back down.

A moment later, Tae-yul joined her.

"We'll leave tonight and find someplace else to stay. You're right, Arthur and the others will find their way here," I said.

Norman said softly, "Em, I don't feel like I could deny him lodging, if he asked me. I know y'all are running from him and you have sound reasons, but still, he's my friend. I couldn't turn him away."

Amy said anxiously, "I don't think he would try to take control of, er, anyone, ah, the situation, here in our home. He's a polite guest."

"I wouldn't want to put you two in any kind of awkward position. We'll leave right after dinner," I said. I looked at

Norman searchingly. "I am going to ask you not to repeat to Arthur what we've talked about with you."

Norman and Amy exchanged a look. They both nodded.

"This sucks," Susie muttered. She pushed her plate away with a spastic, angry gesture. "I'm done eating, I'm gonna pack." She got up and went to the crude stairs that led to the second floor. "Where are we staying, anyway?"

"We'll find somewhere in the Badlands, maybe the new section," I said. "It's pretty crowded over there."

"Pretty crowded?" Norm said. "It's like the gutters of Kolkata over there, swarming with people."

"It'll be hard to find us." I took another big bite.

Norm said, "Impossible to find you."

"It'd be easier if you'd just let Tae-yul deal with the problem his way." Susie scowled.

"No one's hurting Arthur!" I yelled. "Don't think it for one second! This is the last I want to hear of it. I mean it. Susie, if Arthur is hurt, I won't help you get to the camp in Europe!"

Susie made a shoulder motion of acquiescence and trudged up the stairs.

"We should grab this guy Franklin and get out tonight," Tae-yul said. He speared a last bite of meat on his fork and chewed it contemplatively.

"There's no grabbing him. Yeva keeps him on a leash and there are the guards to deal with." I sighed. "Beth, if you're done, go pack your backpack. We'll leave as soon as I'm done eating."

Beth gave me a wide-eyed looked and ran up the stairs.

"You know, Susie's right," Asher said mildly. "You are glowing." He raised his eyebrows at me and then shrugged. "Thank you kindly for the meal, Amy, Norman. I appreciate your hospitality." He bobbed his head with gratitude and then went to the other room to pack.

Amy gave me a small smile. "Norman makes me glow, too."

I took another long, noxious draught of ale.

DEEP IN THE Badlands, we found a two-room shanty occupied by a family of four Africans. I offered them my pair of sneakers from the warehouse and the mother tried them on. She was a full-bodied woman in a turban, and the sneakers fit her perfectly. She grinned widely, told us her name was Chioma, and agreed to let us have one of the rooms. She threw in a big jug of Outpost ale to welcome us to our new residence. Chioma's husband hammered wooden nails into the door between the two rooms to shut it permanently. We had a window to use as a door and a chipped earthenware planter to use as a chamber pot.

Kangee had gone to find Donny and the two of them showed up shortly after we settled in to our new room. I had lit a hurricane lantern and we were making ourselves comfortable on the floor space, which consisted of raw planks glued or plastered down over plywood. But there didn't seem to be many insects coming up through the cracks and we'd be protected from rain, so I was happy with the accommodations.

"Ritzy," Kangee said as she clambered over the window sill.

I gave her a sardonic look.

She smiled and her long black braid danced around her head. "I've stayed in worse." She kissed Beth on her forehead and nodded at Susie in an amicable fashion. She waved at Asher and kind of grimaced at Tae-yul. "Kill anyone today, Tae-yul? You and Susie are a perfect pair."

Susie puffed up to say something heated in response but I waved her to silence.

"So Arthur's here in Outpost City?" Donny asked, in a tired voice. He climbed through the window and seated himself with his back resting against the wall. Asher handed him a mug of ale and Donny sipped it gratefully.

I dug a roll and some jerky out of my backpack and handed both to Donny. "Yes, I encountered Arthur."

Susie made a contemptuous face. "Is that what you're calling it?"

"I haven't seen him or the others," Donny rumbled. "But I know where we can find an airplane. Oshkosh."

"Oshkosh, Wisconsin?" I clarified.

"We went there with Daddy, to the air show, a few years ago," Beth said. She scooted up to the wall to sit beside Donny. "It was a lot of fun."

"Apparently a number of aviation enthusiasts gathered there to protect what planes they could, after the mists went through. Scuttlebutt says there are still planes and fuel there," Donny said.

"That's far away," Susie said. She bit her lip. "Anywhere closer?"

"That's our best bet for finding a plane in good shape, as well as enough fuel to carry us across the Atlantic," Donny said. "You're right though. It's far, over 2,000 kilometers."

"How long will that take us on our horses?" Susie asked.

"Horses can go about thirty-five kilometers a day, from what I've seen," Asher mused.

"That's what, eighty days?" Susie asked, dismayed.

"Fifty-seven and a few hours," Asher said. "But I think Oshkosh is closer to 2,200 or 2,300 kilometers from here."

"You can push the horses some, but not much for such a long time," Kangee said. "They'll need some time to recuperate."

Susie tucked her blonde hair behind her ears and squinted at Kangee. "Can you travel ahead and make sure they actually have planes and fuel? So we don't waste our time."

Kangee nodded. "Good idea. I'll set out tomorrow."

"The longer it takes me to get to Caris, the more people die," Susie reminded us. She glared at me. "That's why we can't waste time dallying with anyone."

"Let it go, Susie," Kangee said mildly. "You might understand one day."

"How about pilots?" I asked, loath to enter a discussion about dallying. "Anyone besides Franklin?"

Donny shook his head. "A couple of small plane pilots, no one instrument rated. They both spoke well of Franklin. Complimented his ability to fly."

"Damn, that's what I was afraid of," I muttered. "It's going to come down to a poker game with Yeva."

"What have you got to stake?" Donny gave me a sidelong look.

"How much money do we have from your outing to the municipal bank?" I asked.

"What? There's a municipal bank here in Outpost City?" Asher laughed.

"It's even more laughable when you walk inside it," Donny said wryly. "Emma, I traded in a few things, not too much, because I didn't know what we might still need. I got us almost 200 credits."

"Think that will be enough to get you into the game?" Tae-yul asked.

I shrugged. "I hope so. I didn't finish the recon."

"That's because you got distracted," Susie snapped.

I gave her a level, unblinking glance. Kangee was right, someday Susie might understand. At least, I hoped so. I prayed that Susie wasn't too damaged to find the joy in a man's arms that I experienced with Arthur.

Susie's accusatory glance fell away.

"I was wondering something," Beth said. She sat with her arms draped around her knees. "We're doing everything we can to get Susie to Caris at the old camp Mama was at. Do they knew we're coming?"

Susie's mouth dropped open in an 'o' of surprise. "I don't know, Beth. Good question. I hope so. I mean, I think so. I know Caris knows we have to be together to face the mists. I know she can feel the same connection I feel."

"Maybe we should find a way to tell them you're coming," Beth said. "Maybe they can help us somehow."

"I never thought of that, but it's a good idea," I said slowly.

Tae-yul asked, "How will we tell them?"

"Kangee," Susie suggested, rising up on her knees. "Can you go to Europe?"

Kangee tilted her head. "I don't know. I've never crossed an ocean."

"Crossing an ocean is a big deal. I don't want you to try anything dangerous that might get you hurt," Donny rumbled. "Kangee, I don't know if this is a good idea."

"She can try and see if it's dangerous. Maybe for her it isn't. Would you be willing to try, Kangee?" Susie persisted. "I think Beth's right, it's important that they know we're coming. They'll want to meet us when we arrive."

"Don't you have a telepathic connection with the other girl? That's what it feels like to me," Donny said. "Why don't you just let her know that way?"

"I'm gonna try, for sure," Susie said. "But our connection isn't exactly telepathic. It doesn't have words. I wasn't even sure of her name until Emma told me. I knew it started with a 'K' sound."

"You didn't know her name yet you're sure you and she together can dissolve the mists?" Asher asked. His voice sounded skeptical.

"Yes, I'm sure," Susie insisted.

"It sounds to me like you bashed me over the head and dragged me away from where I was safe and happy on a whim and a hunch," Asher said stiffly. "Now I'm sitting here in Outpost City, hiding from people and without a clue as to what I'll be doing tomorrow, or even if I'll still be alive."

"Ash, I know what I'm doing, even if I don't have a total telepathic connection with Caris," Susie returned, her fettle and her color rising.

"We've come too far to question our path now," Kangee said mildly. "I don't mind trying to cross over to Europe. I never thought about it. All I can do is try."

"Not if it's dangerous for you," Donny said. He pulled his wife to sit beside him and curled his arm around her shoulders. "That's a mighty big ocean. What happens if you come out of your special travel style while you're over it? You could fall in and drown. I don't want you to risk yourself this way. If Susie can't use her telepathic connection, we'll find someone who's telepathic and get them to send the message."

Asher tilted his head and considered. "Donny, that's an interesting idea. Here in Outpost City, many people have psi abilities, because so many are partly crazy. And many will sell their psi abilities. Everybody works here, right? Maybe we can find a telepath and pay them to send a message."

"Then we'll broadcast what we're doing, and that's not optimal," Susie objected. "Someone could hear about it and interfere. We can't risk that."

"We can word the message carefully," Asher said. "We don't have to say why we're coming."

"I agree with Susie. It's best not to let anyone know our plans," Tae-yul said. "People might try to grab Susie to control her, like Arthur wants to do. Or they might try to stop her because they're crazy. Some of the crazy ones don't care who dies. Some even worship the mists. There are all kinds of crazies now."

"You always agree with Susie," I noted wearily, tired of the bickering. "That's what you're here to do."

"That doesn't mean I'm wrong," Tae-yul replied.

"I can try to go to Europe, to Emma's old camp," Kangee said. "I'll do that after I check out Oshkosh. But it's wise to find a telepath for hire, in case I can't cross the ocean. Or in case I don't come back. For whatever reason. I can swim."

"We'll find a telepath. I'll find one," Donny asserted. He squeezed Kangee a little closer into his side. "Go to Oshkosh and come back. That I know you can do safely. You're not going to Europe. I forbid it."

Kangee looked at him and smiled and cuddled into his burly front. Then she looked at me and smiled with complete equanimity, and just like that, I knew she was going to try to cross the ocean with her special ability. Not just because Susie had asked her to, but because she, Kangee, was curious to see if she could.

I wondered if Donny knew that, too, or if, in the way of husbands everywhere in all times, Before and After, he would delude himself into believing that Kangee would obey him.

THE NEXT MORNING I tasked Tae-yul with doing recon at The Dark Horse. Arthur wouldn't recognize him; I didn't want to return there yet in case Arthur was waiting for me. Tae-yul had strict orders to find out everything he could about the poker game—and not to kill anyone, especially Arthur.

Donny and Kangee strolled out together, arm in arm. Kangee was going to use her marvelous gift for travel to go to Oshkosh and ascertain the truth of the rumors about intact planes. Donny would troll for more information about planes, pilots, and Yeva.

Asher and Susie stayed home with Beth. Beth pulled a book from her backpack and curled up to read it. Asher reclined on the floor with his hands clasping the back of his head. His lids were half open, half closed in reverie. Susie busied herself sharpening knives and tending to her arrows.

I traded a sweater for an orange and green scarf from Chioma and draped it around my head to disguise myself, then went to buy food with a few wooden coins supplied by Donny. A market had sprung up a few streets away on a patch of land scoured clean by the mists, so I didn't have far to go. I kept my head down and my eyes in motion, sweeping from one periphery to the next, vigilant for Arthur or the others.

The market was crowded and smelly and noisy with merchants selling wares of all kinds. They'd set up tables and stalls out of anything available and exhibited their goods in a seemingly random clutter. One or two had laid down a piece of fabric over the table to attempt to create an attractive display. Dogs and cats and goats and chickens and rats threaded through the throngs. People were yelling and haggling and bickering and joking and flirting, and a very fat guy walked around with a ukulele in his arms, singing. It was his size that impressed me most, though his voice was good, a high fine tenor that was pleasing to hear. But how did anyone manage to be that round in The After? It's not like high fructose corn syrup was now part of anyone's diet.

I found a stall selling berries and beans and shouldered my way through the other customers to purchase those. I went in a leisurely way toward another stall selling eggs and roast chickens, and I was looking down to avoid animal poo so I bumped into a stocky, bow-toting soldier. I stumbled and he grabbed my arm to steady me. I looked up into green eyes that seemed vaguely familiar. I tried but I couldn't place him.

"Careful, Miss," he said.

I nodded without speaking. Something about him pinged a distant memory. Who was he? I waved and kept walking. I felt his eyes boring into my back but I didn't turn around. After a few minutes, the magnetic sense of being watched released me. I pulled the scarf closer around my face. I bought two roast chickens and quickly picked my way out of the market. I practically ran all the way back to our shanty.

Tae-yul returned in the late afternoon. He leapt in through the window and grabbed up a chicken drumstick before his feet even touched the floor. "I can tell you about the game," he announced, his mouth full of meat.

"Don't talk with your mouth full," I chided gently. But I sat up on my heels, eager to hear what he'd learned.

Asher sat up also, crossing his legs and steepling his hands in front of his solar plexus.

Susie handed Tae-yul a cracked mug full of water.

Tae-yul swallowed and wiped his face with his arm before sipping the water. "Most nights you have to bring twenty credits to sit at the table. Other nights, it's as high as almost 1,000."

I grunted. So sometimes the buy in was high. Interesting. "What kind of bankroll do most people have?"

"Depends on the night. Most days Yeva holds games where the most people bet is two credits. But a couple times a month she has a no limit game and people can bet as high as they want."

"If your goal is to get that pilot away from her, that's the night to join," Asher said. "The betting will be wild, especially if people are drinking Outpost ale. That stuff's more disinhibiting than tequila."

"Does she play those games?" I asked.

"Those are the only games she plays," Tae-yul said. "The low stakes games bore her."

So Yeva's hunting big game. I said, "I'm going to need more than a couple hundred credits."

"More like 1,000," Asher agreed.

"And a plan for an advantage," Susie said, narrowing her eyes. "We need to make sure you win. Absolutely sure."

"Cheating's not a good idea," Tae-yul said in a matter-of-fact voice. "She and her goons beat anyone who's caught cheating. One guy got caught and he'll never walk again, they beat him so bad."

"So we figure out a way to cheat well, so we don't get caught," Susie said.

"We?" I asked in an ironic tone. "I'm the one sitting at the table."

"Mama, maybe we should let Donny play," Beth said. She laid her hand on my arm. Worry was written all over her lovely young face.

"We're going to give your mom a lot of help, don't worry," Susie reassured her.

"The help you can give me will be taking care of Beth and yourself," I said sharply. "I don't think cheating is a good idea."

"But are you any good at poker?" Susie demanded. "Really, Emma, can you play and win?"

"I believe so," I said quietly, wishing I had more information about Yeva herself. She surely had courage with her cards. She was aggressive. She was probably cunning; she was a successful business woman, after all. The question was, was she a tight or loose player? Did she have a reckless streak? Was she the kind of player who'd chase two aces with two kings, and pray for the third cowboy? Would she be in all the pots, no matter how bad her cards were, simply because she craved action? I'd seen smart people turn foolish that way.

My number one rule of playing poker was not to play a losing hand. Then I wondered if that was what I'd been doing with Arthur all these years, breaking my own rule just to be in the game with him. Did we really have a future, after all? For all his magnificent appeal, for all the depth and charge of our connection, would we ever be able to merge our interests? Not just regarding Susie and the mists. I was still, and always would be, Beth and Mandy's mother.

"You *believe* so?! That's not good enough! We need that pilot guy, Franklin," Susie argued. "When's the last time you even played?"

"It's been a while," I admitted. "But it never leaves you. Playing poker's like, I don't know, riding a bike. If you play enough to acquire the skill, it stays in your body-mind and you never forget how to do it."

Asher said, "You'll have to get all her money that she's gambling that night and then convince her to bet Franklin. That's a big goal. Can you do it?"

That's the question, isn't it? I said, "Maybe a side bet, if I can lure her into one. It's less about getting all her money, because it's not money we're after."

Susie cocked her head in patent disbelief. "Maybe a side bet? We need a plan B. If you lose, we'll grab Franklin. Where does he sleep?"

"At the foot of Yeva's bed, waiting on her all night," Tae-yul said, with a shudder of repulsion. "Emma was right when she said it before. There's no grabbing him. Emma has to get him in the poker game. Trust me."

"Maybe Donny can go to the game also and he can see what the other players' cards are and telepath that information to you," Susie muttered. "You guys are so close he says he can see right into your brain sometimes."

"Hey, he never told me that!" I said with no small indignation.

"Nope, no psi cheating, either," Tae-yul said. He tore off another piece of chicken and ate so fast it seemed like he inhaled it. "Yeva has some kind of loco psychic woman who tells her when psi is being used in the saloon. The woman can't do anything except sense when psi is going on. Yeva keeps her on the payroll. That guy who got beat up? He was reading the other players' minds. Now he's a vegetable."

"So no cheating and no psi," Asher said softly. He peered at me through his thick glasses. "Emma, I'm asking again, are you a good enough poker play for this?"

"I'll have to be." I thought back to my own strengths and weaknesses at a table. I had poor card luck, unfortunately. Luck was a real thing, any serious player understood that, and some people had better luck than others. The key to winning was the amount of skill you could bring to a game in the face of bad luck.

I was good at money management, an undervalued aspect of the game of poker. I had a sense of strategy. Further, in art school, I'd been innocent looking. That naïve affect had served me well, especially when I was bluffing. I always looked sort of wide-eyed, doe-caught-in-the-headlights, and that expression

disguised a whole spectrum of feelings. The implied vulnera-
bility provoked the other players' often ill-conceived aggression. Now I was older and there were some lines on my face;
innocence wasn't going to be a ruse at my disposal.

"Tae-yul, did you hear anything about Yeva?"

"I heard plenty about her, but what do you have in mind?"
he asked.

"What's her style of poker playing, does she express a lot
of emotion when she wins and loses?"

"She likes to win and she gets a little mad when she
doesn't," he said. "She likes big, tall men but when she can't
find anyone else, Franklin has to take care of her. You know,"
he gave Beth a veiled glance before returning his gaze to me,
"in an adult way."

"Did anyone say anything about her tell?" I queried.

Tae-yul shook his head no.

"Did she talk to you?"

Tae-yul colored. "She told me that the girls were two to
five credits an hour and I should quit making goo-goo eyes at
them and go out and earn some money to pay for one."

"You were making googly eyes at the prostitutes?" Susie
spat.

"No!" Tae-yul insisted, coloring more deeply.

"That's disgusting," Susie said. She slugged him in the front
of his shoulder. "Do you know how unhappy those girls are?"

"They didn't look unhappy to me, they looked pretty joy-
ful," Tae-yul grumbled. He rubbed his shoulder.

"They are unhappy," Susie said. "But they smile and act
gleeful because that's what the men want, happy girls who'll
do anything they say—puppets, really. It's all an illusion to
serve the men, don't you see?"

"I wasn't making 'googly eyes' at anyone," Tae-yul said,
nearly whining.

Susie scowled at him.

"Did you by any chance see a small blonde hooker who goes by the name Cherry?" Asher asked softly.

Tae-yul shook his head no.

We all sat quietly for a few minutes. Then Susie said, "Maybe Kangee will find us another pilot in Oshkosh."

I said, "Thanks for the vote of confidence."

15

THREE NIGHTS LATER, I LEFT THE shanty clutching a bag filled with 872 credits. It wasn't as substantial a bankroll as I'd hoped. I'd be playing with scared money, something I never like to do. Having a solid bankroll to bet with meant a player could weather a few bad hands while studying the other players and sussing out the specific tides of the table. It was a serious asset that I'd wanted to have when I faced Yeva.

But all wasn't lost. My biggest win in art school had been on a night when I'd had barely enough coins to make it through a single hand. Somehow I managed to eke through the first few hands and then into a winning streak that lasted for two and a half hours. Then I felt the table go cold, a tangible sensation like a door slamming. I lost the next hand. I cashed out at that moment.

So if I didn't have as big a bankroll as I'd hoped, at least I had the confidence of knowing I'd been victorious in the past despite playing scared. Not that I could let my confidence balloon into over-confidence. That would be worse than playing scared, in my mind.

It was an unusually cool and damp summer evening, with low gray clouds portending rain. I wore a silky black shawl over my shoulders and my bag of money was tied into a leather belt loosely draped over a new dress. Asher had suggested that I wear a dress.

"The more feminine you look, the more you'll be under-estimated," he said. "Being underestimated is a position of strength."

"Asher, those are very practical observations!" I'd replied. I was so pleased with him that I kissed his cheek.

Asher had blushed and hung his head but I could see that his skinny chest puffed up from the praise. I resolved to com-pliment him more often, it made him so happy. And wasn't that an intrinsic part of leadership, after all? Promoting other people's self-esteem, to bring out their best self and their fin-est abilities?

The dress itself was deplorable. We'd sent Tae-yul to buy it, and what did we expect for letting a seventeen year old boy make such a purchase? It was really only appropriate for a showgirl in Las Vegas in The Before. It was clingy and slinky, with pale pink and blue sequins that shimmered like the miasma of a mermaid when I moved. It was cut low in front and back, exposing cleavage that I didn't remember having and an expanse of my back down to the crack of my ass.

In this dress, not only would my opponents underestimate me, but I might underestimate myself. The fall of soft fabric over my body definitely made me feel slutty and instinctual—right when I needed to be in full command of my analytical ability.

The humidity made my recently brown hair fuzz out wildly around my shoulders, so Susie and I wrestled it into a high, ladylike bun. Tae-yul produced a tube of Shanghai red lip gloss that he claimed to have found lying on the ground. Susie gave him a withering glance but he stuck to his story. I blot-ted the tip of the cosmetic, hoping to erase the prior owner's germs, and used lipstick for the second time since the mists had scourged the Earth.

"Everyone's gonna look at you in that dress, Mama," Beth had said, wearing a bemused expression.

"What are you going to do if something goes wrong?" Tae-yul asked abruptly.

"Or if everything does," Susie said. "You know, if you lose and someone recognizes you and they want to hang you again."

If everything went wrong, there were only two courses of action, and both came to me whole and complete in that moment, in one of those lightning bolts of knowing that sometimes struck me. I said, "Susie, if worst comes to worst, call in the mists."

Susie blanched.

"You can also go to Alexei. Whatever else, he doesn't want me to hang," I said.

She shuddered. "There's no telling what he'd do with me."

"Then, Susie, promise me, if it all goes to hell, you'll call in the mists," I said firmly. I took her by the shoulder and looked deep into her eyes. "The mists will be a distraction, if we need one for whatever reason. Worst case scenario."

"Maybe she can't call the mists here because Outpost City is a Safe Zone," Beth said, too somberly for a young girl.

"I can call the mists to anywhere, even into a Safe Zone. But I'll be unleashing hell." Susie shook her head. "I could kill us all, destroy Outpost City. I can call the mists, but I don't know how many will come, and I can't promise I can control them when they show up. My ability is wild and, um, unstable. Caris is the controller. I . . . I just don't know."

"You can do it if you need to," Tae-yul assured her. He stared at my hand on Susie and I could tell he was wondering if he should tell me to remove it. He opted not to confront me. Smart kid. Even if he was making googly eyes at the prostitutes. He said, "Susie, I gotta agree with Emma on this. If it goes bad, you send in a mist. Maybe just a little one. That'll keep Yeva busy and I can grab the pilot."

"I don't know," Susie mumbled, covering her face with her hands. "You don't know what you're asking me to do. I can't be sure only one mist will come. Or that it will be a little one. My psi ability isn't that specific."

"Come on, Susie. Tell me you'll do what needs to be done, and that you'll look after Beth," I said. "Promise me."

Susie gave me a solemn look. "You'd better win, Emma. It better all go to plan."

Donny had set out before me to take a seat at the bar and keep an eye on proceedings. He knew not to connect to me telepathically, but he was going to find a way to give me what information he could gather.

I was going to challenge Yeva in her own den. But I wasn't alone with my card skills. I had a switchblade tied into a garter at my thigh.

ORGAN AND GUITAR music spilled out of the windows of The Dark Horse, and people flowed in and out of the place in a continuous noisy stream. They went in laughing and half-so-ber and came out still laughing and much less sober. Some joked about how much they'd lost at poker. Yeva was raking in the cash today.

Would that put her in a good enough mood to bet liberally?

I loitered outside, watching, before going inside myself. It was bigger inside than it looked from the outside, but then, Outpost City was so jammed with buildings that judging relative size was difficult.

The front room was spacious and filled with wooden tables. It was lit brightly by wall sconces and candles set into candelabra and hurricane lamps and a red-orange fire crack-ling in a fireplace. All the seats were taken and people milled about with glasses or mugs in their hands. In one corner, a slim elderly woman played raucous tunes on the organ, well, tunes that were as raucous as an organ could emit.

I made my way through the milling customers to the bar

and hopped up onto a stool. I looked around. No Donny. Where was he?

The bartender, a stocky, middle-aged guy with an easy smile, set a mug of Outpost ale in front of me. I smiled back and handed him a coin. I lifted the mug to my mouth and pretended to drink though I had no intention of letting myself get loopy with booze. Too much was at stake tonight.

"I'll take your coat for you," murmured a low, throaty voice as my shawl slipped off my shoulders.

I swiveled around on my stool and beheld an elegantly curved, mocha-skinned woman wearing a long blonde wig. She draped the shawl around herself and seated herself on the stool beside me. Then it clicked. I exclaimed, "Lailani! Norman's friend!"

"You do remember," she said, delighted. She gripped my shoulders and smooched the air beside my face and I was struck by her thoughtfulness. Usually people with Adam's apples didn't understand about not smearing a woman's make-up.

"How are you?" I asked, air-kissing back.

"Never been better. Can't complain, wouldn't matter if I did," she said in a voice of molten honey. "But, doll face, don't you owe me a dress and a wig?"

Months ago, Lailani, aka Larry Jones, had lent me a disguise. It had ended up on the floor of a boarding room, torn into pieces by Arthur.

"Yeah, for sure," I grinned at Lailani. "Unfortunately that dress was confetti by the end of the night."

Lailani laughed. "That was kind of the intention."

"Keep the shawl, and you can have this one when I'm done with it," I offered.

Lailani leaned over and ran her long Sylphan fingers inside the neckline of the dress so that the back of her hand slid over my bosoms. "Not bad," she mused, though it wasn't clear if she was referring to the dress or to the soft flesh inside it. She leaned close and breathed into my ear, "Be careful. This place is dangerous. People get into trouble here all the time."

"I'm here for a card game," I whispered back.

"I don't like the sound of that. You carrying something like I showed you how?" she poked her hands up under my skirt and felt around intimately. Her hands came in contact with my knife and her face brightened. "That's my girl!"

"I'm going to use it on you if you don't quit with the gynecological exam," I threatened.

She moved away. "Sure, I'll take that little number off your hands when you're done with it. Try to keep it in one piece, okay?"

I nodded. "Are you working here now?"

She shrugged expressively, even operatically. "No, no, sweet cheeks, I'm still freelance. Yeva lets me drink here as long as I give her a cut if I take anyone home."

"How big a cut?" I asked, not because I had any pecuniary issues with the arrangement, but because I wanted to know how big Yeva's greed was. Her greed could be my ally in the game.

"The standard, 20 percent," she said.

Before I could comment, another girl sidled up to us. She had long pale brown hair and hazel eyes and a voluptuous figure that was fully revealed by the strappy leather costume twined about her. Her fingers stroked down the inside of my arm. "If you're Lailani's friend, I could give you a discount."

"Ah, I——" I choked.

"She's not for you, Trisha, scat," Lailani said, making a sultry dismissal motion with both hands.

"You keep all the hot ones for yourself," Trisha said, not moving. She pressed her front into my side and despite the skimpy garb showing her breasts to full advantage, I looked for an Adam's apple. Nope, she didn't have one.

"This one likes men," Lailani said. Then a wicked smile broke out over her rouged brown face. "Maybe she plays sometimes, you know? Maybe you could tempt her. I never tried but maybe it's possible . . . she has a taste for soft and sweet instead of hard and sweaty."

Trisha dropped her hand to my hip and then traced down along the sequins of the short skirt until her fingertips brushed my thigh.

I took her hand firmly and positioned it at her side. "I like men."

"You sure?" Trisha said, studying my mouth. "After an hour with me, you won't."

"Go away," I said, enunciating clearly. I wished I wasn't blushing.

"If you insist," Trisha said. She pulled my hand up to cup her breast, then winked at me as I exclaimed and pulled away.

"Really, Lailani?" I said, when Trisha had left.

"Oh lighten up, doll." Lailani looked like she was about to say something else, but then her face tensed. "Some guys just came out of the back room. If you want a seat at the table, now's the time. You might get right in. You might have to wait, but you might not." She gripped my arm as I stood. "Be careful, doll, righto? Yeva's poker isn't really a game."

I said, "Poker never is."

IT TOOK ME ten minutes and much random groping by strangers to make my way to the back of the room. A plain pine door was closed and guarded by two bouncers in the style Yeva favored: brawny and large and not overly intellectual looking. I walked between them and took hold of the doorknob.

"Whoa, there, missy, hold your horses," Bouncer on the right said. "Where are you going?"

"There's a poker game back there," I said. "I want in."

"Well now, there's a price for that," he said, grinning broadly. He laid his hand over mine and moved my hand to cup his crotch. "You and I have to come to some kind of agreement, missy."

The other bouncer snickered and didn't intervene.

Surreptitiously I slid my other hand slowly under my skirt and gripped the knife. "What'd you have in mind?"

"What say you and I go to the head and I get a little head?" he asked. Then he laughed because, after all, he was a great wit.

I used the noise to cover the click of the blade sliding out of the handle. Then I had my knife in hand and I quickly pressed it up against his balls. "What say I let you keep your testicles?"

"Now, now," he started, with a condescending smirk. He squeezed the hand he held, hard, drawing a wince of pain from me.

"It's true, you're a lot bigger than me. But ask yourself if you can knock me down before I get this all the way up inside your family jewels." I dug the tip of the knife through his pants. I was pretty sure it scratched him. "You can hurt me, but at what cost?"

The other bouncer howled with laughter.

After a moment's reflection, the bouncer said, "I'm gonna let go of you real slow, and you're gonna put that away." He eased off on my hand.

"You're going to let me through that door," I said.

He released my hand and held both hands up.

I pulled the knife out of his pants with an audible ripping sound.

"You might shoulda taken the deal he offered," the other bouncer said. "You might wish you had a friend in there."

"I've got friends," I said. My bruised hand turned the door knob. Neither bouncer tried to stop me as I went through the door with as much sangfroid as I'd ever possessed. They didn't know I was shaking inside. I hoped.

THE ROOM WAS medium sized, high ceilinged, painted blue, and lit by scores of wall sconces with candles whose flickering lights bounced off three round mirrors, one on each wall without a window. I noted the mirrors first, wondering if they were positioned to show the players' cards. They were high up but I wouldn't be able to tell until I was sitting at the table, which was a long oval wooden affair with a dark finish. Eight seats: that meant no neutral dealer. We would take turns dealing.

Why didn't I think to practice shuffling and dealing? One empty seat beside Yeva, down-table from her—to her left, a prime position, at about 9:00. A good omen. The catch was that my back would be to the door. I went over and stood behind it. While I walked, my brain took snapshots of the people at the table: five men and two women and an empty seat for me.

"You made it past my men," Yeva said, in a loud, accented, and matter-of-fact voice. She was even bigger up close than from a distance, a full-bodied Amazon of a woman whose cotton shirt sleeves couldn't hide her muscles. Her face was broad and placid with a faint wash of rosacea over her cheeks. She gazed down at her cards but I didn't make the mistake of thinking she wasn't scrutinizing me just as carefully as I was her. She had her hair up and coiled, as usual.

"Those goofy boys at the door? They weren't going to keep me from the action."

Yeva tilted her gaze up at me. "There's a chalk board over there. Write your name on it." She glanced over her shoulder at a line of mismatched chairs against the wall. A few people occupied them on either side of a black board perched in the center. Franklin the pitiful pilot sat beside it, head hanging, but Yeva's words caused him to scuff his feet and reach up with a piece of lime green chalk.

"Aren't you eager to take my money?" I asked.

One corner of her mouth lifted. "There's a system."

"These credits are burning a hole in my pocket." I detached the bag with the wooden credits and lifted it to show her.

Yeva sighed. "You gotta wait your turn."

It was time for my first and, I hoped, only gamble of the evening. I shrugged and blew a few stray strands of hair out of my face. "Well, I tried." I turned and walked back to the door.

"Hold your horses," Yeva called. She laughed. "Minimum buy-in is 750 credits. Do you have that?"

"I'm sure I do," I chirped. I turned around and came back to the table.

Yeva scooted over to take the seat, positioning me up-table, to her right, about 7:00. It gave her the advantage; except when she dealt, she would always be in the position to respond to me. She moved her neatly stacked chips to her new seat. She wasn't doing particularly well, but she wasn't doing badly, either. She said, "Must be your lucky day."

Not if you're smart enough to change seats and put me at your right. I sat down and emptied the bag of credits onto the table. "That looks like 750."

"Franklin!" Yeva bellowed.

Franklin tripped over with a big yellow plastic toolbox and set it on the table. His fingers shook a little as he counted my money, which he did aloud.

I took the opportunity to study him. His eyes were bloodshot and rheumy, his nose covered with burst blood vessels, and his face slack with drink. *This is the hero who saved a planeload of people by landing in a field outside of Edmonton?* It was difficult to fathom. He reeked of rancid ale and old puke.

"That's actually 872," he said, an honest answer given almost in a whisper. His eyes lit on me for a second so I nodded. He exchanged the credits for poker chips: white chips were 1 credit, red were 5, blue were 10, green were 25, and black chips were 100. I took one black chip and the rest in smaller denominations.

"You didn't ask about the limits or the games," Yeva commented.

"People talk, Yeva, she musta heard," said the guy to her immediate left, at almost 11:00. He was standard Outpost City-issue thug, a strapping, nearly neckless fellow with a thick dark scrabble of beard, ragged leather breeches and a tee-shirt under a black leather vest, and a large knife sheathed in his belt.

I grinned at him to test his testosterone, which I was pretty sure was considerable and unimpeded by sense or courtesy, given that he'd already taken it upon himself to answer for me. Sure enough, he scuffed his feet under the table, sat up straighter, and grinned back widely. The question of whether or not he would get laid was written on his face. I looked away and he sagged a little.

Yeva snorted. "No limits. Dealer's choice. We play draw and stud poker."

"A classicist," I commented, while stacking my chips neatly for play. She hadn't mentioned Texas hold 'em.

"The lady knows her cards," said the man opposite me, in an admiring tone. He sat at the 2:00 position. He was wiry and maybe in his seventies and wore thin wire-framed glasses. He had some tall stacks of chips in front of him. Either he had started with a fat wallet or he was doing all right tonight.

"What do the classics have to do with cards?" asked the cowboy to my right at the 6:00 placement. He was a medium-sized fellow with outsized callused hands. He had short blond hair and was pristinely clean-shaven. He wore half-chaps over jeans and his woven straw Stetson hat dangled off the back of his chair. He had a few short stacks of chips to show for himself.

Yeva and The Thug to my left, Cowboy to my right, and SmartyPants across from me. I turned my gaze to the worn-looking middle-aged woman at the head of the table, 12:00. She was dark-haired and light-eyed and probably only in her early forties, but life in The After had crushed a lot of life right out of her. I wondered what she was looking for in this game or if she was some kind of ringer for Yeva. She had a moderate amount of money in her pile. She was a question mark. *QuestionMark*.

SmartyPants was talking about how stud and draw were classic poker games, while hold 'em had become wildly popular in the years just before The Day.

I ignored him and studied the man and woman seated between the Cowboy and SmartyPants. The man sat beside SmartyPants at the 3:00 position. He was in his thirties, with auburn hair and hazel eyes that were sizing me up in a good-natured way. He was scruffy, but then, we were all scruffy now. There was a genial air about him I liked, and liking him put me on guard. The poker table was no place to make friends. Anyone who seemed friendly either didn't know how to play or was working the table. He had some respectable stacks in front of him. *You're Scruffy*, I decided.

The woman beside him, at the 5:00 place, was in her late twenties or early thirties, with long, neatly combed light brown hair and highly defined features, the kind of well-delineated nose, slanted eyes, and high cheekbones that made her arresting and would have attracted artists and photographers to do her portrait in The Before. She was also watching me from beneath discretely lowered eyelids. There was something indefinably strained about her striking face but it wasn't obvious. There was also a subtle air of connection with Scruffy, but that, too, was completely in the energy field between them. There was no overt sign of a relationship, just my feeling that they had one.

She caught my eyes and smiled and it was like a bright flash in the room. I thought the moniker Dazzling fit her. I would have been sorry to see how little money she had, but I had learned the hard way not to be too empathic at the table.

"Whose deal?" I raised my eyes ostensibly to look around the table, but really I was checking out the mirrors. They were positioned too high up on the wall to reflect anyone's hand.

"Why it's mine, ma'am," said Cowboy. He took the deck from the center of the table and shuffled easily. His hands moved competently through the shuffle and bridge. He looked at ease with cards, even though he'd asked about classic poker. *A talented amateur, then.* That thought amused me because, after all, that label applied to me, too.

Cowboy's hands paused. He cocked his head, then said, "Five card stud, straight." He set the deck down and scooted a 5 credit chip into the center of the table—the ante.

So I did the same, and Yeva after me, and so on in turn.

Cowboy shuffled a few more times and then laid the deck on the table and turned to Dazzling, gesturing to offer her the cut.

I noted that the deck looked used but not worn. It was a standard red Rider back design deck of Bicycle playing cards. There was no sign of tampering on the backs; the little cupids, hearts, and curving plants all looked normal.

Dazzling took the top third of the deck and moved it toward Cowboy. Her fingers were long and slender with perfectly trimmed nails but her hands had reins-calluses, so she'd been riding a lot and recently. From where, to what purpose?

Cowboy recombined the deck and dealt my first card, face-down. He dealt around the table and then laid out the first face-up cards.

"The lady gets a bullet," crowed Cowboy.

So I was high with the ace of hearts, and I didn't like that out of the starting gate. It smelled bad to me when the new kid was dealt a sucker card. But I kept my face neutral. Yeva got the ten of spades. Queen of diamonds to the Thug. Seven of clubs to QuestionMark. SmartyPants got the four of hearts. Scruffy got the one-eyed black jack. Dazzling took the diamond deuce.

"Check," I said, without looking at my hole card.

SmartyPants raised his eyebrows. Scruffy smiled amiably. Dazzling's eyes flicked to me with curiosity.

She's weak. Then, *what's she doing in this game?*

Yeva laughed out loud. "This is gonna be fun. Five credits to play."

"Raise you to seven," said Thug. *So he has a lady down, making a pair, and doesn't care who knows it.*

SmartyPants folded, but the others, in turn, put in seven credits.

I peeked at my hold card. Ace of clubs. A warning bell went off in my head. I called anyway. Should have raised. I took the hand with trip aces. It made me a little nauseous. I was terribly superstitious about winning the first hand, and I sent out a prayer to Humpy Sherwood, whom my grandmother had told me was the patron saint of poker. "Don't let this be the last hand I win," I silently begged as I raked in my winnings. I was fairly certain ole Humpy was entirely fictional, an invention of Granny's, but it never hurt to prevail upon the auspices of heaven.

"You don't look so happy to win," observed SmartyPants, who knew not to chase his ante with bad cards.

"I love to win." I smiled prettily. "Look, I got the deal, too." I gathered the cards and shuffled the deck. My fingers remembered how to do it; it was like falling off a cliff to hold a deck of cards in my hands, it went so easy with the natural flow of things. The physical feel of the cards in my hands reminded me, with an ache, of my time in art school, in The Before, when everything was shiny and easy and simple.

Yeva watched as I shuffled, noting the bruise where her bouncer had grabbed me. She must have felt my gaze, because she nodded. Not once did she take her eyes off my hands.

"How about draw poker? Are there any special house rules concerning that?" I asked.

I folded early for the next few hands. It gave me ample

opportunity to study the other players. Yeva wasn't as flashy a player as I'd expected; she had some self-discipline, and she watched the other players closely. The Thug next to her was a walking disaster, betting carelessly and exercising poor judgment if any at all. QuestionMark played evenly, though once when she raised, the corners of her lips trembled the teeniest bit, and I knew she was bluffing. There was something odd and hangdog about her, something not right, but I couldn't pinpoint what it was.

SmartyPants played tight and cool. He adjusted his glasses once after folding and I wondered if that was an expression of emotion, and if so, was that impatience or frustration. His cards weren't particularly bad, but then again, they weren't good either.

Scruffy won both hands. He kept playing as stolidly as if he'd lost and didn't mind. Nothing emanated from him except peaceable good will. He was almost certainly playing the percentages, just as SmartyPants was and as I planned to.

Dazzling stayed in on lousy cards, which puzzled me. *Why hasn't Scruffy taught her how to play?*

Cowboy played almost as tight as SmartyPants. He was polite and occasionally made friendly comments, as if he was trying to elicit conversation, which wasn't forthcoming.

QuestionMark got the cards. She looked down and said, "Seven card stud, threes wild." Her eyes darted to Yeva, as if checking with her.

Yeva didn't respond or otherwise acknowledge Question-Mark.

This was my first game with a wild card. It was kind of a girly game but what the hell, I was kind of a girly person. At least, I had been back in The Before. I thought I might have some fun this round. I hoped I'd get the cards for that.

While QuestionMark shuffled, Yeva called for more ale for the table. Franklin skittered to the door and then right back in, and seconds later, a girl came in with a tray, a pitcher, and fresh glasses. She was dressed in a way that revealed all her assets, two of which nearly fell out of the skimpy bikini top when she leaned over to pour our ale.

"You better stop before you're broke if you want some time with Helena," Yeva said to the Thug.

The Thug grinned, continued leering at Helena, and drained his ale in one long, single, shamelessly loud gulp. Little rivulets trickled down the sides of his mouth, and he waggled his glass in the air, asking for more from Helena.

Helena obligingly bent low to pour.

"I'm feeling lucky this hand," the Thug said loudly, never taking his eyes off Helena's boobs.

"You always *feel* lucky," Yeva said scornfully, "you never are."

"Aw, Yeva, I always get lucky one way or the other," the Thug said. He turned in his chair to watch Helena as she sashayed out of the room.

Scruffy caught me watching the Thug's display, and he raised his eyebrows in amusement.

Figuring it might be the right time for me to move the game in the direction I had in mind, I said brightly, "Hey, Yeva, how about a little action on the side? Twenty credits says I get a better hand than you do."

Yeva grinned. "Make it fifty, and you're on."

"That's not too rich for your blood?" I asked playfully, testing her.

Yeva snorted.

I shrugged. *Let's see how far you'll stretch, Yeva. Once I get your money, I'm taking Franklin.* "Then let's make it 100." I pushed my 100-credit chip past my elbow and toward her.

Yeva smirked and pushed her own chip toward me.

QuestionMark dealt the first two cards down. As she went around the table, dealing the third card face up, I sneaked a sideways glance at Cowboy and caught him peeking at his hole cards. Just for a moment, he flashed his six of diamonds—a rookie mistake—and the card was no help to him unless he had a lot of diamonds or a little straight.

The only face card dealt up were jacks. SmartyPants opened the bidding with the first one. Scruffy and Dazzling called with a ten and seven, respectively.

Cowboy's breath caught, so subtly that only Dazzling and I caught it. He had a black deuce showing, but I wasn't sure if he was pleased with his hand or afraid to call. "I call," he said evenly, answering that question.

I had a wild card and a nine in the hole. "Call."

Yeva had a piddly six. She said, "Call."

The Thug said, "I call. I have my own jack so I'm not afraid, and get that hot girl in to pour more ale."

QuestionMark called and dealt the next card.

The Thug got the ace of diamonds, so he was high. He chortled and bet. QuestionMark and SmartyPants called.

Scruffy, who didn't have much showing, raised to ten credits. He counted two red chips and pushed them to the pot. But Scruffy hadn't counted his chips when he'd won the two hands, he'd just pushed them out without counting. He'd had the cards then—and he didn't now. So he counted chips when he was anxious. That was his tell. I was a little surprised he'd bluff with only a ten and a two showing. It didn't seem to fit his thoughtful persona.

Dazzling pushed in ten credits with way too much enthusiasm for a single king. She either had a wild card or another king in the hole.

Cowboy said, "I call."

I called. My hand wasn't all that great, but I did have a wild card, and I wanted to see the next card.

Yeva had nothing showing and called anyway. Why would she do that? Maybe she had a pair of something in the hole. *Maybe the ale she's drinking has loosened her up. Then again, she could be trying to scare me into folding so she can take my 100-credit chip.*

My fifth card was another nine, giving me trip nines with that nine and the wild card in the hole.

Yeva was high showing with a pair of sixes. The corners of her mouth twitched a little as she leaned forward and said, "Twenty credits plays. And you, missy, care to raise our side bet to 150?"

The game was about to get interesting.

I said, "Money's cheap. How about something meaningful?"

"Shit, let's make it twenty-five. I got face cards showing," the Thug interjected, yelling. Just like that he told me, SmartyPants, and probably Scruffy and Yeva that he didn't have anything in the hole. He also didn't have much money left, so bluffing was stupid.

Yeva turned in her seat to look at me. "What's 'meaningful' to you?"

Something benign, to start with, something that doesn't give anything away . . . "I drink for free in your saloon for a month."

Yeva crinkled up her face. "And if I win?"

"I'll work for free for a month, but only as a bartender or a waitress," I said, stressing the "only."

Yeva toyed with a chip and considered my suggestion while QuestionMark and SmartyPants called.

"Raise," Scruffy said. "Thirty'll make it even more fun." He counted out six red chips and shoved them to the center.

"Thirty?" Dazzling said. "Call." She counted her chips, and I found myself hoping she had more than a pair of kings.

Then I mentally kicked myself for wanting to take care of her.

"Call," Cowboy said, and I knew he had too big a spread for anything meaningful, but I didn't hope for better for him.

"Raise. Forty," I said, putting out a red chip, a blue chip, and a green chip. I looked at Yeva. "So? Our side bet stands, 150, or a month of free service or free drinks?"

"Both," Yeva said. "The extra fifty for sure. Make it *six* months though. That's real meaningful."

Six months? As in . . . 180 days, half a year? If I lose, that's going to slow down the mission. I'll have to drop out, send the others on to Europe without me. And what about Beth? What will she do in this hellhole for six months? My heart sped up as I answered, "You're on, ma'am."

"I can use a good waitress or barkeep around here, especially one I don't have to pay." Yeva smirked. "I call your bet too."

Everyone called again, and we were all still in.

Last card up.

Dazzling was high, with a pair of kings granted her by a wild three. "Twenty credits," she said.

Cowboy looked at her wild card and then at his own natural pair of kings. He shook his head. "I'm out." He turned his cards over and leaned back, crossing his arms over his chest.

I had four nines, only two of which were visible. I wasn't backing down. "Raise to thirty credits."

Yeva looked at her pair of sixes and cast a cursory glance at my wild card. I figured her for two pair. She should have figured me for three of a kind. She took a swig of ale. "Call."

The Thug said, "See what I've got? Three face cards showing. I raise. I'm all in!" He shoved his remaining two stacks into the pot.

Mildly, SmartyPants inquired, "How much is that exactly?"

"Let's see . . . thirty-six credits," the Thug said. He gulped the rest of his ale.

"I fold," QuestionMark said and turned over her cards.

SmartyPants folded right behind her.

Scruffy had a pair of jacks showing. He called.

If Dazzling stayed in, we'd be playing with a community card, because there were only four cards left in the deck and five people still in the game.

She chewed her lip. "Call." She pushed in the additional credits she owed the pot. She only had a few credits left.

I stayed, pushing in six more credits.

Yeva drummed her fingers on the table. I found myself wishing she would fold. The last thing I wanted was to stay put in Outpost City for six months because of a gambling debt. Susie, Donny, and Beth were counting on me.

Yeva said, "Let's raise the stakes on our side bet, missy."

"To what?"

"If you win, you drink for free *forever* in The Dark Horse." She chuckled and clarified, "Well . . . as long as you're in Outpost City. Alive."

"And if *you* win?" I asked cautiously.

"You work for me but as *more* than a waitress." She didn't look at me. "You're one of my girls. Just for a few months. You're not young but you've got some appeal and my regulars like fresh meat."

"I'd pay for an hour of that!" the Thug said enthusiastically.

"An hour? Pssh! You wouldn't last more than two minutes, if you could even get it up after all you been drinking," Yeva scoffed. She finally looked at me, daring me to back down from the wager.

I felt a little nauseous at the scope of it. The four nines soothed my stomach a little, but I still felt sick. *Does she really think I'll turn tricks for her? But I can't back down now, can I? Not if I'm going to wrest Franklin from her.* Keeping my voice steady and feigning a confidence I didn't have, I answered, "Sure, Yeva."

"Pot's right," the Thug announced. "Dealer?"

QuestionMark turned over the ace of spades on top of the pot.

I knew I'd won, and I sent out a prayer of gratitude to Humpy Sherwood.

Scruffy turned over his cards, folding.

Dazzling looked at me and Yeva and the Thug in turn. "I'm all in." She pushed her credits in. "That's sixteen."

My heart sank a little for her. This was my pot. The ace was a mismatch with Yeva's hand, and the Thug couldn't possibly back up the ace, queen, and jack he had showing.

It was now about strategy. If I bet too high, Yeva would fold despite our side bet, and I'd get no more of her money. I wanted to take as much as possible, as leverage to maneuver her into wagering something else, Franklin in particular. I had to position my bet to entice her to stay. I said, "Twenty credits."

Yeva examined my cards: ten of spades, four of hearts, nine of clubs, three of spades. Sure, I had a wild one showing. But what was I so proud of? She said, "I call."

"Hell, I've got a pair of aces showing. *I* call!" the Thug thundered.

"And what have you got to guarantee the bet?" Yeva asked in a silky voice.

The Thug squirmed in his seat, then stuck a handgun on top of the pot, crowning the ace. It was a small, double-action revolver, oddly feminine looking for a guy amped up on his own testosterone.

"Well? Are you staying or what?" Yeva asked Dazzling.

She nodded, reached around her neck, and withdrew a locket on a golden chain. She slowly swirled it down over the ace, into a spiral on the card face. "Three kings," she said. She then flipped over her hole cards and showed a king and a deuce.

It was a great hand but not good enough. I wondered what was in the locket, whose prized photograph she was going to lose. "Four nines." I flipped over the hidden nine and three.

Yeva cocked her head. She flipped her cards down without showing them. "Got me."

"Aw hell," the Thug said before swearing vociferously for a solid minute and a half. He turned over an eight and a four, proving that he was just as stupid as I'd thought. He pushed back his chair with a loud screech and stomped out of the room.

"I'm done too," Dazzling said. Her voice was neutral, but there was something wistful about her eyes as they lingered on the golden chain. She got up and left the room with considerably more grace than the Thug had exhibited.

I picked up the gun and checked to see if it was loaded. Nope. Still good to have. I pulled my winnings toward me and stacked them without counting them, then pushed the necklace and gun to one side.

Yeva put her fingers on the 150 credits of chips and pushed them out to me. "Good hand. Lucky you. I serve the best Outpost ale in town."

She was thinking that I played smart but real tight, and that I didn't like to bluff.

I was thinking that it might soon be time to disabuse her of that notion. I said, "Maybe we can bet for real now that the amateurs are gone."

Yeva chortled, and even contained SmartyPants cracked a smile. Scruffy raised his eyebrows again. Cowboy straightened in his chair, pleased to be counted in with the cool kids.

"You just took enough credits outta this game to live comfortably in Outpost City for a year," Yeva said. "You'll drink for free for the rest of your life. What do you consider a 'real bet'?"

"Real stakes, *life* stakes."

"I'd like to see some real life stakes," said a man who'd walked through the door while I was stacking chips. "I heard there'd be some action here tonight. Penny ante stuff doesn't interest me."

I knew this would be a problem when I'd taken the seat, that I wouldn't see who passed through the door until they were all the way in.

Yeva turned bodily and scrutinized him, running her eyes up and down his tall frame, liking what she saw. Of course she did. Arthur was gorgeous. "Well, why don't you sit here by me?" Yeva said, patting the Thug's chair.

"If you don't mind, I'll take that seat," Arthur said. He walked around the table and sat in the chair left open by Dazzling's exit.

"Yeah, I can see your pretty face over there," Yeva said with a giggle.

Was that her idea of flirting? I felt a wave of repulsion.

Arthur smiled back at her.

I lowered my eyes to my hands, which rested on the table. In poker, as in horseback riding, quiet hands were a must.

"Who we got for this place? Franklin!" Yeva hollered. "Read the board!"

"Garfield," Franklin said.

A small, lithe man with wispy, pale hair and bulging, hyper-thyroid eyes rose from the line of chairs against the wall. He walked stiffly, almost robotically, over to the empty seat. He nodded once in greeting, then plopped down jerkily and pulled the chair up to the table.

"Franklin, chips," Yeva said, in a loud, reproving voice.

Franklin scrambled to the table with his box of chips.

"You got a buy-in of 750, friend?" Yeva asked, grinning at Arthur.

He set a bulging canvas sack on the table. "Arthur."

"Well, Arthur," Yeva said, almost in a coo, "looks like you've got what it takes."

Arthur grinned widely at her but didn't answer. He dumped the contents of the canvas sack onto the table, and a lot of wooden credits slid out.

Franklin set to counting the credits.

SmartyPants and Scruffy chatted, a collegial postmortem of the last hand. Cowboy rose and stretched his legs and arms. Helena returned with more ale. Yeva went to the door to speak to someone who stood at the threshold.

Garfield took out a small, hand-carved rosewood box. He kept his head down and waited for Franklin to finish with Arthur.

I watched Garfield closely. There was something odd about him, something strange about the way he moved and especially about the wooden box with its unrevealed contents.

What's in it? Surely not enough credits to buy in to this game. What's his story? He doesn't look like someone seeking a thrill in a poker game. His affect is all wrong.

A white-haired woman rose from the line of chairs against the back wall. Leaning on a polished brass cane, she treaded heavily toward us, watching Garfield intently.

When she neared the table, Garfield lifted his head. He looked directly at her, and the old lady recoiled and crumpled over her cane. He then turned his head and stared at me. Out of his blue eyes peered someone else, a crafty and unbalanced intelligence I knew all too well.

If I wasn't sitting at a poker table, if I hadn't schooled myself to impassiveness, I would have cried out. As it was, I stiffened. An exclamation froze on my lips. I forced myself to speak quietly. "Yeva, don't let him open the box."

"What?" Yeva said, wrinkling up her nose as she strode back to the table.

"Emma . . ." said Garfield in a tortured voice, his larynx contorted by the personality who was using it.

"Yeva, him!" the white-haired woman declared with a gasp. She shifted her weight about on her feet and lifted her cane to tap Garfield's shoulder.

Garfield swung his head around and stared balefully at her.

The old lady dropped her cane and listed before collapsing.

Yeva put her fingers to her lips and whistled.

Several bouncers from outside charged in. Yeva pointed and they grabbed Garfield by his arms and dragged him toward the door.

"I am Alexei," Garfield said in that strangely accented voice. "I am near . . . for you." He didn't struggle in the bouncers' grip but let them drag him out.

Franklin reached for the rosewood box.

I leapt up and threw myself over the table, slapping both hands down on it. "No! Do not open that thing!"

Arthur leapt to his feet, gripping a nasty-looking blade.

"Something you want to tell us, Emma?"Yeva asked, enunciating my name loudly. She had gone to help the elderly woman rise and regain her cane.

I raised both hands in a pacifying gesture. "All I know is that whatever's in this box can't be good. It's dangerous. I'm sure of it."

Yeva placed her arms akimbo. "How do you know? Who was that character?"

"I don't know that guy personally, but I know he was being used by a psychic maniac," I explained, then sat back down.

"Yes, that man was being used by another entity," the white-haired woman said, nodding in agreement. "The entity is strong and ruthless. I've never felt anything like it. The box holds something . . . malevolent. I don't know what, but I would prefer not to find out." She stared inquisitively at me. When I didn't say anything, she turned and hobbled back toward her chair against the wall.

"You know this entity?"Yeva queried.

"I've run into him before."

"What did he mean, saying he's near 'for you'?" Yeva pressed. "I do despise riddles."

"He wants something I have," I answered, shaking my head at Alexei's unpredictability. *Susie?* I thought. *Possibly me, Beth, all of us. Damn.*

Arthur sat back down. He was listening carefully, his gaze on his chips. His handsome, symmetrical face was neutral but I could feel him brimming with questions. I wondered if my fingernail marks on his back and chest had healed, or if he still wore, however faintly, the residue of our afternoon of passion. If I closed my eyes and inhaled, I would take his scent inside me, the open sky-lit tang of his arms and his flesh.

One half of his mouth lifted in a small smile, as if his own thoughts were similar.

I thought if he looked at me this second, it would all spill over, everything he wanted to say to me, everything I wanted to tell him and couldn't, yet, because of my commitment to Susie.

The elderly woman paused and started to turn. Was she sensing the connection between Arthur and me?

Break the spell, I thought urgently. I still had to win this game, still had to get Franklin free from Yeva so he could fly us to Europe. I couldn't allow myself to be distracted by Arthur. I couldn't allow myself to get thrown out of this room.

"Get your bouncers to take the box out of here unopened," I suggested brightly. "One of the guys who was standing at the door earlier has a big knife hole in his pants. He should change."

Yeva's broad face contorted into a gleeful smile. "He does, does he? That knife hole have anything to do with how you got past him to enter into my poker game?"

"What me, carrying a big ole knife that could rip apart a man's pants at the crotch?" I blinked my eyes in mock innocence. Out of the periphery of my gaze, I saw the elderly woman returning to her chair.

"I never blame a woman for being prepared," Yeva said. She sat down and whistled again.

A few blustery bouncers returned, their arms and legs chugging.

"What dolt let this woman in? You? Take the box out of here. Don't open it. It's dangerous. We'll deal with it later."

The bouncer gave me a surly look before fixing on Yeva. "What should I do with it?"

"Put it in my office, unopened . . . like I just told you," she answered, rolling her eyes as if he was the biggest idiot she had ever addressed.

"Are we playing?" Arthur asked.

"We still need one more player," Yeva said. She looked around the place and yelled, "Franklin! Who's next on the board?"

16

IT WAS LATE AT NIGHT, MAYBE EARLY next morning, and I was slowly but steadily increasing my winnings.

Cowboy had gone bust and left the room.

A Chinese man named Liu Xiang took the seat vacated by the Thug first and then Garfield, but he left after six or seven hands, having lost his bankroll. I got the feeling he had reserves but was reluctant to dip into them. He was smarter than he was skilled at poker.

QuestionMark went broke but remained in her chair, arms folded, watching us play. No one suggested that she vacate the premises. I was pretty sure I saw her casually swap out a card from her discard pile, but I didn't mention it, and neither did anyone else, so it might as well not have happened. It still didn't answer the question of why she was in the game in the first place; not once did QuestionMark's participation seem to yield any discernible benefit to Yeva.

It was down to the five of us: Yeva, SmartyPants, Scruffy, Arthur, and me.

Arthur was doing well. He played the way I thought he would, with skill, intelligence, imagination, and occasional flashes of unexpected inspiration, just as he did everything else. Was there anything that man wasn't good at?

Yeva and Scruffy were low on funds, but SmartyPants, like me and Arthur, was slowly gaining ground.

First things first: I had to draw Scruffy into something he couldn't win so he would leave. Poker stakes went up every time someone went bust. Bets were big enough now to draw a sweat.

I had to admit that I was enjoying myself.

Arthur got the deal. He sent a veiled glance at me. "Five card draw, jacks or better, progressive."

I wondered what, if anything, he was trying to tell me. *Why did he join this game anyway? Did Norman and Amy tell him what I'm up to?* I wouldn't let the tendrils of my mind curl around him, because I couldn't risk drawing the attention of Yeva's hired psi-sniffer. The elderly woman was frail but good at her job. The mists had given her a useful gift.

"Let's make the ante more interesting," Arthur added. "Say . . . fifty credits?"

"Fifty? What are we, Silicon Valley billionaires?" Scruffy joked.

"I'm here to play for real," Arthur said, "for real and for keeps, no bullshit."

There was a moment of silence. Out of turn, SmartyPants said, "I'll play fifty."

"Fifty? Okay," I said, thinking that Arthur was certainly communicating with me now.

"Why the hell not?" asked Yeva. She tossed in four blue chips and two reds.

We all put in fifty.

Arthur shuffled, offered Scruffy the cut, and dealt.

"Arthur and Emma," Yeva said, taking up her hand, "you two know each other?"

"We've met," I admitted. Stick as close to the truth as possible with the psi sniffer around, right?

Yeva elbowed me and leered. "Was it good for you, too?"

Arthur laughed easily.

"Not bad," I said.

"Not bad?" Arthur drawled.

I looked at my cards to stop myself from blushing. It didn't work, but I was able to see an ace and a bunch of drivel through the haze of feeling. I cleared my throat. "I can't open."

"Me neither, but I'd like to hear the truth behind 'not bad,'" Yeva said with a gleam in her eyes. "I bet Arthur was a helluva lot more than 'not bad.'"

"You'd win that bet," Arthur told her with a wink.

"Can anyone open?" I asked primly, before the repartee went any further.

"Not me," SmartyPants said. His eyes glimmered with mirth, and he emanated amusement, despite his bland affect.

"Nor me," said Scruffy, in a thoughtful tone.

We all threw in our cards and anted another fifty.

Arthur dealt again, reminding us that we had to have a pair of queens or better to open.

I couldn't open, but I had another ace. I'd stick.

Scruffy said, "I can open. Thirty credits." He pushed the chips in without counting. So he had the openers, a pair of queens, kings, or aces. He felt good about his hand. He didn't count when he was confident.

"Raise to fifty," Arthur said evenly, pushing out fifty credits.

I had an Ace. I looked at Arthur. What was he so proud of? I surveyed his face, which I knew so well, trying to discern his intention. *Is he trying to scare me out of the game?* I said, "Call."

"I'll raise you to 100," Yeva said. She pushed in the appropriate chips.

Arthur approved. "That's a good bet, Yeva."

The woman grinned. "What say you and I have a side bet, Arthur? One with real life stakes, like you said you wanted."

One corner of Arthur's mouth lifted in a sardonic smile. "What'd you have in mind?"

"An evening," Yeva said. "The kind that starts with drinks and leads into a night. You know what I mean? Whoever has the higher hand decides what kind of quality time we spend together. If I win, I decide; if you win, you decide."

Arthur's eyes twinkled, and I wondered if I could stick Yeva with my switchblade before she hit me. Maybe if I moved really, really fast and jabbed her deep in the throat or the heart immediately. I'd only get one shot before she came at me swinging. Or I could puncture a major artery so she experienced rapid blood loss, that might do the trick.

On the other hand, Yeva was betting with some imagination. That presented an opportunity.

"Yeva, that's an interesting bet, and I'm tempted, but I'm here for more than an evening. I'm here for a life. With Emma. Who chooses to stay with me." He fixed his gray eyes on me. His gaze was filled with such immense clarity of love and desire that it rocked me.

Focus, Emma, I told myself. *You're here for a mission*. Still, I couldn't tear my eyes from Arthur's.

Yeva sighed. "So, no, Arthur? Too bad. You're missing something special."

Arthur didn't answer because he was still staring straight into my eyes. I didn't have to use any psychic abilities of the human biomind to understand what he was telling me: He loved me, he wanted me, he wasn't going to let go of me so easily. He was here to make that point and to gather me to him via the card game, if that's what it took. He conveyed it all with that look.

Not now. I have a bigger mission than myself. With an ache in my chest, I tore my gaze away from his. *Sorry, Arthur. I love you, but this is just something I have to do. The moment I came for has arrived. Now is the time*. I swallowed. "How about a real-life side bet with me, Yeva?"

"You already won a lifetime of free booze here at The Dark Horse. Besides, you're not my type," she said.

I held up my hand. "You're not mine either. But there must be something I have that you want. Something I can do for you. I'm a healer, thanks to the mists. I can put my hands on you or someone you care about and fix an ailment, bring them back to health."

Yeva fixed her eyes on me. "Interesting. What do you want?"

I didn't want to reveal my endgame so quickly, but I didn't see any other way. I steeled myself and blurted, "Franklin."

Yeva burst out laughing.

"What?" Arthur exploded. "The drunk?"

Chortling, Yeva held up her hand. "Emma, I'm the healthiest person I ever met. But if you're looking for a pilot and you want to wager, you do have something I want."

"And what's that, if not healing?"

"Susie."

Too shocked to speak, I just sat there with my mouth hanging open. How did she know about Susie?

"You're not the only one who gathers intel," Yeva said. "I got friends all over Outpost City."

"No!" Arthur said tightly. "Emma and I are playing for her, and Susie comes with Emma. If I win, they're mine . . . both of them."

So that's why Arthur's here: me and Susie. Both of us. It's another attempt to position Susie so he can use her. Will he never understand about the mists?

"Sorry, Arthur, I didn't hear Emma accept your side bet, so mine takes precedence," Yeva parried. "Long as we're betting, Emma, let me tell you the real life stakes for our side bet. If your hand is higher than mine, you walk outta here with Franklin. I'm sick of his drunken whining. He's pathetic. But my hand is higher, you give me Susie. She's young and real gorgeous and fresh and my customers will enjoy her. I turn you over to my friend Rolf. That's what I promised him." She pointed to the row of seats by the wall.

I turned and scanned the people sitting there.

One man leaned forward, out of the shadows, and held

up his hand. "You don't remember me?" he asked in a steely voice.

I recalled the green-eyed soldier from the marketplace.

"After all the fun we had when I caught you trying to steal a horse here in Outpost City, all those months ago?"

Recognition permeated me like a toxic gas that kills cells in its wake. Rolf was the soldier who had originally greeted me at the gates of Outpost City when I came here en route to rescuing Beth. He was the same soldier who had caught me attempting horse theft. And he marched me out to the gallows to hang. I was sure he'd been killed in the chaos surrounding my escape.

I said hoarsely, "No side bet."

"Then I'll just let Rolf take you when we're done playing for the night," Yeva said. She winked. "This is really your only option, Emma."

"You have a date with a noose, sweetheart," Rolf said, smiling. He stretched out his legs before him in a position of ease.

Arthur started to speak, but I interrupted him, talking fast. I said, "Leave Susie out of this. You can have me for your customers, as you suggested in our earlier bet. Why should I hang when you can get some use out of me?"

Yeva pursed her lips and examined me the way a trader looks over a horse. "As I said, you've got some appeal. You must be something in bed if Arthur wants you so bad. But Rolf reminded me of the deal I made with him. When I make a deal, I keep it. That's what keeps me in business: Trust. My word is my bond. That's what Outpost City runs on. That, Second Life ale, and my hookers. So, Emma, if you win, you walk out of here with Franklin, and Rolf stays here in this room for least an hour. That's my bargain with you, the last offer I'm willing to put on the table."

"I don't like any of this," Arthur said in a cold voice that I knew boded poorly for Yeva. And Rolf.

I stared at my crappy hand with its single ace. A sick feeling roiled my gut. What choice did I have? "I accept."

"Damn it, Emma! No!" Arthur said. He quivered as if trying to restrain himself from jumping up and hitting someone—or worse.

Yeva must have thought the same thing, because she whistled sharply, two short, piercing blasts with her pinkies in the sides of her mouth.

Instantly, the door banged open, and the bouncers ran back in.

"Keep watch, fellas. Make sure no one gets . . . boisterous." She looked at SmartyPants, who had gone a little pale. "For you, 100?"

"I call," he said. His voice was composed.

"I call." Arthur, too, looked composed. Knowing him as well as I did, I knew he was steaming.

"This is all pretty rich," Scruffy said. He looked directly at Yeva. "As long as we're making side bets, Yeva . . ."

She sneered. "I know, I know. You want that girl back. What's her name? Ginger, the other one's daughter."

Scruffy's mouth tightened, and he nodded.

Yeva shrugged. "She's not working out so well as a hooker."

"That's because she's only twelve."

"You and the woman must have rode hard to get here so fast," Yeva commented. "It's been, what? A week since I bought her from the raiders?"

"I'm pretty sure child slavery isn't legal, even in Outpost City," Scruffy answered. His genial face remained impressively composed.

Yeva grinned and leaned back in her chair and glanced at the chairs along the wall. "Rolf, tell me, what's illegal here in the finest town in what remains of the world since the mists destroyed everything?"

"Stealing a horse or a firearm," Rolf called back.

Yeva scooted forward. "Right. What I do with my merchandise is my business."

Scruffy started to speak but she talked over him. "Don't worry, I love a good side bet. But what do you have that I want? I can't think of nothing."

Scruffy reached into his pocket and drew something out to lay on the table, a gold sheath with a protruding bone hilt. When he pulled the dagger from the sheath, it was all the more impressive. The tapered, double-edged, gold blade was carved at the base with animal scenes. The bone hilt was enhanced by gold beadwork, bezel-set with rubies and emeralds and turquoise trefoils. It was antique and it was beautiful and Scruffy had somehow seized it out of the spoils of The After to wager for a child's freedom in this game that wasn't a game.

Yeva's whole face lit up with naked greed. "You're on."

It took me a moment to refocus on the game. We were all in, with our various side bets, and the pot was right.

Scruffy threw down three cards. He had a pair of queens, kings, or aces.

"Dealer takes three," said Arthur, discarding three cards and dealing himself three more.

I showed my ace. "Four."

"Humph," Yeva grunted, then discarded two. "Gimme two."

SmartyPants discarded three.

I was looking at my hand and a lightness pulsed through my body before I could contain it. Another ace, a pair of fives, and a jack. Two pair. A good hand. A really good hand for five card draw, nothing wild.

Scruffy said quietly, "I'm all in." He pushed in his chips without counting.

So he has a good hand too.

"That's 246?" Arthur asked. "I call." He shoved a few stacks of chips into the pot.

Is he bluffing? I couldn't tell. If I connected myself into him,

I'd know. But I didn't dare with the psi sniffer sitting nearby. I said, "Raise. Three hundred."

Yeva pursed her lips and surveyed me. Then she said, "You got another ace to go with the one you showed us?" She drummed her fingers on the table, thinking. "I raise you to everything I've got." She counted quickly, then pushed her chips into the pot. "That's 334. I'm all in."

I stared hard at her broad face and noted a flash of triumph as she handled her money. Just like that, seeing her confidence, my heart sank. Yeva wouldn't go all in unless she could beat a pair of aces. That meant two pair or, more likely, three of a kind.

SmartyPants didn't betray a flicker of anything. "Fold." He placed his cards down on the table.

"Call," Scruffy said. "I've got this to guarantee the bet." He took off his wristwatch and held it up for us to examine.

"Does it work?" Yeva asked.

Scruffy nodded and tossed it onto the pot.

"Call," Arthur said, adding what he owed.

"Call," I said, knowing I was going to lose. I added chips worth thirty-four credits.

We all looked around the table, realizing that the pot was right and the moment of reckoning had arrived.

"Two pair," Scruffy said, flipping over queens and eights.

I shook my head. "Aces over fives."

Yeva laughed outright. She leaned back, tilting her chair onto two legs, and guffawed. "Not good enough! Three fours and a pair of sixes. Full house!"

No! Susie, I thought. Then I looked over to where Rolf was happily rising from his seat.

"Not so fast," Arthur said. He turned over his cards one at a time. Seven, eight, jack, ten, nine—all clubs. "Straight flush."

"Okay, okay. You win the pot." Yeva waved, dispensing with the money as if it mattered not at all. She crowed, "I got Susie

and that beautiful gold dagger!" she crowed. "And Rolf . . .
He's got himself an outlaw to hang!"

Barely breathing, I stared at the table.

Scruffy left the room without a word.

Arthur rose to his feet. The bouncers behind Yeva moved
about restlessly, like guard dogs waiting for their master's
attack command. He looked at QuestionMark and said evenly,
"One moment, Yeva. How do you think this town will react to
hearing that you run a crooked game? Where will your trust
be then? How do you think all the people who've lost credits
here will feel? Maybe they'll want to draw and quarter you.
That's not illegal in Outpost City."

Yeva stopped laughing abruptly. She glared at Arthur and
then motioned to the bouncers. "Get him out of here . . . and
make sure he stays quiet!"

With his preternaturally fast reflexes, Arthur knocked
down the first bouncer as the guy dived onto him. He spun
and landed a right cross on the next guy's chin, sending him
into a slumping heap on the floor.

Yeva whistled, and a new horde of brutes raced into the
room. Arthur was doing well but they were going to over-
whelm him sooner or later—he couldn't stand against so
many. I had a bad feeling about Yeva's command to make sure
he stayed quiet. Then again, Arthur always had a back-up plan,
and I assumed the others were probably waiting nearby to
come to his aid. At least I hoped that was the case.

Rolf stood behind my chair and reached one hand down
to caress my neck.

I felt my bile rise, and I restrained a gag.

"Careful, Rolf," Yeva warned. "That one carries a knife."

"C'mon, sweetheart," Rolf said. He grabbed my upper
arm and yanked me up from my chair. He bound my wrists
behind my back with a leather strap. Then he ran his hand up
my inner thigh and commandeered my knife.

Arthur was holding his own, but six men jumped him at once, and he disappeared under the scrum.

"Let's go! Everyone out!" Yeva barked, leading the way out of the poker room.

Several men came up with Arthur bloody and unconscious and hanging in their arms. They hustled him after Yeva. Rolf shoved me ahead of him, pushing me out the door. The whole mass of us paraded through the tavern, which was still half-full at this hour, about four in the morning. Yeva led us out the front door into the night.

On the street in front of The Dark Horse stood more of her men, with Susie and Donny closed in between them. Susie was struggling and furious but looked unharmed. Donny's face and chest were covered with blood, his lips split and one of his eyes was swollen shut. He'd been badly beaten, and he was swaying on his feet.

One man stepped forward, and draped over his shoulder was a limp, unmoving Tae-yul. Was the boy dead?

I exclaimed. Then I had a sickening thought: Have Yeva's men taken Beth too?

Susie gave me a furious look, and I wondered if she'd been told about my foolish wager. There couldn't possibly have been enough time since the game ended for Yeva's men to collect her. Then a cold, clear realization clicked inside my head: *This was all planned! My side bet with Yeva wasn't something left to chance, something thought up on the spur of the moment. Donny must have been taken early in the evening, probably right when he arrived at The Dark Horse. They must have taken Susie from our shanty after I left. The game was fixed . . . but how?* I knew Arthur had alluded to something, what had he noticed? I had kept all my senses alert, expecting Yeva to cheat, yet I'd noticed nothing amiss.

What of Beth? A frantic worry clanged through my being.

Yeva gestured, and the pack of men led us down the street and across another street. Rats skittered around us in the dark.

Susie brushed up close to me when the man holding her had something to say to Rolf. She whispered, "Beth's with Asher."

I wondered how that had come to pass, but Susie was jostled away before I could ask.

We arrived at a small, empty patch of dirt that was likely a market during daylight hours; now it was host to small forms that resolved into a herd of goats. The men holding Arthur dropped him. He thudded to the ground and rolled, groaning and bleeding. The man carrying Tae-yul dropped him alongside Arthur, and I saw how grievously the boy had been beaten.

"I'll make sure they never talk," one of the bouncers said. He pulled out a knife from his belt and looked at Yeva.

This is it, our position of last resort. Everything has failed.

"Susie," I cried, "now! Do it!"

Susie froze, and even in the wan light of the torches in the street lamps, she went pale. "Emma . . ."

"Don't wait!" I cried. "Remember your promise!"

She took a deep breath, and the whole world went silent, as if muted by the hand of God. The sky broiled crimson.

Yeva and the others looked up. Across the scarlet heavens, a thick blanket of glowing white cotton scrolled, blotting out the moon and stars and irradiating us on the ground below. The white writhed and churned the red sky. Several pieces broke off and gathered into themselves, compacting like clenching fists. Slowly, they descended toward us. They were roughly the size of small cars. The sweet aroma of honeysuckle and the caustic stench of sulfur wafted downward; it was the smell of mists, the smell of death, and it enveloped us where we stood on the empty lot. The goats screamed and bounded away.

One man cried, "Mists!"

Someone yelled, "Run!"

"Kill the girl!" Yeva commanded. "She's calling them somehow!"

Most of her men fled without obeying her, but Susie's captor just froze, staring at the sky and shaking.

Behind me, the snick of a blade emerging from a sheath told me that Rolf meant to follow her directive—to kill Susie. I didn't think but I turned sideways and shoved my shoulder into his chest. He wasn't expecting that, and it caused him to stumble, but he quickly righted himself and drew his blade all the way.

Donny had been released and he lurched toward Rolf. Before he landed, though, a lean figure stepped out of the dark and pointed a gun at Rolf's head.

"Easy. She's loaded," Scruffy said. "I'd just as soon not have to kill you with my second-to-last bullet."

I knew he didn't have any bullets, or he wouldn't have counted them. But Rolf hadn't been playing poker with Scruffy, so he didn't know. Rolf raised his hands, letting the knife dangle from his fingers. Scruffy plucked the knife from his grasp, then kicked Rolf in the back of his leg, forcing the green-eyed soldier to his knees.

Dazzling appeared behind Yeva and pointed a gun at her head.

Yeva said, "Are you crazy, woman? The mists are coming! We're all gonna die."

"If you don't give my daughter back to me, you'll die sooner, right here, right now," Dazzling said coldly. "I'm willing to die for her. Are you?" Her exquisitely molded face was white, but her shoulders and jaw were set, and her hand holding the gun was steady; everything in her spoke to fierce resolve.

The mass of mists localized and hovered over the empty lot. A dozen balls of mist dropped to a few meters directly above our heads. The deadly flower-and-rotten-egg scent intensified, making those of us left in the lot gag and choke. A slurping sound ensued, as if the mists were suckling, and my hair rose and floated upward. I was nearly overcome with primal terror. The man guarding Susie fled, leaving only Yeva and Rolf, Scruffy and Dazzling, and Susie, Donny, and me to stand there, with Arthur and Tae-yul still crumpled on the ground.

"You can have the damn girl!" Yeva yelled, her eyes wide with fright. "Just let me go!"

Dazzling yelled back, "You're not going anywhere until she's here!"

"I've never seen the mists do this. It's as if they want to suck us up into them," Scruffy said, looking upward in terror. His face was taut, and his eyes were huge with fear, but the gun in his hand didn't waver. It stayed trained on Rolf.

I felt a flicker of admiration for Scruffy, who was standing cool and firm with an empty gun in the face of the mists. I'd want him at my back in a fight. Right now I had other things to focus on. I walked over and stood beside Susie and yelled through the tumult, "Are you with us?"

She stood erect, stationary, and bathed in white light from the mists, like some kore, an ancient Greek sculpture. Her eyes were huge and bottomless and unfocused. Red laser lights beamed from them.

The mists continued to descend until they were only a meter above us. Around each of our heads, our hair floated wildly, struggling upward. My inner terror accelerated. Would Susie halt the mists before they consumed us?

"You gotta let me go get the girl, if you want her," Yeva said. "You better do it quick, before the mists eat us all. It'll be too late then. We should all run, before they get us! Stop that girl before we're dead!"

Yeva was right. I grabbed Susie's forearms. "Susie!"

A faint light of recognition flickered in her face. The mists rose a few centimeters.

"Not you, Yeva," Scruffy said. "Someone else. Emma, will you go get Ginger?"

"They won't listen to her," Yeva argued. "They'll release

the girl only to me, since she's mine. Let me go now, and you will see her again!"

"Emma can't help you, and neither can I," Donny said and fell to his knees. He spat out a sticky string of saliva and blood and a few teeth. "You folks better work this out. The mists are here. Emma, can you do something about this before we all die?"

"I'm trying," I said. "Susie, where are you?" I shook her gently. "Come back. We need you here. Please don't go away on us. We have the mission."

"Him! Rolf can go. They'll listen to him," Scruffy said. He stepped back and gestured with his empty gun. "I'll go with him." He looked at Dazzling. "Can you cover Yeva?"

"No one goes anywhere," Susie said in a high-pitched voice several octaves higher and more menacing than her usual bright alto. "Yeva keeps women as prostitutes. She uses children that way. She was going to use me as one."

The whole world blurred red around us with a roar of rushing air. The balls of mist swirled at even higher speeds and coagulated around Yeva's head. Dazzling leapt backward as the mists merged and dropped to encircle Yeva like a giant white tube. Yeva screamed, but the mists swooshed into her mouth, a forceful stream of white effluvium gushing into her. There was a mini-boom, like thunder. Yeva vanished and fine yellow sand sprayed everywhere.

Just like that, the mists were gone. Their unnatural radiance snuffed out, leaving us in the pale light of moon and stars and some torches on posts that served as streetlights. The sky calmly resumed its normal indigo color, as if the mists had never visited at all.

Susie pitched forward in a dead faint. I caught her in my arms.

Rolf dropped to his knees. "Please don't kill me with the mists," he begged, sobbing. "Please! I don't want to die that way."

Scruffy stared around blankly, then visibly pulled himself together. "We want Ginger. Where is she?"

"Yeva's dead, so you can have her. I'll take you to her. They'll give the girl to you if I say so. I'll make them. I–I . . ." Rolf babbled. "They won't argue since Yeva's dead, right? Besides, Yeva was running a crooked game. That woman, Nora, can throw a glamour over a card and make it appear to be something else. Sh-she did it in the last game. Emma had three aces, a full house. She beat Yeva, and since Yeva's game was crooked, she forfeits all her winnings. That's the unwritten rule in Outpost City, the only thing that keeps games straight."

"Full house?" I muttered. "Trip aces? Never saw it."

"That's the point. No one sees it when Nora does her psi thing," Rolf said.

Scruffy exchanged a glance with Dazzling, who walked over to stand beside him. "Get up then, scumbag," Scruffy commanded, "and take us to Ginger."

Still weeping, Rolf scrambled to his feet.

"You folks all right?" Scruffy asked.

I was holding Susie, and poor bruised Donny was struggling to rise to his feet. Tae-yul and Arthur were still on the ground, blacked out and oblivious to it all.

"We'll be fine," I assured them. "Go get your girl."

Scruffy stared at me. "You still taking the pilot?"

"As soon as we're all back on our feet. I won him fair and square, didn't I?"

"I'll hold him for you then," Scruffy said. "We'll be waiting for you at the saloon."

"I appreciate that," I said gratefully, kneeling so I could situate Susie on the ground comfortably. She was a tall lass, too big for me to carry.

"Then what?" Scruffy prodded. "Once we've got Ginger, there's nothing to hold us here, in this godforsaken hole of a city. I'd be happy to put Outpost behind us. Perhaps we could accompany you to wherever you're going."

"Might be good to have the company," Donny agreed, finally ambling to an upright position. He swayed a bit, but he looked pretty good to me. "Emma, is Susie okay?"

"God, I hope so," I muttered. I checked her pulse and found it fast and steady, which I thought was normal for her.

"We're going to Oshkosh," Danny said.

Scruffy cocked his head. "You got a pilot, you're headed for Oshkosh, you're going after a plane. Why? Where do you need to get to?"

"France," Susie said softly. She sat up, circled her arms around my shoulders, and pressed her head into my neck like a young child snuggling with her mother. When my skin felt wet, I realized she was crying. "We're on a mission to save the world."

Scruffy said, "Consider us partners."

17

SUSIE WAS GROGGY AND DISTRAUGHT but physically fit, so I worked on Tae-yul first. He was a mess of broken bones, including a shattered jawbone and two fractured clavicles, but the healing current flowed through me and mended them in a short time.

Tae-yul rose and stood beside me. "Good. Now I can keep guarding Susie."

"You're welcome," I said dryly. I then squatted down beside Arthur, who was almost as badly off.

Tae-yul put his hand on my shoulder. "Maybe you should leave him. It will slow him down enough to let us get away. All the way to Europe, maybe."

I pushed the boy's hand away. "Very funny. I love Arthur. I'm not going to let him suffer. Got it? He's going to be healed."

"Then we have to deal with him immediately," Tae-yul said as he moved to Susie and helped her to her feet.

I barked, "By 'deal with him,' you do not now, nor ever, mean 'kill him.' Do I make myself clear, Tae-yul?"

He nodded, and he and Susie walked over to stand near me and watch me work on Arthur. Susie leaned heavily on Tae-yul, but whether that was for physical or emotional support, I couldn't tell.

I put my hands on Arthur's chest to let the healing current flow into him. "Susie, how did Asher get away with Beth?"

"That was my doing," Donny said mildly as he limped over to stand at my back. "When Yeva's guys grabbed me, I realized it was a setup. I crept into Asher's mind and sent him out of the shanty with Beth. You were out, I guess, or he'd have taken you too."

"I went to get some food," Susie said. "The men grabbed me as soon as I got back, but how come you didn't contact me that way? I might have gotten away."

"Yeah, why'd you let Susie get taken?" Tae-yul bristled.

Donny chuckled. "I can't get into Susie's mind. Yours either. Susie's connected to that other girl so tight that it's like a deadbolt locking her mind from mine. I'm not sure what your story is, Tae-yul. It's like your mind belongs to something else, something big. Are you part of—I don't know— some kind of mental collective?"

"We help Susie," Tae-yul said, his voice neutral.

Donny cleared his throat. "'We' meaning the little kids?"

Tae-yul didn't speak but he must have nodded.

"Do we know where Asher and Beth are now?" I asked. "Have they been hurt? Donny?"

"They're fine. They went deeper into the Badlands and are hiding out at a group home sort of place, a place where people crash for the night," Donny answered. "I've been keeping an eye on them." He chuckled softly in his Danny way. "Inner eye. I'll send Asher a message to collect our gear from the shanty and meet us at The Dark Horse."

"Is Arthur going to wake up and give us grief?" Susie asked, clearly worried. "Is he going to bring the others to follow us and force us to stay with them?"

I shook my head. The bruises on his face were receding, the broken zygomatic arch was mending. Next, I would work on his hands, arms, and kidneys. Arthur had taken some blows. "I can leave him sleeping."

"Let's not leave him sleeping here," Donny said. "God knows what the goats and the rats would do to him."

"We'll find suitable lodging for him."

"Sure. We can tell them he drank too much ale," Tae-yul suggested.

Susie asked tremulously, "Can you keep him asleep for two days? I don't want him tracking us. Please, Emma? We've got to get away from him."

"I know," I said. "I don't know how long he'll sleep for, but he'll be out."

WE LEFT ARTHUR comfortably ensconced in a semi-clean bed in the first lodgings we found. Luckily, Donny had credits in his pocket to pay for a few nights.

The last one to linger in his room, I took a moment to look at Arthur's long form stretched out on the bed. His handsome face looked much younger with the lines of care and time erased by sleep. He would be out for a while, then wake to find himself whole and rested. At least I had made his body whole.

His heart was going to hurt because I'd run away from him again. I couldn't help the hurt he would feel any more than I could persuade him that he was thinking incorrectly about the mists. I was too conflicted to say anything aloud, and he wouldn't have heard me anyway, so I just touched his cheek and went out quietly.

The Dark Horse was only a short distance away. It was mostly empty but still brightly lit, and we found Scruffy and Dazzling waiting for us. Rolf was nowhere to be seen, but a red-haired girl who could only be Ginger was burrowed in Dazzling's arms, so I knew Rolf had broken the news about Yeva.

Franklin sat slumped over a table, with a mug of ale standing in front of him. I walked over to him and shook his shoulder.

"Yeah? What ya want?" he slurred. His bloodshot eyes tried to focus on me.

"You're with us now, Franklin," I said.

He smiled drowsily and wriggled his mouth beneath his moustache. "So it's true, huh? That bitch Yeva's really dead?"

I nodded. "Totally true. And, Franklin, you'll never have another drink again." I pushed the mug away from him. "You're done."

"Aw," he started.

Tae-yul glided over to stand beside me. "Mr. Pilot, if you drink any alcohol, we'll kill you. *She'll* kill you," he said, pointing at Susie.

Susie waved, looking a little perkier at the pleasant thought of killing someone.

Tae-yul went on, "She's bloodthirsty. She makes Yeva look tame."

Franklin groaned and shuffled his feet beneath the table.

Scruffy trudged over. "Never got the opportunity to introduce myself properly. I'm Mark," he said, gripping my hand firmly in a solid handshake.

"I'm Emma, and this is Tae-Yul. That's Susie, and over there is Donny," I introduced, gesturing to each of my comrades in turn.

"That's Mel and Ginger," he indicated, pointing to Dazzling and her daughter.

"Good to meet you all . . . officially," I said.

Mel nodded over her Ginger's head but didn't break free from the total meld with her child.

"Do you know where Yeva's office is?" I asked Mark.

He pointed to a door off to the side.

I opened the door and walked into the dark room. I walked back out and grabbed a hurricane lamp off one of the tables, then walked back into the office. It was a small, neat little room, occupied by a desk with a sheaf of paper on top of it. A few jugs of ale sat on a small bookcase. Beside one of the jugs was the box Alexei had sent to the poker game via Garfield. Carefully, without opening it, I gathered up the box and wrapped it in a shirt I found on a lower shelf. I carried the bundle back out to the main room of the saloon.

From the door, a quizzical voice called, "Is this where the party is?" It was Asher, holding Beth's hand and wearing Susie's bow and several backpacks, including mine.

"Mama!" Beth ran from Asher to hug me.

I clasped her close to me as I set the box down on a nearby table. "Sweetie!"

"Did you get the pilot man?" she asked eagerly.

I squeezed her. "Yep, we sure did. We got him." I peeled a finger off her back to point at Franklin.

She turned in my arms and peered at him, then wrinkled her nose. "Ick. All that trouble for *him?*" She looked back at me. "He looks kinda . . . stinky," she whispered, albeit loudly enough that everyone heard her.

"Don't worry. We'll fix him up," Donny said, ruffling Beth's hair.

"Where to now?" asked Scruffy; I found it difficult to think of him as Mark.

"Cypress Hills. They have our horses."

WE GOT ALL the way out the gates of Outpost City before they came after us. Arthur must have awakened and realized we were leaving town, then gathered his people.

In the pink, pearlescent light of dawn, I saw the group heading toward us, and I knew what I had to do. They were my beloved friends, but I could not allow them to obstruct our journey.

"Uh-oh, a confrontation," Donny said. Franklin's arms were draped around his shoulder, and he was half-dragging, half-carrying the drunken pilot. "That's Arthur and the gang. This is gonna slow us down."

Susie started to nock an arrow into her bow.

"Susie, no."

"Emma—"

"This is something I have to do," I said, "something I have to choose to do. You told me that, remember? That I have to choose what is important. Right now, what's important is getting to Cypress Hills and then to Oshkosh with Franklin, then to the camp in Europe so you and Caris can do your thing. It's a long shot, but it's the only chance we've got. That's what I'm choosing."

Susie nodded.

I held up my hands and relaxed, calling forth the current of energy. My hands warmed and tingled. My heart constricted with sadness. *Oh Arthur*, I wondered, *why do you have to be so intent on controlling the mists? It's madness. I can't permit your madness to interfere with our mission. I won't, no matter how much I . . .*

A stream of bright energy erupted and shot out of my hands. I was so connected with Arthur that I felt it when the beam met his chest. I felt his collapse, I felt his heart stop. *Arthur, I love you. How could you have brought us to this moment?*

The End

ACKNOWLEDGMENTS

I WOULD LIKE to thank all the Book Review bloggers who have supported my books through the years. There are many and I am grateful for their time and thought. Careful book reviewing is an art and these reviewers deserve praise and appreciation. In no particular order, these reviewers and blogs are: Rebecca Skane at Seacoast Online; Leslie Wright at Blog-Critics; Sandy at The Reading Cafe; Dianne at Tome Tender; at the Paranormal Romance Guild, reviewers HC Harju and Chinyere Etufugh and administrator Gloria Lakritz; Marga-ret Marr at Nights and Weekends; Delhia Alby at Between Dreams & Reality; Audrey at Drey's Library; Debbie at Crys-tal Reviews; Jen at No Market Collective; Ashley at Game Vor-tex; Stéphanie at Tynga's Reviews; Lydia at The Lost Entwife; Evie from Paromantasy; Layna from Lunar Haven Reviews and FreshlyBakedBooks; Night Owl Reviews; Mandie at Tak-ing Time for Mommy; Jen from Emsun and From Gutter to Gilt; Jackie from Housewife Blues and Chihuahua Stories; Melissa at WereVampsRomance; and all other book review bloggers who have published a kind word about my books.

Many thanks to Lori Stone Handelman for her brilliantly insightful editing and kind support.

Thank you to Drew Stevens for his beautiful book designs, and for being great to chat with.

Thank you to Gwyn Kennedy Snider for her absolutely beautiful book covers.

Thank you to Michelle Czernin von Chudenitz for too many reasons to enumerate.

Many thanks to Marc Tsavaris and Allen Strassen.

Thank you to Dr. Jane Ely.

Thank you to Christine Rodriguez.

Many thanks and much love to Gerda and Mark Swearengen, Stuart Gartner, Harrison Howard, Geoffrey Knauth, Kristin Gamble and Charlie Flood, Jan Broberg Carter, Debra Jaliman, Linda Hillebrand, Komilla Sutton, Lynn Bell, Thomas Ayers, Sarah Miniaci, Ying Li and Weidong Huang, Stephanie Maloney, and Don Steelman for the warm support. Thank you to Mark Weaver and Fred Nadler.

Much love always to Jessica and Naomi Hendel.

All of my love and the deepest gratitude to Julia and Madeleine Howard and to my husband Sabin Howard.

TRACI L. SLATTON is the international bestselling author of historical, paranormal, and romantic novels, including IMMORTAL (BantamDell) and BROKEN; the award-winning dystopian After Series which includes FALLEN, COLD LIGHT, and FAR SHORE; the bittersweet romantic comedy THE LOVE OF MY (OTHER) LIFE; and the vampire art history romp THE BOTTICELLI AFFAIR. She has also published the lyrical poetry collection DANCING IN THE TABERNACLE and THE ART OF LIFE, a photo-essay about figurative sculpture through the ages. Her book PIERCING TIME & SPACE explores the meeting ground of science and spirituality.